I0675612

Vanayan Dreams

The Singers of the Dark
Book 3

Peter Yard

ISBN-13: 978-0-9944514-8-4

Contents

Prologue 1

one 3

two 9

three 26

four 39

five 60

six 82

seven 113

eight 135

nine 164

ten 181

eleven 206

twelve 236

thirteen 257

fourteen 282

fifteen 293

sixteen 313

seventeen 328

ACKNOWLEDGEMENTS 345

Prologue

The galaxy is old and vast. Everyone knows it and ignores it like faded graffiti. Few understand the meaning of deep time and three hundred billion stars, where every story that can happen has happened, yet each is still unique.

Once there was a civilization that constructed a history of the galaxy, trying to make sense of it all. Over time, it included detailed appendices to enable translations for various sentient beings, always striving to be understandable and a boon to those that followed. Then the torch would be passed on down and down through the eons to others who would refine it further, adding new histories, languages, technologies, and cultures.

This is the story we soothe ourselves with to make the dark abyss between the stars less frightening.

It is a lie.

Humans saw their civilization fall, then re-emerge after a global dark age into a new enlightened culture called the Nexus. When humanity reached the planets, they found several derelict alien probes in the asteroid belt from different times and civilizations. Strangely, all of them had included designs for the same technology: beacons and jumpships. The beacons enabled faster than light interstellar travel, and the jumpships performed the traveling. When humans discovered the Mirrish, they had their appalling introduction to the Galactic Calendar; the sad and ancient history of the galaxy.

But there were also hints in the Calendar of an exception. A civilization that was lost or hidden. They were called the Vanaya, a scintilla of hope, for the one lesson running through the Calendar was that all civilizations fall—except one, maybe.

Raymond Tans had seen the fragility of civilization and the frailty of humans out in the Dark. He knew the cold reality of the Calendar, a bucket of ice water thrown on sleeping contentment. He knew it; he lived it.

That time is long gone and humanity has seen a new dark age, this time not of its own making. Now on the world of Neti, where humans are rekindling the vision, a decision has been made by the ultimate outsider. Soon it will change everything.

one

The medic moved on to treat someone else, so he didn't see Maria stand, look about, then stride fearlessly towards the raging inferno. Too late he saw her. The burning city dazzled his eyes in the dark, the heat stinging his face. He couldn't approach it. He watched helpless as her rippling silhouette advanced impossibly close to the wall of flames and then merged into them. Breathless and stunned, all he could think about was how he would explain this tragedy to Master Mikel. It made no sense. Just another pointless death this terrible day.

Maria looked back, but no one could see her. Now she stood wreathed in white fire, her clothes flashing in a moment, curling, blackening, transcending to incandescence, then away to nothing. She stood naked, untouched, pristine, eternal. The superheated air blowing her long dark hair like a cool spring breeze. She stretched out her right hand among the caressing flames, reaching for some invisible thing. A vertical slit of brilliant blue shimmer appeared, about her height but almost without width or depth. A razor of light from an opening door. She stepped towards it and into it and disappeared from the world of Neti.

The room awoke. Her mistress would arrive soon, and before then the room needed to prepare the man.

There was light; soft, yellow, comforting through his closed eyelids. He was Here. No name, no memory, not even a sense of being a 'he'. He had not taken a breath, and he must breathe. It was important, vital.

He opened his slowly responding mouth. All actions sluggish. A deep yellow calm everywhere. He forced his lungs and diaphragm to take in a breath and felt—nothing. No charge of oxygen, no rising panic for air. Just calm.

He was standing without effort, though his eyes were closed. It seemed strange. The action effortless even while he had been struggling to take a breath.

Opening his eyes revealed a massive room, beyond palatial, perhaps a dozen stories high. Not unheard of. Some vague memories flashed past: crystalline cities, vast spaces, improbable landscapes. A fantasy that memory said was real.

Vines and flowers draped the room with sparkling flecks of every color, as if the petals were flakes of sister metals of gold and silver, now shimmering in waves of green, silver, gold, blue, and much more than a mere spectrum. In the center of the room near the ceiling was a huge ball of yellow light. A sun. Miniature prominences gracefully erupted from its cool, dim surface. At his feet the floor was a mosaic of colored leaves, as if every season had passed in minutes creating a soft green and autumn carpet now turned solid—a clock tick of an age-old forest.

Then he remembered. His name. Ray. Raymond Tans.

He remembered things: his brother, his sister, High Noon. He was sure there should have been pain remembering his brother, but there was only peace. There were other memories, hard to recall, like strange faded photos from an old trunk, but oddly they were the more recent memories. He looked down at his hands, turning them. The back of his hands, young, unwrinkled, free of age spots that those fading sepia memories insisted should be there.

How did he get here?

High Noon. Memories of loss and sadness returning like an inevitable tide. A space station hovering above the ice world of Reshox. A misplaced human colony, surviving by maintaining a beacon so starships could visit it and nearby systems. While down below beneath the ice, an old secret lay waiting to trigger an interstellar war. The rookie humans caught between two ancient civilizations of immense power while he navigated that minefield. Most of the humans didn't care.

In the end he did what he could, and he wasn't responsible for what came later. He did well, but fate wouldn't let him be. He'd lost Avril and Ranei. Only his memories remained to torment him. Grief threatening to swamp him again.

He shook himself. Self pity wouldn't solve anything.

He looked at his arms and body. He was dressed in a white t-shirt and faded jeans. It was odd since he rarely wore either, but right now there was an abundance of weirdness.

A vertical sliver of intense light appeared in the room with the color of a lightning bolt, yet without a sound. From the glare stepped a woman. She was naked and didn't care. She looked at him and smiled. Clothes appeared on her. Everyday clothes he would see anywhere in the Nexus. Her hair was long and black, framing an unfamiliar, pale, intense face. A knowing look in her eyes.

"Hello, Ray. It's me. Ranei."

Just the mention of her name was a knife thrust into his chest.

Perhaps she had some mods, changed her looks, it wasn't uncommon, but this woman didn't resemble Ranei at all. And how did she appear here like that?

"I have a new name now. You can call me Maria."

"What is this? Where is this? Ranei?" He barely knew where to start. He froze, overwhelmed. None of this was right. He took a deep breath; it didn't help.

She walked over to him. She wasn't the same height as Ranei, and it jarred against his memories. She was taller. She put her arms around him and hugged him, rocking him gently from side to side. The scent of roses in her hair. Then she pushed back a little, still holding his arms.

"First, let's start with, when is this? The year is 3049, if you use beacon synchronization, and I have just come from Neti. As for, *where is this?* That's a hard one. But your first question is actually the correct one. What is this?"

"3049? How? Have I been cloned with inserted memory modules? I've seen it done. I guess that's what it is. What this is?"

"No, you were not cloned. The Nexus no longer exists. Human civilization has, well, you could say it is down but not out. A resilient fighter. This place is not High Noon, or a cortex construct. This is the Dream."

"Which means what? Could you stop speaking in riddles?"

She moved closer and kissed him on the cheek.

"I'm trying to soften the blow. But you are still the same, thank heavens, we will need that. Ray, you died 700 years ago. You didn't live to see civilization fall. Three Dawn Ships came through the portal near Neti and crippled human civilization, even damaging the Mirrish. Now human civilization is on a path to recovery. I would normally be happy and confident, but I believe humanity and my people are in danger. We need you now, so I have—reincarnated you—for want of a better word."

She let go and took two steps back. He could finally see her more clearly.

Breathing deeply still didn't help. He wanted to sit down somewhere with some hard liquor and talk this through with Ranei. Or Maria.

"You expect me to believe all that? And who is we?"

She smiled. "Oh, Ray. I thought you would have guessed by now. We are the Vanaya, and I am Vanayan. And you are now in the Vanayan Dream, the continuing collective consciousness of our civilization."

She was so close yet, as he now understood, so alien. Perfect skin, lustrous, thick black hair flowing and framing her pale face. Her deep brown eyes staring at him with a gaze that fixed him to the spot. And now he knew she was a goddess. Not like the demigods of High Noon with their simulated virtual power. She was the real thing and he was her cat's-paw. He wanted to wake up, but he knew this was real; it had the unmistakable feel of the World when you have woken. There was no option but to take it at face value.

"If the galactic gods want to toy with me, why wait until now?"

"I was busy on Neti. I had a copy of your memories, and other things, your consciousness, if you will. You wouldn't understand. The important thing is I have discovered a threat to both of our peoples."

two

Vanaya.

She said the name differently to the sound he remembered from the rare translations in the Calendar. He heard it as 'van-eye-ah' with the barest hint of an exotic accent, and it was still magic. She might as well have said Gondor, Narnia, or Valhalla.

"The Vanaya? You mean the myth? And what is the Dream?"

He was ignorant and vulnerable. Even his questions made no sense. He had little choice but to trust Ranei, or Maria. He looked at the back of his hand again, an old trick to tell if he was dreaming—no change. This was reality, or a reasonable imitation.

"The Vanaya were the people from Corvena, after they regained space flight, successors to the Mavanaya. You remember the game on High Noon, don't you?" she said.

"I remember. Seemed like just another fantasy RPG. So, how much of that was true then?"

"More than you would believe. Your people had neural links and the shared hallucination of High Noon—remember all those personal domains, the

9

shared hallucinations?—well, the Vanaya have
something vaguely similar but on a vaster scale. The
Dream is All, remember it. You are in the Dream now,
or my dream; everything you see, touch, experience, is
part of it. Is this room real or virtual? Or both? When
you teleport, you are in the Dream. But the Dream
intersects with the physical in a way your link
hallucinations do not or did not. You can move from the
Dream to the Now and be in the real world and
influence real events."

Crisp memories flashed before him like a drugged
fantasy. Ben and Ray reclaiming the space station amid
the shared hallucinatory domains. So long ago, if this
woman was right, and a glance at the room told him he
better get a handle on this fast.

This place should have unhinged him, or maybe
he was more resilient than he gave himself credit for.
Another quick look at the room suggested he was doing
well. The worst thing was not the room, but the way
she played with his notion of reality. Crafting an
irresolvable paradox with such ease.

"Come on. Is it real or not? And you know what I
mean, is it physical?" he said, surprised by the tension
in his own voice.

"Some is physical. And some is virtual. But wait
awhile, and those things that were virtual may be
physical and vice versa. Even the things that stay
physical may have attributes that are virtual. If
everyone sees the same thing, and it affects the
physical consistently, then by any reasonable
definition, it is real. The paradox is an illusion. Move

beyond it. The rules of logic still apply. Time travel is still impossible, for example, though there's a way around that too."

"You can do time travel?"

"We can fake it is all I meant. Like reading a good period novel can, but so much better. You can't change the past, though you can experience it in representational interactive form. Want to go back and live through the sack of Troy? See the fall of New York? We interpolate some of the experience, smart guesses, some of it is based on vast amounts of reliable data and personal experience. The level of authenticity of the experience is available, you can't ignore it so you know if it is a guess or as real as living it."

"The Dream is All," he repeated as if it might wake him up, "sounds more like simulation than dream to me. Yeah, interesting, but you said someone destroyed Earth? That's more important to me than all this talk of dreams."

"Not annihilated. Blasted back to the stone age would be closer. Or maybe a feudal era."

"So, who did it?" he said, faking as much determination as he could, waiting for his courage to catch up.

"No idea yet. That's why you are here."

"Why me? You could have brought back lots of people, and not necessarily human." An anger was rising in him, but his body refused to respond. "You can do that, can't you?" he yelled in her face.

Instant regret. He missed Ranei and wanted her back, but not like this.

It didn't seem to bother her.

"I love you," she said. "And I am alone. You cannot imagine how alone. You know what loneliness is like, I monitored you closely. We can do this together."

"Finding dangerous enemies is not bonding material, Maria."

"Oh, it would surprise you. Been there, done that, ad infinitum," she said.

"So this Dream, or whatever. I'm in it. How do I get out? Because no offense, I don't want to be here. I'd rather return to Earth and help."

"You can't return, not without my help, and I need you here. I tell you what. If you succeed, then we can both go there. Help rebuild civilization. What do you say?"

"Just like that? Defeat the Dark Lord and return to the Shire. Read the book. Seems to me that task was a little difficult," he said, trying to maintain aggressive sarcasm, but the resolve wasn't there. "For God's sake, I just want to get out of this alive and help my people."

She gave him a hug and walked a few steps away from him. It felt too random to be comforting. Then, as if remembering something, she turned and faced him.

"About the Dream. Sure, it is a ridiculous statement. The Dream is not truly All. But it is the closest thing you will find to it. Before we leave here, you must understand this idea. Understanding is vital, do not think of the Dream as an illusion. Think of it this way. Humans live in two worlds: the world of the fictional mind, and the world of physical reality. Because the fictional world is so seamless you often mistake ideas as part of the physical world. It results in notions like luck, magic, and the supernatural. If words and ideas are powerful within, you could say, then they should be powerful without. I should be able to fly by wishing it to be so. Not unreasonable since the outward world that you know is part of your inner representation—but it still isn't reality. You can't step off a cliff and fly, but I can. The Dream is different, this fictional world is not fiction, not completely anyway, it is real and directly affects the real. Thoughts here translate into real-world events once you have the power and knowledge, though you will find the Dream and Reality have many levels. Here magic is real, as in the game we role-played on High Noon."

"Was that the lesson of the game? The magic of the characters was manifested through the ancient tech?"

She gave a smile so big her eyes were squeezed by its expanse. Then he knew she was Ranei.

She stepped away from him. Her demeanor was different. Now she was serious, not the oddly teenage persona of before.

"Something has changed. You know the portal at Neti? There are two neutron stars in close orbit with each other, and Neti's sun Mellis is gravitationally bound to the system but at a considerable distance. The portal is a construct using the close orbits of those neutron stars, and it is not possible to dismantle the portal without causing a supernova sized explosion, which is why the problem persists. The Dawn Ships should not have emerged from the portal when they did. We monitor exactly how many ships remain in the temporal flux of the portal and when they would exit. These ships were not due to exit for many tens of thousands of years, so what happened?"

"Ranei. I mean, Maria, or whoever you are. If you know this, why didn't you stop them?"

"We manage the galaxy. On the surface it looks like a game, of sorts, where the gameboard is the galaxy. A very serious game. The Game: the enhancement of life and civilization in the galaxy. Nothing less. Done with the minimum of interference. You need to balance interference and freedom, otherwise you end up with dead worlds. We learned that lesson the hard way, so now we change the fate of civilizations without being noticed and are awarded merit for our performance. A personal reward. I got merit for my work on High Noon and Neti but got points taken off for—other times."

"Okay, a mythical civilization of enormous power whiles away the millennia playing a gigantic game of chess with the galaxy? I find the whole idea hard to swallow, Ranei. Much easier to think it's a lie. Convince me I'm not somewhere else. Perhaps back in one of those cortex hallucinations? Maybe I never left," he said.

"Maria." She corrected him. "Disbelief is a natural defense against a shocking truth."

"Or bullshit."

She turned away, but he saw a momentary smile. She was playing with him.

"Tell me, Ray. What was the largest industry of the Nexus, your civilization? Was it starship construction, surface transport, terraforming, or what?"

Silence.

"Entertainment," he muttered.

"What kind of entertainment?"

The room became stifling, airless. She knew exactly which buttons to push. He had always despised much of the telepresence content. He thought people should explore reality themselves as much as they could. Not soak themselves in other people's undiluted, uninterpreted experience. He was probably being unreasonable, but he wasn't about to change his mind.

"Telepresence reality. Live or re-live exotic or dangerous adventures." His own words left his mouth dry. Humans had moved so quickly to living other people's adventures. If humans had the option of safely watching one of their own save an alien world, they wouldn't even hesitate. Could he resist?

"Why didn't the simulated experiences make you decadent and go extinct? How could you survive geological ages?" There was little conviction in his words, and he knew she had convinced him even as he spoke.

"We didn't succumb to it, we embraced it. We remade it and it remade us."

"Great. More aphorisms."

"Do you still doubt who I am? Don't you humans have a saying, 'seeing is believing'? Why don't you look up? There's your 'seeing.'"

How to deny that cavernous spectacle? Aladdin's cave on LSD. But the most convincing thing—the gilt-edged proof—was something he least expected.

"I can't feel my neural link," he said with an icy calm he reserved for life-threatening moments. The link had always been part of him since his teens when it was inserted, its combination of hardware and tissue growing into his brain and becoming a part of him. It had been a rite of passage, his coming of age, and the basis of his social existence. Now it was gone.

He took a few moments. Maria seemed to have endless patience—as she would.

"So what is your real name?" He said with a composed voice.

"Emari Ya Irenni Lak, is the closest with a human throat and vocal cords. It has a meaning, but never mind. The civilization that named me and the world that raised me no longer exist. That was about 1.8 billion of your years ago..."

"How old are you? I mean, did you say you are billions of years old? I misheard, right?"

"You heard right, 1.8 billion. It makes all Vanaya an anachronism. We don't belong anywhere anymore, so we adapt to wherever we are," she said.

He looked about searching, trying to find some chink in the world, a clue to the truth, something nonsensical that would say to him, "It's all just a dream."

It was all too real.

"Your name, 'Emari'? Reminds me of Helen Amaris, one of the first investigators on Neti. Don't tell me you were her as well?"

"Of course not. I'm usually good at what I do. I disappear without a trace, in most cases. We rarely intervene directly, though we inspired the construction of Neti. In truth, we did a bit more than that. It was laxness in our attitude, a fashion of letting Nature take its course that allowed the Tarkoi to rise to power. The creators of the Dawn Ships, the Thousand Tyrannies, as your archaeologists called them. Our fault, so we fixed it, without betraying our role."

"Except Earth is in ruins now," he said, and it hurt. He had visions of burning cities with friends and family lying dead on ashen streets. All his pain centuries too late. Forgotten by everyone except him. A memory of his last minutes on High Noon intruded for a bitter moment—déjà vu reflected on itself.

"Someone changed the exit times for three Dawn Ships," Maria said. "Only we can do that. There must be a faction within the Vanaya that wants to destroy humanity. Who or why is unknown. We obey a Code of Transparency and Involvement, we must never hide actions from each other and we must avoid involvement with those in the Game beyond our character's role."

"How does this involve me at all?" he said.

"So I thought who could investigate this and challenge a galactic civilization? It was either Mikel or you. Mikel was busy, and I loved you, so you won out," she continued, oblivious to his words.

"You love me?" he said, surprised. The words were unexpectedly hard to say.

"I told you that before. You didn't even hear it, did you? Do you doubt me?"

"Why? I'm like a pawn to you. A mayfly alive for a day and then gone."

She looked at him as if about to say something, then changing her mind.

"No, don't think like that. Now is the only time that matters. Now is when we live, when we plan, when we do things for those that matter," she spoke to reassure, but part of him felt patronized.

"The Code of Transparency, doesn't this conversation violate that Code?"

"Yes, and it troubles me, but this is too important and I need an ally who can change the fate of civilizations. I could have picked Mikel or you, but I love you, so you are it. Besides, he was busy rescuing a world or something," she said.

"And who is Mikel?"

"That's something for later."

"Are you still in your role? Is your love just a part of your character? Is this another part of your Game?" His voice was more certain. He had questions that needed answers, and he might as well barge in, 'better to be hung for a sheep as a lamb,' as a remote ancestor may have said. Curiosity was part of his being and it was waking up. Inwardly he smiled.

"I understand your doubts but the answer to all of those is no. I love you because it is just part of my nature. I have a human, well body isn't the right word, I have a human form. I am capable of physical love, yes it is part of my human aspect but my desire is not because of my role, it is because of who I am. I have been many people of so many strange and wonderful species. Sometimes I have been male, usually female, sometimes something else. Right now I have a human form with human instincts and I am female and I love you. Don't complicate it," she said, smiling as if she was discussing her choice of desserts.

"I'm having a real problem seeing how this works. How does a mere human act as an ally to a god? I'm just a pet, aren't I?"

"No, no. You must enter the Dream beyond this bubble of mine. There are ways to do it. Then you will have access to, I guess you would say, godlike abilities and I will be there to make sure you don't overstep your bounds."

"Maria, have you done this before? Resurrected me?" The notion made him queasy.

"Only simulations," she said.

"And then you killed them."

"Huh? No! The map is not the thing mapped. Wasn't that something one of your mathematicians once said? Eric Temple Bell, though I prefer Korzybski's later twist on it, 'the map is not the territory,' more poetic. Simulations are like useful descriptions. If I describe a rock, then the description isn't a rock. Or, I can simulate a human walking, it isn't someone walking, but if I build a robot that walks then it is real and the walking is real. The simulation is a map, the walking robot is the territory. You are not a map, you are territory. But still virtual—patterns of energy—for now," she said.

He stopped. Looked about. Closed his eyes— black, not even random images—then opened them again to the same gargantuan room. The delusion persisted, perhaps he was insane, perhaps these were the final hallucinations of a dying brain. But it was so vivid and consistent, and he supposed he had better treat it as real.

"How can you get away with this? Won't the other Vanaya see me for what I am?"

"I can hide you. It is common or rather typical that most of us take the form of our last character in the Game, or some favored identity, often masquerading in all aspects as that being. You can go unnoticed unless someone questions you in detail. Don't worry, we don't use memory sharing like your people did, that is a one-way path to the Kamoi, the Hive Core, where our egos dissolve and the Dream is truly All."

None of what she said made sense. Still, what choice did he have?

He looked up to the distant ceiling. Intricate like a baroque work of art, but the forms and artwork spoke of an aesthetic that was nothing like any culture he had studied. There were patterns and fractals, sometimes a hint of simple nature and other times artificial forms. It was hard for him to tell them apart. It looked like a glittering mechanistic forest as if Nature chose metals to work with rather than lowly carbon. The walls of this vast room, dwarfing the two of them, covered in something like scintillating paintings, as if pointillists had designed them with masses of faint pulsed LEDs. Waves of color rolled across and changed what he looked at, and then there would be a drastic rearrangement ruining his LED explanation. All the time he watched the spectacle there, in the high center of the room, a pale sun kept erupting, reaching for him, bidding him to pray to it as his kind had done once long ago.

With an effort he looked away and down to meet Maria's eyes. She waited while he calmed himself. He could imagine his wild, deranged face.

Change topic, he thought. To anything.

"I don't mean this in a bad way, but why do you always seem so young in your mind, like you aren't mature. Oh, that sounds terrible, I mean..." He wanted to blush but couldn't, worrying about that at least distracted him from his faux pas.

"Easy, it's all right. You need a super positive outlook to change the fate of worlds, to see your work often fail, or to succeed and then leave your friends. You can't forget it all. Any agent needs to believe that their effort and sacrifice is worthwhile, and paradoxically to live in the moment. Do you imagine I can have the memories of a billion years in my head when I walk among humans? I'd go insane and lose my identity before that. The fact is sentients survive by forgetting. The Vanaya don't take that path exactly, we store large sections of our memory away and then forget non-essential things. If I need more memories, I can access them though it is painful. I mean really painful, and even a million years is an unbearable burden. Without selective amnesia, we would all choose true death. So, I create memories of being human and a sizable chunk of memories of being Vanayan. Some try to forget all of their Vanayan identity, but one day the memories will come back and you risk the horror of full remembrance, unfiltered and unedited. It can destroy you for millennia."

"A billion years? Really?"

"Really."

"There's something I don't understand. I expected more wisdom and insight from a goddess."

She laughed. Ranei's tinkling laugh he once thought unique. Now he recognized a touch of the alien in it.

"I'm definitely not a goddess. Though, I'm a close imitation, I suppose. Here's the thing, just as we limit our memory, we also limit our intelligence. Too much intelligence disconnects you from interacting with other sentients, which is the whole point of The Game, so we limit it. The Game is not just entertainment, it is our mission, our life."

"I thought. No, not just me. Everyone I knew imagined that a highly advanced civilization would do amazing things. Megastructures, learn the secrets of the universe, understand the big questions, increase understanding and wisdom to great heights. Not playing a game!"

"And when you have done all of that? Several times? To live millions of years is to lose all connection to the things that once made living worthwhile. When you climb those heights of understanding you find it doesn't help. What do you do? You go back to the things that matter, helping others. As I said, the game is serious."

"Was it related to the RPG on High Noon, somehow?"

"The role-playing game on High Noon was one way of influencing the participants, I added features that interfered with the Castan memory effects. So it was part of the True Game. The True Game influences the fate of civilizations, without it far fewer would have survived for as long as they did—we are a positive force. We try to be like Maxwell's Demon, an invisible agent that by small actions over extended periods of time can change the state of a system."

He wasn't buying any of this yet. Her certainty fed his skepticism.

"Maxwell's Demon was a fiction though, a thought experiment intended to demonstrate a paradox in thermodynamics. Later work showed that it still obeyed the rules," he said.

He was going through the motions, trying to discuss and gain an intellectual handle on the situation. But like the Vanaya, he suspected he might get in too much trouble if he thought too clearly about all of this.

She didn't buy it. "It was only an analogy. Most analogies are flawed, they aren't mathematical isomorphisms where you can prove a kind of compliance. That doesn't mean you can't discern the truth in it though."

"I looked for you after on High Noon, you know, but the Cortex said you never existed," he said. "I figured it had wiped your memory and given you a new life to protect you."

She smiled, a soft nostalgic smile. "By that time I had changed the Cortex itself so it forgot me. Its memory of me postfaded, as they used to say on High Noon, which I thought was a lovely bit of irony. You would have found the truth if you had spoken to Jody because he still remembered me and knew I was missing. Avril sussed out a bit of who I was but I swore her to secrecy, she only wanted the best for her adopted son/brother/boyfriend."

There was a sudden pang of grief. As if he had forgotten a great loss until this moment. He had traveled far and had lost contact with so many people whom he admired and loved. And Avril was gone. Now joining many others.

It was heart wrenching. Coming home was never the same, his world-line looping back displaced in time never to reconnect. Casual goodbyes fixed in stone.

He needed time to digest all of this. He needed to lie down and have a nap, tired or not, sleep on it and let his subconscious come to some resolution. Maybe he would wake up to his real life. He turned and there was a bed where none had been before. Was it there because of dream logic or Dream logic? He lay himself on it, feeling the patterned quilt underneath with its soft and rough patches; the starched white pillows cushioning his head with the delicious scent of fresh linen—while he stared up, up to the far hallucinogenic ceiling where that pale sun floated against a silver-gold background, and flocks of small, silent multicolored birds arced around the burning globe like a swarm of planets.

He closed his eyes and took a calming breath.

In closing his eyes he had merely opened another set of eyes. The black void was gone. He appeared to be suspended in a bland matrix of softly glowing dark blue panes and lines of light extending in every direction. Like being in an infinite set of mirrors but none of them reflecting him. A vampire in a mirror-maze. He was undead.

He opened his eyes.

Around the sun above, the birds now joined by what looked like a flying iridescent snake ribboning around the flocks like a flowing opal, undragonlike and hypnotic in its sinuous progress. He got off the bed with zero effort, as if gravity was only a formality. Maria was still there watching him, waiting.

three

"Come on, Ray. Time to go," Maria said.

"Where?"

She lifted her left hand, palm open as if to karate chop him, then pointed to an empty part of the room a few meters from him. A door appeared unconnected to any wall. The sight was a paradox on the autumn leafed floor, floating a few centimeters from the ground as if caught on a protruding tree root. An aura of soft white light acted as the door frame. Carved into the burgundy wood was a glossy tangle of curling vines, leaves, and strange animals.

The door opened toward him, and light poured out. A soft yellow welcoming glow while the light in the doorway had turned solid, resembling a radiant wall of snow.

She grasped his left hand and dragged him towards the door with unexpected and irresistible force.

He didn't remember going through the wall of light. Yet before him was a city. Perhaps 'city' was an outmoded word here, because what he was looking at didn't match the word. 'Bizarre theme park' would be a better fit. There was nothing in the Galactic Calendar, the 'official' history of the galaxy, that compared to what was before him.

Then he looked up.

He struggled to think what it reminded him of, then he remembered seeing Togore prepare for war. Buildings and structures flowing through the air of the massive habitat. He imagined if he stretched and twisted a transparent Togore into an infinite helix and then twisted that into a kind of pretzel, then it might approximate either his confusion or what he was seeing. It was like a city version of folded DNA, or in this case its alien equivalent, an XNA, wrapped around invisible histone proteins. A deranged and imposing vision of the nucleus of a single cell. The comparison might even be intentional.

He could use that. It gave him a way of seeing the whole without being drowned in the detail.

The land and buildings in the foreground spread out into a wide ribbon of endless length; a 3D children's diorama by immortal youngsters. The ribbon twisted in odd curving directions. He could see in the black sky the land-ribbon looping and coming back. The whole thing twisting back so there was no start or end, finally obscured by a dazzling sun in the black. The sight made him dizzy, and he feared at any moment he could fall up and hurtle along that tract of land like an out-of-control ride on an old amusement park, his hands slipping from the handholds and flying up and out into the endless spaces.

He looked at the surrounding area, something to anchor him while before him were floating buildings and suspended pieces of land with towns. A fantasy land.

There were few people about. In ones or twos but not large groups.

He tried to focus on the buildings or distinct places that stood out. What was in those areas he saw: a park, an office building or similar, strange structures more art than architecture, a floating forest, and more? And then. And then he was there. In each place, walking through the park, the buildings, the forest, the museums, and others—all at the same time. Many places and many instances of himself. This was parallel consciousness, something humans rarely, if ever experienced. He understood this as he experienced it as almost an afterthought. His sense of self seemed as if it would be washed away at any moment in the flood of being, and he might wake up as something else.

With a jolt, he was back in his one-self. He gasped but old instincts didn't help here. Some primal part of him rejected the experience as too strange. Intellectual cowardice? Perhaps, but if asked to say which of those selves was real, he could not give an honest answer and that repelled him. Maybe another time. For now it was best to take small steps.

"Is this real? I mean, is it physical or virtual?" he said. The same question he had asked before. He feared he would get the same answer. Deep down he wanted this place to be an illusion and his experience dismissed.

"Welcome to the city of Eklus," Maria said, "It has a thousand other names, some not uttered for many thousands of millennia. Is it real? Is it matter or does it matter?" she laughed. "As far as you are concerned it is as real as New Shanghai. As I said before, saying 'where' we are is problematic. In fact, some of these places are virtual and some are not spatially contiguous, meaning parts of the city are in different places at the same time, but it is all real enough. Come, let me show you my home town. I'll be your guide. Don't wander off, some places here have over three spatial dimensions. You'll get lost there, even if you come back the same way you went in. Human minds tied to three dimensions and you are still too human."

He looked about again, this time focusing on their immediate surroundings. They were standing in a park. An area large enough to have a lake about two hundred meters across and a small wooden bridge at this end over a creek entering the lake. Several rustic buildings stood nearby on the other side of the bridge and forests defining the edge of the park. Nothing about the park was normal. Eklus might as well be in the realm of Alice in Wonderland.

How much of this was real? She said, 'levels of reality', he didn't know what that meant. At the moment he faced a waterfall at this end of the lake which issued from a piece of land floating ten meters above the ground with nothing supporting the apparition. It looked like a fragment of a mountain with trees and clouds. Something was messing with the perspective because it looked distant with cloud topped summits and a magnificent waterfall falling from the floating land, but it was also obvious that the floating land close, the waterfall churned the water just twenty meters away. A few steps from him, waves from the impossible waterfall lapped the lake edge while underneath the floating mountain was nothing. His eyes refused to focus on what must be below the mountain. He couldn't say if underneath was rock, or dirt, or clouds, nothing was visible. A familiar tactic used in a class of games called 'excursions', open world and often alien where the links would conspire against you to divert your attention away from various things, but excursions had never been this convincing.

Around the lake edge near him grew many plants and trees—not only the distinctive red vegetation from Corvena—he recognized some from Earth and others from Mirr and Term. Biological domains that were incompatible with each other. Many more were new to him. The scene left him with the impression of an alien Monet with a sky straight out of delirium. The park had animals, too. Some familiar and large. In the distance, on the other side of the park, a shape moved that tugged at a childhood memory.

"Is that a dinosaur, I mean a dinosaur-like creature?" he said, while his eyes followed the two legged massive creature on the far side of the lake. The animal was unique to any representation of the creatures he had ever seen, yet so reminiscent of them. Beautiful, nasty, and powerful. Ancient fears rippled through his mind. He hoped the creature was alien.

"It's a real dinosaur. We visited Earth many times over its history. We sampled. This is a close relative of a Tyrannosaur, actually it is one, but they were more diverse than you imagine. I grew it just for you. You need not fear anything here, apart from being found out, everything is controlled and safe."

The creatures, dinosaur included, wandered about with blissful calm as if the strange sights, sounds, and beings were normal. He fought a momentary temptation to pursue and ride the beast.

He saw people, maybe twenty, spread about in ones and twos, and by 'people' he meant—as was common in the Nexus—any sentient. Among those he saw several having picnics, of all things, while others walked about unaware of the sights above their heads. He saw many unfamiliar species, and almost everyone represented a different world. Nothing here was what it seemed.

Ahead of him he saw that the area of the lake where the creek entered. A sudden ripple broke the creek's surface. The watery shadow looked like a fish, though he didn't know from when or where. The creek meandered into the distance up the slope. Not the slope of a mountain but the arc of this place. His eyes followed the line of it in the distance as it climbed and climbed the curve of the real.

Thank heavens I'm not human or I'd throw up, he thought.

He followed her as she proceeded across the wooden bridge. Maria's steps on the bridge made a familiar rattling wooden sound. He wanted to clutch the solidity of that sound and embrace it, but even that could not allay the strangeness here. He listened for his own footsteps, he didn't hear them, he was a ghost. A ghost that cast a shadow. In the opposite direction of his shadow hanging in the sky blazed a sun. Not an actual sun because across the lake he the shadows of trees pointed in a different direction.

Maria must have seen his confusion.

"It's not physical. If you move much further the sun will jump to a different place. A physical light source is pointless. Though there is real light, you know, with real photons here. We use whatever is most appropriate," she said.

"At least a sun is something I'm used to. It doesn't make my head spin," he said. A weak excuse, but he decided he'd stick to it.

She ignored him and turned towards a building, a tavern. It looked normal. Earthly. Tudor style, rough black wooden beams with lime-washed walls and a worrying lean, as if the place might topple over mid-drink.

"So much in this area is familiar. Why is that?" he said.

"My creations. Temporary, but I hope my fans enjoy them. Little souvenirs of past escapades."

"You have fans?"

"Time is long and obsessions help us cope. We can't all play the game for high and noble purposes,

32

otherwise it would never have lasted as long. The Game must also serve other needs," she said.

"I see. Distraction and forgetfulness. Let him who is without sin—."

Inside, the tavern was dim, suffused by a warm orange light from a blazing fire at the other end of the room. There were about twenty people in the room in small groups in animated discussion, yet he could not hear anything being said. Instinct drew his attention to the fire, but there was no heat on his face. It was fake, like so much here.

The customers seemed to be drinking mugs of ale or beer. There were various alien races. Some he recognized from the Calendar—extinct species and civilizations mingling and having a beer or a rough equivalent. All perfectly normal, he thought; a sarcastic leer on his face. Some of those races can't breathe this atmosphere, and the beer is probably toxic. Another lie.

A young human male came up to them. He was wearing clothes that hearkened back to ancient texts, but he couldn't place the culture. Persian? He missed his neural link.

"Hello, Emari, we're all looking forward to experiencing the sack of Tanten. See, I've even copied the looks of a trader. You haven't released it yet. Why not?"

He understood for the first time since waking he had not been speaking or hearing Nexus English. Emari spoke to him in Vanayan from the beginning, and he did not realize.

"You will get it when it is ready, or do you want to experience every day in the Library? Anyway, Amur, this is Rayma, he has been assisting me. Not his real name, he is practicing his incognito role. A bit too dedicated, maybe. He has volunteered to be an agent. Giving up the comfortable life of the audience. I think he is crazy, but what would I know."

Amur's piercing eyes examined Ray. An icy dread should have crept up his spine, knowing that at any moment this being could expose his identity; all he felt was a dispassionate concern.

"Brave. We must have met but I'm getting no ID. That's dedication, how do you do that? Never mind, just curious. Though I wonder why? The audience is safe while being an agent is about pain. Extreme pain. Are you a masochist like our dear Emari?" he looked at Ray, evaluating, calculating. "No, I guess not. But there is pain, a lot. Are you prepared for the experience?"

Without warning, Ray spoke, his own voice with a different persona, not under his control, talking with knowledge about things he had no idea about.

"Too many agents retire from duty. Some have to step up, do our part, and take their place. We chose the path long ago, and that is what we have to continue. Do we abandon the galaxy to chaos? It isn't just about them, we are also saving ourselves," he said. There was a confidence and conviction in his voice he wished he could capture, hold, and never let go. It faded in moments.

Amur chuckled, unable to keep his cynicism to himself, "Well, Rayma, rarely you hear a pep talk in the style of the Zuxeh Tefa. You must be one of the originals. If you feel happy, then good for you. Yeah. We all thought that once, when the Vanayans sold us that line, some later than others. Remember how we got here, or even better, the lies we believed?" He stopped for a moment with a tightening in his face. In a human, Ray would interpret it as anguish. "I know, I know, we treat the Game as a distraction, forgetting the 'why,'" he looked to the side, distracted or thinking, perhaps hoping to find someone more interesting to talk to. "Anyway, good luck out there, I hope to see some of your adventures soon."

Before Amur left, he whispered something to Emari, Ray heard it all, but it seemed meaningless, something about her next destination and a leader board. He wasn't sure how accurate the translation process was. All of this seemed crazy. Perhaps he was insane, being treated by Nexus medics for a neurological disease or toxin. How could this be a powerful civilization? Had he wandered into some delusional Esports convention? Both might be true, sentients were masters of paradox and idiosyncrasy everywhere you looked.

When Amur left, Emari turned to Ray, which he took to mean there was a secure communication link between them.

"It's an endless game to many. A giant reality show. I reminded Amur of our origins, and he didn't like it. Sorry I took over your voice. I had to. Amur is more alert than most, despite appearances."

"This is not how I envisaged a super-civilization. You have amazing achievements but on a personal level it seems ordinary and unsophisticated."

"Complexity is the origin and death of civilization. We keep our society simple otherwise we would add endless detail and destroy ourselves despite our power."

"Sounds like Joseph Tainter. An anthropologist and historian who wrote about the collapse of complex societies. He lived before the collapse of the Globals. Read his stuff once. Talked a lot about how societies use complexity to solve problems, but such complexity has a cost. The more advanced the society is the higher the cost, eventually the energy cost is overwhelming and the energy-complexity spiral has to either go up, the rise of civilization, or decline, which we call collapse."

"Yes, Ray. None of that is new. I've seen it happen many times. Your world had the clues but didn't act. Like many others. Just look in the Calendar for too many examples. So, now do you understand why we simplify?"

"I don't know. Even so, I expected more sophistication and more individual achievement, I suppose," he said.

"Here we can offer you a close version of your Heaven or Nirvana. What does it mean for humans?

Often an eternal, blissful, unthinking existence. It isn't about being smart and changing things, rather a bliss filled dream or sleep. But that would be death to a civilization. No matter how much sentient beings want to live the blissful escape they can't because it will lead to death. The death of everything. On the other side of those scales, if we are too aware, we will see the shortcomings and frailties, all the flaws in our society, and the tensions that could boil over. If all of that was revealed it would bring us down. Many of us sleep for an age then wake trying to find new meaning, but if you are too smart, that won't fool you. So, wouldn't it be better to dial down the intelligence and live a peace hovering above the envelope of bliss?"

"It sounds like the fine print of your Heaven was written by the devil."

They left the tavern and walked back to the path via an alternate route.

"Why did you take me there? There was no point," he said.

"I had to press the flesh, as you say, to talk to my loyal fans. Popularity is important for accruing influence and power, or mana as you might call it. I also wanted to show off my new protégé. Set the tongues wagging. The Kamoi will know. It is a gesture to them so they don't kill you on sight. Just joking." She laughed.

They came to a vivid green area in the park. The green was not grass but something like moss, resembling a sponge with the color of fresh spring leaves.

"Time to go," Maria said.

"Can't we just stay. I feel bewildered. I need some time, it's like delirium."

"No. We have to go."

"Why? Where?"

"The Kamoi. It is a long way away. I'll show you some sights on the way but we must get moving."

"Why there? You don't seem to be in much of a rush to find those who killed my home. We're wasting time."

"We can't do anything until this is done. Relax, we will get around to it. You are disoriented from a big shock. Don't worry you will adjust to all of this faster than you think."

Another vertical slit of silent light appeared.

"How do I?" he said.

"You don't have to walk into it, that's simply for dramatic effect."

"Okay..." he started to say and was gone.

four

Black space, a sprinkle of stars like a frozen moment of night rain caught in a streetlight, all humbled by a swirling hurricane of glowing dust and gas ahead, bright and glaring near the center where a hole should anchor the scene like an ancient vinyl record spinning on an invisible spindle. He knew without knowing how he knew. Correction: of coursehe knew how he knew.

Above the brilliant maelstrom arose a jet of matter, like a high-speed photo of glowing steam escaping from a leaking valve. Somewhere underneath the disk would be a matching jet. The whole scene motionless while knowing all the things in front of him here were defining examples of the word 'extreme,' including velocities.

This complex, tortured expanse of matter and energy was the neighborhood of a black hole. A cute, safe name for humans to paste over its true nature.

The closer in towards the center you looked, the bluer and brighter the light became, pushing into the invisible burn of x-rays. Somewhere at the center of that cyclonic blinding eye lurked the much smaller pupil of the event horizon. Unseen, yet his senses told him that, 'there be dragons,' the edge of the world, oblivion.

He was bodiless, yet there was a visceral sense of wonder. He tingled with a delight he thought his jaded mind had lost under the weight of too many days.

"Am I still virtual, or whatever I was back in that room?"

As he asked information flowed into him. The Vanayan bodies, or forms, were not simple or restricted to what was visible. And he occupied a small part of Emari's Dream or processing envelope, however he preferred to name it. He was an egg, unhatched and without agency.

Too many questions. Concentrating on the now was his best bet. "It's wrong," he said, trying to deflect his own concerns. "It looks like a disk. There should be gravitational warping of the light. Shouldn't it be a lopsided, something?" A textbook image from his past appeared before him challenging what was before him. There should be a breaking wave. A wave of light breaking over a black hole in a cosmic surfing movie of the surreal where the path of the light from behind was bent as if traveling through a lens.

"It isn't a supermassive black hole, just a stellar mass one, about 12.7 solar masses. The event horizon isn't very big, about 75 kilometers in diameter and invisible to us, so there isn't any gravitational distortion visible from here. And, yes, what you are seeing is modified, anyway. Even if we were closer, you would see a sanitized version, suitable for young minds and humans. Any other questions?"

Information about the black hole appeared in his mind, including its size, which was all about the vast circling accretion disk—the place where all the action occurred. The temperature of the black hole surface, the event horizon, was close to absolute zero. However, the surrounding accretion disk had temperatures ranging from cold dark gas on the dark outer fringes to x-ray searing temperatures in the millions of degrees near the inner edges.

The disk in front of him was more chunky than he expected. A memory that wasn't his told him human scientists once called such black holes Polish donuts. Not all the gas lay in a thin accretion disk, rather it formed a diffuse torus, the inner edges blasted back by ionizing radiation pressure and a storm of fast sub-atomic particles, a vast fiery eyewall in a hurricane of light. Within that eyewall was the classic flat spinning disk on a mind numbing scale: size, energy, temperature, velocities. At the poles of the disk, the glowing jet flamed outward, resembling a snapshot of the escape valve of a celestial furnace. A fury of radiation pushing particles in its way forward accelerated to a good fraction of lightspeed. This was no place for living things, and cowering behind the insubstantial walls of a starship was futile. Humans had shields that could reflect a large fraction of neutrinos and dark matter, reverse engineered from the defunct alien probes found in the asteroid belt, but they were useless here. In that maelstrom, they would be no better than using plastic wrap to protect against a tsunami.

He was the first human to witness such a sight. There were no beacons near such dangerous places, and sublight ships to them would only contain automated probes. No one wanted to travel sublight, and no one was crazy enough to want to get close enough to a black hole to eyeball it. The Calendar had reports of beacons being 'hopped in'. They set a beacon up, allowing a jump closer to a black hole where another beacon was placed. Expensive, dangerous, and it never ended well for anyone.

The thing about jump transport was that beacon-to-beacon jumps were worth the risk if you didn't do it too often. If you jumped further away from beacons, then the level of risk rose from worrying to courageous and then to suicidal. The probability of a safe jump resembled a normal distribution or bell curve. Near to the beacon it was all somewhat good and wonderful, venture too far away and it got ugly fast. The safe distance depended on the quality and power of the beacon and human beacons were budget level things. Humans then took the incorrect analogy with the normal distribution curve further, people calculated a fanciful variant of the standard deviation as a measure of the shape of the curve. No one in their right mind would travel out a full 'sdev', or 'essdev' as the pilots pronounced it. Instead, the distance was often measured in thousandths of an sdev. The beacons knew where the other nearest beacons were and could show you on a starmap, but outside their immediate areas it got difficult and dangerous. This solar system must be remote from any beacon.

He shouldn't be able to notice anything unusual at this distance, yet there was something else. A tracery near where the disk thinned and flattened before brightening to a dazzling intensity; an indistinct filigree like a spider web decorating the eyewall part of the accretion disk.

He looked closer and closer, his sight noticing impossible detail. No longer spider-web thin but vast structures made of—what? Knowledge appeared in his head. Not matter. Some artificial substitute for matter constructed out of mass and energy and other things. The entire thing turned the spinning accretion disk into a giant turbine powered by the faster spinning hot dense plasma nearer the center with its tangle of trapped rotating magnetic field lines.

Now he knew the name of this place—Sayel 378.

He thought of Earth, trying to plant at least one virtual foot on a grounded memory.

"Around Earth we had orbital mirrors to cool the poles. It helped restore the temperature difference between the poles and the equator. They harvested enormous amounts of solar energy, beamed to ground receiver stations. Where does this energy go?" he said.

She was beside him, but disembodied. Just a voice in his 'head'.

"This is one of the power sources for the jump system. You didn't think your little jump engines could really enable travel across the galaxy did you? The energy is re-routed through, well, let me explain.

Energy, or more properly its form as something like information arising from symmetry, is a massive abstraction that the cosmos uses, but in various forms. The one true currency. This is one form, but still the same thing deep down."

"The information interpretation of quantum mechanics, or maybe the Bayesian version, QBism I think they called it. It was popular back when, yeah, back then," he said. He was a child again, trying to impress an adult by saying something almost intelligent. The talk about energy and symmetry was incomprehensible; he was lost. All while staring into the majestic power of nature mixed with the works of true gods.

"Not completely wrong, but not even close either. You should try to abandon your prejudices and allow yourself to understand much deeper ideas and abstractions. Anyway, our work doesn't disturb the dynamics of the system, our structures are tiny, trying to blend in and not be broken by the enormous forces. We don't even break conservation of energy at this scale."

"Tiny, right. Are there any habitable systems nearby?"

"Unlikely. They wouldn't survive long here. This is a hazardous area."

"What would happen if a rising species evolved nearby?"

"We would alter the flow of infalling matter to create an asymmetrical jet. Push the powerstar out of the way. It would take a million years or near enough.

Besides, at this distance from the galactic core habitable worlds are rare, though sometimes rogue systems are deflected from their orbit around the galaxy and find themselves in this region. It is a dangerous place and often ends badly for life. Think of it as a heavy industry area. Non-residential. Let's get in closer."

There was another sensation of zooming with a flurry of data, schematics, strange multidimensional animated charts, and images. He was seeing Ranei—correction, Maria—viewing relevant details, passing encryption checks, receiving permissions, and getting jump co-ordinates.

Everything changed as the universe blinked. They were in a forest, non-Earth. The plants were reddish rather than green, like vibrant autumn colors where the color was not that of dying leaves but of a different form of chlorophyll or an equivalent. They were on the edge of a clearing about the size of a football field. Scattered about were strange new animals passing through the forest and the clearing. Most of them the size of mice or rabbits, but a few the size of wolves. He was invisible to them.

Every plant he looked at he knew; its origin, history, biology, and how it got here. He looked at another, and another. At an animal, then more. Each time knowledge like familiar memory poured into him. There was a vast procession of ideas and information for everything he looked at. He had no problem knowing when to stop; he was a veteran of many readings of the Galactic Calendar. This was small stuff in comparison. The basic lesson from the Calendar was: stop and put what you learned to one side lest it drown you, take a breath, and move on. Plenty of time later to understand it.

"Where are we? I would like to have seen more of the powerstar," he said.

"You are. Remember the faint lattice in the accretion disk? We are at a node in that."

He walked ahead into the clearing and saw the sky. He was in a great cavernous area. A cavern that held the sky. The sides, so far away, blued into misty shapes stretching up tens of kilometers or more to clouds and blue sky with a fake sun emitting real light. The faint silvery metallic cavern receded into the blue distance to his left and right, and another similar passageway facing him but filled with machinery if that was what it was rather than abstract artwork on the scale of mountain ranges. He wondered if the gravity was the slow spin of the lattice, then dismissed it as a folly. Part of him completed the logic anyway, since the rotational velocity matched local gases in orbit; he should be weightless. None of his clever ideas or sophisticated experience meant anything here. The grandest technologies he knew were just flint knapping in comparison; useful, but out of place.

He wondered what it looked like outside. Then, for a moment he saw.

There was blinding light everywhere; a glowing hot dense plasma, hotter than blue, burning in the ultraviolet. Somehow it cleared like a rising fog. In the distance he saw the surface of the lattice. A vast plain of metal, or something like it. He knew it was superconducting and ridiculously tough protecting the inside from the vast electromagnetic and particle assault. Looking up through the now transparent plasma, he saw that he stood on the surface of a massive silvery mesh. The surface was so enormous that this filament seemed flat around him while it stretched on and disappeared into the distance. The tracery of the mesh was a spider web that could capture worlds, and from the mesh there were filaments rising towards the invisible black hole far away in the center of the blazing sky. The filaments didn't seem substantial, and they weren't; part solid, part plasma, they would interact with the flowing plasma, extracting energy from the rotating magnetic field and the infalling matter. It was like sipping water from a waterfall.

He was back in the strange forest.

"That is what it looks like outside. Again, not actual light. No visible light can penetrate the plasma. Its charged particle density gives it a high resonant frequency, anything below that including visible light can't get through," she said.

His curiosity was almost overwhelmed. Almost. "Oh god, does this architecture run through all the lattice? How on Earth did you build it? How much does it mass? It can't be stable. What happens if something hits the lattice? Do you mean there is nothing between us and the black hole?"

"Calm down. Nothing to worry about."

He didn't need to calm down. Nothing Maria had said or done had made him feel so real as he did right now. His exuberance came from asking questions. They validated his sense of self.

"Not upset. I'm just excited, I guess," he said with a touch of delirium. He craved a calming breath.

"This is not typical of the entire structure," she said, "Anything rigid would be destroyed in an instant, some parts flow and move, more like a liquid or a controlled plasma. This is a familiar part. How was it built? Look it up, you're a big boy, you can do it. How much does it mass? Measure it in many Earth masses, again look it up. The lattice rotates at the orbital speed of matter here, most objects approach slowly and are easily deflected, others are too small to do damage or are destroyed, or deflected through the lattice. Answer to the last question is 'yes, but so what?'"

He spent a few seconds absorbing the engineering details of the construction: plans, targets, the sequence of gas collectors trapping gasses for raw material to build the various phases, fabbing planetary scale fabbers that grew the structure. Layer upon layer of development taking millennia all absorbed in the space of three breaths.

He had run out of superlatives. After a while 'wow' and 'amazing' became empty. This was far beyond human experience. In fact, it was beyond Galactic Calendar experience. That frightened him more than anything else. It meant the Vanaya were not just hiding from the other cultures, cozy in their remote worlds, they were the masters pulling strings from the shadows like the gods from some bronze age pantheon.

"Maria, why did you bring me here?"

"I suppose so you could see the nuts and bolts behind the magic. To remind you it isn't magic despite what you see. Powerstars like this aren't the only power source, we sometimes even use enclosed black holes, using something your people once called the Penrose process. Surround a fast-spinning black hole with a mirror and fire in a beam of light into a region around it called the ergosphere, where spacetime is dragged along by the rotation. You get much more energy out than you put in, extracting energy straight from the black hole."

"Whoa. Do you do that often? How do you even control such a thing?" he said. His head was spinning with possibilities, all of them nasty.

"It's tricky. It isn't practical to move a black hole, so you have tomove the shell constantly. I mean in theory you could dump excess charge into it and move it electrostatically using an opposite charge to attract it. But for a mass measured in suns, it will not work well. And then you have containment. The thing can rapidly go critical and blow up the solar system as amplified light gets fed back into the system. We use it, but it isn't as reliable as this."

Now this powerstar seemed much more inviting. Almost like a country brook and a water-powered mill. The analogy suggested all the weirdness might be messing up his thinking.

"We will leave here in a moment and once again jump to a point outside the accretion disk. You can't jump straight here. The black hole interferes too much with the jump precision, so we break up the trip. This powerstar was along the way, so I thought I would show you."

"This forest. How old is it?" He wanted to hear her say it to have a personal connection with the understanding. Facing knowledge with companions was better than learning it alone.

"Millions of years old. Over that time we control the rate of infall of matter to the event horizon otherwise there would be enormous shockwaves spreading through the disk. The station is not invulnerable, so we manage the star, keep its feeding even and steady. When the flow of inbound material becomes erratic, then the supporting forces will be turned off and the lattice, as you call it, will collapse and fall into the singularity, and all of this will disappear. Until we create a new one. Don't worry about sentience arising here, we monitor the evolution of various species and cull as necessary."

He looked at the forest with the odd sadness of leaving a new and charming friend. Knowing you would never see them again.

The sky blazed with brilliant stars of almost every color. The sight reminded him a little of the overwhelming experience of seeing the Ice Queen's Palace on Reshox. No sun was visible, yet the night sky dazzled him. There were so many stars it seemed as bright as an overcast day on Earth.

Then the suns came up. Fast. An impossible double vision of two giant arc welders in the sky.

From the horizon on his left, a brilliant blue-white light spilled onto the gray, pebbled plain they stood on, casting infinite linear double shadows. In the distance, a low mountain range reflected a fearful glare.

The light should have seared his skin. But then he should also have died in the near vacuum. He was not human anymore, or perhaps not even physical.

His eyes adjusted in seconds.

Maria stood next to him. He looked her over, noticing her clothes for the first time. Was the choice random? Could he learn anything from her preferences? The most striking thing was an electric blue scarf around her neck over a charcoal shirt and navy blue slacks. Maybe she liked blue. Shoes? Barefoot. That made no sense, but it shouldn't either. The shoes became an odd detail circling in his mind like Ouroboros the snake devouring its tail: shoes were unnecessary in their form, but clothes weren't either, or a human shape, so why the rest and not the shoes.

"Ray, are you all right?"

"It's nothing. Really nothing." Except he wanted to know.

Before he could ask, Maria explained.

"This star system has five stars with only the central binary visible at the moment. We are now in the galactic core. It is a monstrous volume of space. An enormous multitude of stars with few life-bearing planets. A harsh place for life. Life needs billions of years of relative peace to mature, and you won't get that here. Our destination is near the center."

"Hold on. Are we heading for the supermassive black hole? Sagittarius A*?" He had to pronounce it properly as 'Sagittarius A-star.' The name sounded weird. Something you rarely said aloud but only read or wrote.

"No. I said, 'near the center' not 'at the center'. Sagittarius A*, as you call it, is too unstable for construction, and all those thousands of stellar size black holes orbiting it don't help. Though there are monumental works around some of them, not all were changed you will be happy to learn. We strive to conserve them. The galactic core is central, so it is a natural region to put the Kamoi and other things in but it can also get hectic what with supernovae and matter accretion events."

What would a matter accretion event look like at this distance? He had seen many simulations and many old clips by long gone civilizations of the huge glowing frozen arcs and jets of gas and high-energy particles erupting from the core. Like a snapshot. Videos of short term eruptive events could also be found in the Calendar that happened millions of years ago, color-corrected for humans, some magnified infrared images of the events, but nothing close up, everything recorded from a remote vantage point. The center of the galaxy was too risky. At least that was what everyone thought. Those standard arguments he heard again and again: too dangerous, therefore no beacons.

Yet this was the center of operations for the people who designed the beacons. Something seemed wrong. He needed to think about it.

"Aren't there huge eruptions from the galactic core? That would make living here a problem. You said yourself life can't mature in this region."

"The eruptions don't happen all the time, and we have counter measures. We have ways to protect our planets. It also keeps nosy neighbors to a minimum."

They could protect entire planets from core events. It seemed fanciful, but so was the spectacle before him. Such power and sophistication to stand here unharmed was humbling, and a warning. He was a child mingling with the adults and had no inkling who friends and enemies were. He had to take things carefully, gingerly, one step at a time across the minefield. There were no other options apart from trusting his guide. He dismissed the train of thought, back to the here and now, whatever that meant.

"Tell me about the Kamoi, the Hive Core. Does that name mean what I think it means?" he said.

"Your people hadn't worked out the details of group consciousness and group minds, but that doesn't mean it can't be done, or done properly. Come on next stop, the Hive Core."

"Wait. If I am incognito why am I going to the center of power? Isn't this the opposite of what we want?"

"The Core is on our side. I am sure it also wants to resolve this, and it isn't as if it will be the first time it has sought the temporary assistance of outsiders."

All he heard was the word 'temporary.'

It was a garden, or a manicured open forest, similar to the one near the powerstar. Night had fallen, but there was no darkness here under the spectacle of tens of thousands of suns, some so bright they startled him. No constellations, rather fingerpainted smears of many colored intensity. Not as bright as daylight on Earth, but still humbling to face the overwhelming immensity. He didn't know where in the galactic core he was but he suspected they were quite a way from the center, otherwise the planet would roast under an x-ray glare.

Looking about the garden he recognized some plants and animals, many reminiscent of Earth, some remarkably similar though not identical. A few he remembered from the game on High Noon. The ecosystem of Corvena. Above, the sky was a glittering spectacle as if he was standing on an illuminated stage, air turbulence sparkled the starlight like a million small searchlights. He saw patterns. Not constellations but something more; greater, nearer. Many of the stars were not stars but parts of orbital structures gradually obscuring the distant stars as the planet rotated, producing a massive three-dimensional effect that made him giddy.

With an effort, he looked down at Maria, trying to break the spell.

"Didn't you say this region isn't good for life? I mean, I'd guess you could get a gamma ray suntan here." They had ways to protect themselves from radiation storms, but living here seemed like tempting fate.

"The entire planet is an artificial garden. The planet itself is also artificial. Though perhaps not in the way you imagine. Just as you can control ecosystems to supply certain services: oxygen, waste disposal, water recycling and so on. You can also re-engineer planets to have predictable tectonics that maintain atmospheres and seas. To provide long term stability for an advanced society. Planets are already in a stable state, and if there is life on them, then those conditions will probably last for geological ages. Habitats are temporary things, like a tent. Just thought I'd add that before you asked."

"What happens when there is going to be a nearby supernova? You must get a lot of them here. Oh right, you just move the planet out of the way. Bloody hell. I'm surprised you people haven't made Dyson Spheres and reworked the entire galaxy."

"Ah, naïve beliefs applied to advanced societies. Apart from the impracticality of Dyson Spheres—they don't make physical sense—you think we would do what you would do? So, did the Nexus go on a war of conquest to the stars, like their ancestors would have done? No, because the reality was different to the imagined one. A culture imagines achieving some goal, but by the time it achieves that ability they have become something else. Same for individuals too, I suppose. Think about it, if we needed to build a Dyson Sphere or a Dyson Swarm, and rip apart our worlds so we can trap all the light from our sun then it would mean our population growth would soon exceed the limits for such a sphere. It assumes we wouldn't understand that growth was the problem and not the physical limits of a planetary surface. Advanced civilizations are advanced, they don't think like you do."

She seemed angry, more than he had seen her. So human.

"Okay. I get it. I suppose it was annoying hearing all that arrogant bullshit for so long and not being able to say anything."

She smiled.

"One of the greatest inventions of your Science was to validate the answer, 'I don't know'. Speculation is fine, but too many people want to run too far with it or assume too much."

"Ha. Back in ancient Rome when a conquering hero entered the city, a person would be assigned the duty of standing next to the hero and whispering into his ear: all worldly glory passes. Perhaps there should have been a similar ritual for speculation: I do not know." He laughed some more before wondering what Vanayans would make of him. Ridiculous? But he was masquerading as a Vanayan, so with luck they would not get the opportunity.

"I remember Rome. Your culture idolized it too much. The Nexus was far better."

He would have to get a handle on 'being surprised' by her. It seemed like it would be a regular event. Sometime he must ask her about Rome. And what about Egypt? Or China? Ancient Sumer or Norte

Chico? Stonehenge? He could just look. If he wanted he could see and understand it. But he was still taking baby steps and needed that guiding hand. And knowledge gained too easily is undervalued.

One thing at a time.

The 'garden'—a large forest—richer than his memory of Earth's natural places. He had never visited the rejuvenated rainforests, perhaps they rivaled this, but he had doubts; this area seemed optimized for maximum diversity and had probably been this way for many millions of years. Long enough for legit evolution to work its wonders. If this world resembled Earth in diversity, then it would be before the rise of humans. Looking within, he saw the region extended far more than he thought. Not a forest, but a wilderness of wildernesses, including forests, deserts, rainforests, coastal regions with climates that were tropical, temperate, or arctic. He found other biomes that matched nothing he had seen on Earth or on other worlds, though he had seen them in the Calendar, but never in real life. These visions of this world whether augmented reality or telepresence or something else felt more real than his experience with neural links. He had lived in those forests and deserts, swam in those seas. The knowledge was personal.

The terrain included many trees and rivers and stretching from one end of the continent to the other. He saw a view of the geography of this world, the systems maintained with great care: seas, atmosphere, the planetary defenses, and the incredible mechanisms to move the planet if needed. The planet's artificial day/night cycle left him incredulous. His mind tingled with life like blood flowing back into an anoxic limb.

"Clarke was right. And this is well beyond 'sufficiently advanced technology,'" he whispered to himself.

Yet it was all window dressing, while beneath him was the Hive, the central core of the Vanaya within the core of the galaxy. All aptly recursive.

It was only a node.

"Why did we come here? This is just a node. Central yes, but a node. We could have accessed the Kamoi from anywhere," he said.

"The body you have at the moment isn't real, and it isn't virtual. It is a construct that is useful but limited. The Core only allows construction of new bodies after it validates the process."

"Why?" he said.

"Really? With Earth's history you must have seen when a system isn't transparent, there is always someone who will use it for nefarious ends. Vanaya may have less of your species' faults, but we still need checks and balances. The last thing you want is a trickster god. Your world loved them but never had to deal with real ones," she said.

"It must take enormous amounts of energy to move our bodies here." He was missing something. Within the selected locations they had visited, was there any need for the system to move him physically?

"That's right. The body you are occupying is not the thing you had before we left Eklus. We only transferred your mind and consciousness, as you call it. In fact then you didn't even have a physical body whereas now it is about halfway. As I said, the Dream Is All. When you get admitted to the Dream officially, you will be assigned a 'form,' a physical construct. Then it will be moved physically because it would be more difficult to rebuild. Then you can interact with the universe as a physical entity. That interaction is hard to describe, believe me once you begin to use it, it will become natural."

He was no longer surprised. Not even that she could read his thoughts.

five

The Kamoi is everywhere and nowhere, so he was told. Typical mystic mumbo jumbo, far more romantic than describing it as a distributed system. Being spread out like that can be a problem with any processing system, signal speed forces the components to be physically close to each other. Well, that is the usual argument, but then the processors Ray knew about communicated at light speed, and the Kamoi didn't have that limitation. In the cosmos the speed of light governed all determining the order of events in time. Space and time bent to it. Faster-than-light travel should cause nonsensical aberrations to the order of events, and lead to impossibilities like time travel. But the beacons didn't enable FTL 'travel,' you didn't travel the distance, it was more like the way an electron doesn't travel when it quantum tunnels across a potential barrier to appear 'instantly' on the other side like a rabbit pulled from a magician's hat. That was only an analogy, the closest thing his old self could think of that reflected what the beacons did. Now he understood now. It was nothing like that. The truth was far stranger and impossible for human minds to understand, and now he could play with dozens of those concepts and their mathematical formulations at once in his head without effort. Was he being lazy and timid holding on to his old self image? How long could he still remain himself?

His attention had drifted from the real into the endless library inside him, more wondrous than the Calendar he had known and been humbled by. Superluminal communication and the nodes that was the topic. A sharp memory intruded, of shared laughter with colleagues in friendly 'what-if' sessions about where technology was headed, the topic of faster-than-light communications would always come up and everyone would laugh. A joke in the Nexus while the Mirrish—in secret—only thought it workable between beacons.

Sometimes when talking to the Mirrish the subject of FTL would be mentioned and they would smile, their dinosaurian eyes hiding deep histories and dark secrets. The Mirrish no longer resembled an elder race, instead he imagined them wearing a tarnished crown atop a flawed head with too many memories and errant passions—so human.

Here at the Core, the worlds that made up the Kamoi spoke to each other via methods he couldn't grasp unaided. The concepts slipped from his mental fingers like shiny liquid mercury; dangerous, bright, and intangible. If he drifted back into that mental realm then, yes, they would become obvious, easy, old tech.

He had been used to the Calendar, resistant to that siren. But the inner view was far more enticing and always with him. It called to him the more he peered into within. He took a deep pointless breath and focused on what he called the Real World.

The biggest question was the one he dared not ask aloud. How could he understand yet remain human?

The world about him looked the same but so different. He didn't need to open a comms session with a Lobe or Cortex, and he didn't need to specify protocols. He was already a part of the protocol, a part of the machine. Even in the real world he was being drawn in, that after all was why they were here.

"It's all right. Just relax. The Kamoi will wait until you are ready," Maria said.

He relaxed. Why should he even be tense? That was a physiological reaction, and he didn't have a physiology, did he? At least now he could ease up and think straight. He was too busy before. So much new experience was confusing. Was that the point?

"Maria, have you been distracting me by keeping me busy?"

She smiled. It was becoming annoying and condescending.

"Great."

Well, he was here. There seemed to be only one direction. He might as well take it. He was being manipulated, a slave with an invisible collar. And slaves have no choices.

"I'm ready," he said, and even as the words were coming out of his mouth the world changed.

Color leached from the world.

Everything went gray, then black.

He was falling. His mind wrapped the disconnect from the real with the analogy of falling. It didn't help. He relaxed and let the experience happen. Random thoughts and images flitted about his vision or mind, he couldn't tell which any more.

He walked the streets of cities long turned to dust in forms alien and familiar at the same time.

Saw spires rising greater than the height of mountain ranges all suspended in space with a dazzle of stars reflected on the structures, making them look slick with water.

Great arcing glows of contained plasma jets harnessed for an unspoken purpose.

Starships the size of cities before the era of jump technology.

A million million scenes of families and friendships all faded almost to oblivion.

Lives without count.

He understood them all for an eternal moment. Then they were gone and so was his understanding. Just a fading echo. Was it over? What did it mean?

There was more.

Like a virtual reality movie, a story unfolded before him. He was part of it, yet apart. It seemed to reach into the true source of his being so much he feared if he mis-stepped, he would be lost and never return.

But it was so hard to stay himself.

It was more than just a story he had been told or remembered. He had also lived this. Deep down he prided himself as the intrepid adventurer finding a cracked, yellowed scroll and being the first to read it in thousands of years. It fitted like a key into the lock of his life; Atlanta, Pavarr, High Noon. The Kamoi knew him so well.

There was a town by the sea. He knew it.

Jau and Aukee lived in the town of Cejine in the last days of the Chedzee Ascendancy, a nation on the western shores of the northern continent of Liya of the world later named Corvena. The corvi, the people of Corvena, averaged smaller than humans and often covered with a fine almost invisible down that gave them a false gentle look. Each of them sported a stunning mane of feather-hair made of thin hair-like ribbons often with spectacular colors seen on few sentient species. Jau sported black and red hair. Watching him walk was like seeing the last embers of a midnight fire being stoked. As for Aukee, more about that later.

Aukee's birthday was in five days and Jau wanted to buy her something special. So he attacked the problem in the single minded way many adolescent males would for someone they loved but feared to tell.

He walked to his uncle Nais, a jeweler in the small market near the docks. Cejine was a small seaside town so Jau never felt overwhelmed or daunted strolling through the place. He knew he should have some guilt; he had returned home now that his studies had finished. Loafing with no plausible excuse not to do something serious with his life.

"Jau!" His uncle's voice carried across the market murmur.

Jau started as if a snarling predator had just rounded the corner. He sprinted over to Nais's stall, not because of his great affection for his aging uncle, though there was that, the larger issue was Nais had no problem discussing Jau's faults at full voice.

"I'm here uncle. I know what you will say…"

"When are you going to start up a stall or work for me? Eh? Today, you said? Or perhaps I misheard."

Jau would have blushed if his biology allowed it. Instead he gave his usual hangdog look hoping for a favor.

"I want to get a present for Aukee. I thought maybe you could make something. I have a little money," he said to his uncle.

Nais looked at him. He loved Jau like the son he never had and envied his brother for the family the gods had gifted him—especially for Jau. He wanted to teach Jau his trade and perhaps he could take over his shop one day. A legacy for him, but the youngster was too unfocused outside his studies. Aukee would be good for him, 'too good' many had said. Nais thought all he needed was to believe in himself. An idea occurred to him.

"Do you think a little trinket is worthy of Aukee? She's a girl like no other. I have a better idea."

Jau shifted nervously running his hand through his ribbony hair. He didn't like it when his uncle got creative.

"Do you know the Misty Rocks?"

Rhetorical question. Everyone knew it, a known hazard to all ships entering or approaching the port. Often shrouded by mist the low rocks had sunk many a vessel. No one sailed there, officially.

Nais didn't wait for a reply.

"The Rocks are a hazard? Yes, for large vessels, but not for small fishing boats. They are shallow draft. Not a problem in a mild sea. They say the Rocks are all that remain of an ancient temple which foundered during the Sea Change. It is also said if you are daring enough you can find jeweled offerings. Or if you aren't so brave there are plenty of shellfish, they say contain pearls. Go to the Misty Rocks in your skiff and get me a jewel or pearl or something, even a piece of shell. Prove to me and her you can do something wonderful. Or," he paused for the habitual dramatic effect, "you can come and work for me and make a piece for her yourself. How about that? Please Aukee and learn a skill at the same time."

Nais thought that presenting a daunting task next to a merely boring act like working with him would motivate the lad to front up and learn a trade. Maybe he would one day be a scholar and philosopher as his teachers had thought, but philosophy wouldn't feed a family, not in this coastal village. The trouble with Nais's logic was that on the topic of Aukee, Jau was not logical and he decided to do the opposite.

Next day the sea was flat with a rippling of waves, as if the sea shivered. A useful breeze on a flat sea—ideal. He set out in his little boat, raising the single sail and set course for the Misty Rocks.

Everyone knew The Rocks, but for most people they were to be avoided. Most boats hugged the shore, coming into the harbor to get as far from the almost invisible danger. Youngsters, when they first learned to sail often took a forbidden trip out to the Rocks, would touch them then rush back with a piece of seaweed or shell. Only the brave did it. He remembered stories about the spirits of the dead that haunt the area, discouraging most. Aukee had gone to the rocks when she first learned to sail. She was clever, brave and strong, and more daring than anyone cared for, often taking crazy risks. She had mellowed in the passing years and had fallen for hapless Jau; an issue of perennial mystery to the local gossips. Many wondered what she saw in him, but Aukee would reply with characteristic fierceness that they must be blind. His good points were crystal clear to her, though no one else saw it, including Jau.

The rising and setting swell would hide and reveal the town in turn when he looked back. The sight teased his fears.

He reached the Rocks. Some seemed hand carved. He couldn't see anything of value. He looked for shells or loose rocks or jewel encrusted stone; nothing, it was bare. He threw a lasso over the central mount, which was only a meter high, the entire rocky outcrop being only two meters across. The skiff rocked with a hollow sound against the lone pinnacle. Now, having secured the skiff, it was time to get serious.

"I can't go back empty handed. I must get something for Aukee," he said aloud.

He looked over the side of the boat to shapes far below. The water was rippling cyan glass today.

"There's nothing else to do. Have to do it." He barely knew what he said as he focused on the play of light below.

He plunged into the water with a lungful of air.

The Rocks were a building, more of a square tower than a temple. Like everyone in his town, his eyesight underwater was as good as in the air. He swam down along the side of the building at arm's length, past seaweed windows and growth encrusted statues. Shafts of light around him made it look like he was descending into a sacred place as he passed between vast colonnades of shifting light. No jewels encrusting the rock, but there were shellfish. He grabbed at one but it would not budge. Using his short knife, he dislodged it. He started counting the shells as he pocketed them. One, two... his lungs screamed at him. A third one went into his pants pocket with the others with trembling fingers. He pushed for the silhouetted skiff above with a fierce desperation and slumped into the boat, gulping deep breaths while he opened the shellfish. But there was nothing except the tasty meat. A brief distraction. He could take the shell back, knowing it was all that was necessary by his Uncle's rules, but it didn't reflect his feelings for Aukee. He had to give it another try.

This time he took care. He calmed his mind the way the village elders had taught him, taking several lungfuls of air, waiting for the buzz of hyperventilation to make sure there was enough oxygen in his bloodstream, then he dived. He couldn't do this a third time, he would not have the endurance, so he pushed himself to go deeper beyond the obvious places. He passed tufts of greenish weed and sank further into the darkness. The mounting pressure squeezed his head, wanting to compress the air-filled spaces in his skull. Then, without warning, the bottom appeared. Pale blue with dark seaweed clumps growing over fallen masonry, all color except blue drained from the scene. Here and there were some beautiful life-sized statues of people in strange clothes; untouched by corrosion or living things. He couldn't waste time. In moments he found a bunch of large shells the size of the palm of his hand. He pried a few off the rock with shaking hands.

Something out of the corner of his eye. There circling almost at the limit of the visible was a large mikra, a predator like a cross between an eel and a shark, three times longer than he was high. It was a monster. Despite his preparations, his lungs screamed for air now. As he tried to ignore his lungs and fear, with slow care he moved to the opposite side of the building. Would he make it? Panic was almost on him. He swam for the surface, lungs screaming, repeating his mantra so that fear and desperation didn't make him panic. He fixed his gaze on the rippling light at the end of that dark watery tunnel. Either the mikra or drowning would get him, or with luck if he kept calm he would live.

Focus. Stay calm. Steady strokes. He thought, barely able to control the urge to breathe.

Then he surfaced. The air exploded out of his lungs and inhaling as if it was the only thing that had ever mattered in his life. Even the daylight seemed dim in his anoxia.

Shaking. Afraid blood-soaked teeth would clamp on his legs any moment. He hauled himself onto the boat, weak and desperate for air.

There he lay, gasping and shaking unable to move. He could not go back down again—it wasn't a question of bravery. Whatever he had would have to do.

After he got back, he waited most of the day so he could recover. Back home he saw his face in a mirror and was thankful his parents were out. He looked like he had fought the mikra and lost. Later down the street at the market, Nais saw him. Did he notice his unusual lethargy? He didn't care what anyone saw. He wanted to sleep for a whole day, but first, there was the matter with his uncle.

Nais made no calls to him, rather he zeroed in with a concentrated gaze. He met the gaze without compromise as he walked to within an arm's length of his uncle.

"Here. Can you make this into something?" he said, handing over a large blue pearl.

His uncle's face froze looking at the jewel placed into his hand. Jau was sure he had never seen him like this before.

"Jau, you—you really went out there? I didn't mean for..." Nais said flustered. "What did you see?"

"That understanding is only for those who do it?" He was too tired to bother translating his thoughts into everyday language. "If I said I saw carved rock, seaweed, and shellfish you wouldn't understand. Can you make something for my Aukee?"

"Yes, yes. I'm proud of you, my boy. I only wanted you to get moving and work with me. Never mind, though your father will have words with me when he finds out."

Jau put his hand on his uncle's shoulder, "I don't think we need to tell my parents about this. Do we?"

Nais laughed. "I have an unfinished ring that this will match quite nicely. Give me two days."

When it came time to present the ring to Aukee. She was standing by the sea, near to the market. The small waves lapping around her bare feet.

Corvi hair is like thin ribbons a few millimeters wide, often falling down below the shoulders. It is reminiscent of feathers and often has iridescent colors of great beauty. Aukee had blue iridescent hair to below her shoulders, swept back like a mane it transfixed Jau. Her face was more typical: cat like ears with small tufts of fur at the tips; the line of hair from the ears sweeping down to meet the eyebrows; and a fine, almost invisible down gave her face a softness others never saw.

He said nothing, approaching her. Willing his hearts to slow down. Her presence always dazzled him and though they had grown up together, his passion had only intensified over the years. With a slight nervous tremor in his hand, he held out the ring to her without saying a word.

She took the ring and blushed as the females of her kind did when they experienced intense emotion.

Without a word but with exaggerated slowness, she picked up the ring and placed it on the finger of eternity. The message was clear. She leapt forward and hugged him so hard it was almost hard to breathe. She eased back still holding his arms.

"Where did you get it, Jau?"

"My uncle said he would make a ring if I got something from the Misty Rocks. See, it's blue just like your hair."

"There's nothing at the Rocks, Jau, not anymore. Wait, did you dive? Don't tell me you dived in that place. How deep? For this, this must have come from the bottom. Do you understand how dangerous it is?"

She stepped forward and hugged him again, holding him close. It seemed like time had stopped.

Almost a year later they were betrothed.

They walked along the same sandy beach. It was a Spring morning just before midday and he had closed his stall early for lunch. Just as well Uncle Nais had gone to visit Jau's aunt in the mountains, otherwise he would never have gotten away with it. Everything seemed so right and perfect. Then he saw the imperfection, the sign of an end to many things. Ships in a line coming over the horizon, not fishing boats but the sails and form of warcraft.

They ran back up to the market. Yelling warnings and pointing. Breathless. The sight of fear in Aukee's face by itself caused some to flee. It took no convincing for the rest. The news from far places had been desperate in recent weeks and now those bottled fears poured into their peaceful town.

Aukee stood in the middle of the deserted market, frantic and taking rapid breaths, agony on her face. "We must defend the town. I need my bow and sword," she said. The voice of a soldier being overrun, wanting to die with a sword in her hand.

"Are you crazy? You'll die for nothing. Quick, follow me," said Jau. Trying hard to think of what to do. But the solution turned out to be obvious. Flee to the Misty Rocks where the big ships would never go.

They ran to his skiff and pushed off. At the other end of the beach, the first soldiers of the invaders waded ashore from their beached vessels. They ignored the tiny lone boat sailing seawards almost out of bowshot. A waste of arrows.

The wind ran out as they reached the Rocks. The multiple jagged points like teeth of a rabid animal waiting to rip out a hull. The main pinnacle stood clear a meter higher than when he last saw it. More of the submerged building was above water. It would hide them from the invaders.

"Did they pick low tide so they could see the Rocks?" Aukee said.

Jau didn't answer. Even through the thickening mist and smoke a spreading red glow of the burning town reappeared with the ocean swell, and the endless screams blended into a pulsing wall of distress.

They both thought of family but couldn't say their fears out loud.

Soon the terrible sounds faded away. Only the sounds of the sea and noises from the warships in the distance on the other side of the rocks.

They ate shellfish after Jau dived. Hunger made it seem like a feast.

Next morning not a single warship remained. They had gone. There was only the sound of the sea now, but they waited anyway.

After two days, weathering the cold each night under the uncaring light of the Three Clusters, they had had enough. They headed back rather than succumb to thirst or exposure.

On the beach, only a few marks in the sand remained of the ships. The town was black, smoking, and empty. Jau had never experienced such complete silence. There were bodies everywhere through the streets of the small town. A terrible stench of smoke and burnt or rotting meat threatening to choke him as they entered the market. Some of the dead they recognized, but most they could not identify at all. Everyone was dead including their parents, others fled, he hoped, which was a good idea. Survival in the end trumped grief.

His mind was a flurry of desperate thoughts.

"We have to go, there's nothing here now. Those ships are likely traveling further down the coast towards Melray. My aunt has a small farm in the mountains. They would welcome family willing to help tend the fields," he said.

They didn't leave that day. There was too much grief. Family and friends and a way of life turned to dust. They couldn't bury their family in time, so they gathered them together onto a funeral pyre and set it alight. They slept that night in fits between tears in an untouched hut at the edge of the village. In the morning they left never to return.

The journey up to the small mountain farm and the time they spent there is the basis of many stories. There in their little hut Jau would come to write his Annals of Change, a philosophical treatise that would in time form the philosophical foundations of the global Mavanayan Union, and later still, would underpin the Vanaya culture.

A faint voice spoke. Beautiful, but somehow not human. It was neither male nor female.

"It is said while they were waiting on the Holy Rocks, Jau collected many more but smaller blue pearls. He fashioned them into a necklace and presented it to Aukee. The Core Truths he discussed in the Annals are often referred to as the String of Pearls, but the first and greatest among them is the first one, Aukee's Pearl, the one made into a ring. It represents love and compassion, the start of the Path to Understanding."

He stood in the Garden, the fading dream now burned into his memory. His skin tingled, as if sea salt still stung his dry and cracking skin, his eyes and nose still smarting from the acrid but oddly sweet smell of old burnt wood from smoldering homes and the stench of death. He breathed out as if to expel the odor and cleanse himself, and if lucky perhaps exhale the pain and memory.

Now he was different.

He took in a breath by instinct while still shaking and at last a slow calm and ease settled on him. He felt the weight of his body on the soles of his feet. The slight breeze against the hairs of his bare arms. He was real.

But not his old self. Now he was physical and full of sensations while his body craved a moment of joy. There was a sour tinge, fleeting, as he sensed something else at the limits of his inner sight, slippery like an eel, it eluded him.

"From what I see the Kamoi approves of you." She smiled, trying to encourage him without success.

"I had a—vision. Is that normal?" he said with effort fighting back the traces of memory.

"Nothing about the Hive Core is normal. What was it about?"

"You know the Story of Jau and Aukee?"

She stopped for a moment as she searched memories long since buried away in some dark, guarded vault of her mind. A grimace of pain, passed across her face, then quickly, or urgently, replaced by a smile.

"Odd. Why would the Kamoi show you something from ancient Corvena? Never mind, now on with my task..."

"No. I mean first, I think I got a clue or something. In the last part of the memory a voice spoke. Here listen," he said.

Without knowing how, he touched Maria's mind. It was like a still pool with pretty lotus flowers scattered on the surface, their large green calming leaves and bright blossoms inviting a closer look, but as you approached, you saw the pool's depths descended to a bottomless abyss, unknowable, and frightening. He took a deep breath then grabbed—in some way—the memory and gave it to her, as if he was passing a flower.

"I don't understand," she said.

"It seems to contain a clue or something. It seems a bit strange."

"A clue all right. Odd, it's like an answer to a question never asked. There are myths that after Jau and Aukee died, the gods placed their spirits and ideals among the stars. The first being Aukee's Pearl, which leads on to the String of Pearls. The necklace. There is no known set of objects called the String of Pearls, well there are many that came long after the legend but none match the era of the story so no one knows what it means apart from being symbolic. The String of Pearls doesn't exist is the main conclusion. But Aukee's

Pearl is real, or something has the name from those times."

He scratched his chin.

"Ranei..."

"Could you call me Maria? I got to like it on Neti."

He saw her differently now and would recognize her anywhere in whatever form or name she chose. Names no longer mattered to him.

"Right. Sorry, I forgot. Maria, is this a clue to who or what destroyed the Nexus? It can't be random. Is Aukee's Pearl a star, or perhaps a planet?"

Why was he asking her? He could find this out for himself. Which he did.

"What, a globular cluster? That's crazy. How many stars are in Aukee's Pearl? Millions. Well, I guess the clue is nonsense. I thought it must have meant something but apparently not."

Maria ignored him as she stared at the ground distracted, trying to make sense of it all. She talked, but as if she was talking to someone else.

"I wouldn't dismiss it. Coherent visions for people in your situation are rare."

"What situation?"

She didn't answer, so he continued. "This is important so I think we should pursue it. Just maybe the Kamoi is trying to help you out, Maria."

"Doubtful but it appears the Core wants you to do something," she said.

"I thought our priority was to find out about the Dawn Ships?"

She ignored his question.

"You seem to have been recruited into the Game, temporarily. Strange, it's weird, why pick an outsider? A novice? Perhaps we will find out at Aukee's Pearl. Lead the way."

'Lead the way.' Those were her words. He didn't know where the place was or how to jump, or 'vip' as they called it. Surely, they didn't call it that, it must be a translation into his vocal cords. Common Standard conversion no doubt straight out of the Galactic Calendar. That reminded him.

"The Galactic Calendar. That's your work isn't it? The Vanaya."

"Certainly is. There are several levels with only the highest level being uncensored, well almost."

"The Mirrish thought they were custodians of the Calendar," he said, remembering Jayarn's confidence.

"There's always someone advanced and arrogant enough to think they own the Calendar. They don't but we let them believe it."

"Why do you censor the Calendar? Removing all those tech references. You could help so many people."

"Allow them access to technologies much more advanced than their understanding? How do you imagine it will work out? It's a recipe for disaster. Unless they sort themselves out, sentients go to space with the same instincts that allowed them to triumph over their rivals with a club in hand. Not good at all. It's also why we hobble the jump system."

"What do you mean, 'hobble'?"

"Jumps are dangerous because there is unavoidable and fundamental damage to jump engines. It can destroy ships at random, it is unpredictable, and it means you have to repair your engine before you can use it for another jump. We built the limitation into the design. It doesn't apply to us so we can make jumps in safety but for other civilizations it restricts their growth, slows them down, prevents easy empires that spread misery and ruin," she said with an angelic smile.

The universe went a shade or two darker. No one, as far as he knew, had ever suggested this.

"You know just what to say to make me feel more depressed. It sounds like you cultivate the galaxy the way you cultivate this planet, just a pretty garden."

She tilted her head to the right, her long black hair falling down as far as her upper right arm. Her gaze was steady and annoyed.

"Rubbish. Civilization is rare and fragile. Ecosystems can withstand enormous disasters, they've evolved for hundreds of millions of years, but civilizations are new and shaky. They often destroy themselves because of their own blindness. They are a rare and temperamental plant. We try to give them a decent chance."

"Have any civilizations ever reached a level where they can challenge you?" he said.

"No. If they did, we would enter into negotiations to unite with them. There are protocols, but we have never used them."

"Could that have anything to do with your manipulation of the jump system confusing any experiments they do on it?"

She smiled. "Well done. Yes, casual experimentation will send them down the wrong theoretical track, but if they are really smart, they won't trust it and will instead go back to basics. Fundamental research, it's what makes civilization advance. Trust it, human," she laughed.

He tried to find another question.

He was hedging and procrastinating, putting off doing the impossible. She said he could teleport—he had no idea how to do such a thing—he must tell her.

"Are you going to jump or not? Don't be chicken, Ray."

She was reading his mind again.

"I still don't see the relevance of this to our actual mission."

But there was only one way to find out.

He looked inside and just imagined the act of jumping to Aukee's Pearl. In his mind he saw the destination: a mass of details, co-ordinates, and a stream of understanding that translated it all. He reached out and a silver blue shimmer appeared before him—a path to Aukee's Pearl, to the Default Origin in the cluster. Without hesitation he stepped forward into the thin rippling light.

six

They stood on a small world, or a vast machine. The 'ground' was an etched silvery maze flowing with energies he sensed but couldn't see. At various distant places on the metallic plain emerged spires and shapes like small buildings. He knew somehow they were not living spaces. This worldlet they stood on, an asteroid-sized body, was a machine. Above, the sky blazed with more stars than he had ever seen at once, even in the core where the glare obscured most. Once his people had called deep space The Dark, but being here gave the lie to that, for now. Nowhere did he find a nearby star he could pretend to call a 'sun' yet the sky here would never be dark while the etched mirror plain about him sparkled with the reflected light of many tens of thousands of stars.

"Jump system infrastructure," Maria said from behind him, unaffected by the spectacle, "there are many such structures in the inner galactic halo used to fine tune the jumps within the galaxy. Turn around and look. We are at the Default Origin for this cluster."

He turned to face a huge glowing deformed disk, stretching from below the horizon up to his right, almost to the zenith, fuzzy-bright near the center, like a strong light through a thick fog. It looked like a flat glowing creature gently undulating as it swam through space. The galaxy is not a standard spiral galaxy, it has been perturbed, and now the dance of gravity has left it slightly warped by some past encounter. Across the center of the disk a barred structure, a twirling glowing barbell caught in an eye-blink complete with motion blur. The center of the galaxy. He had been there moments ago. Moments. Now he was in a realm where moments and ages blurred into one.

"There are over 150 globular clusters in the galactic halo. How many haves this kind of technology?" he said.

"Not all of them. A few. I forget the details. No one comes out here there's nothing to see or do. The low metallicity means there are few planets that can develop life and civilization."

By 'low metallicity' she meant astrophysical 'metals'; any element beyond hydrogen and helium. The vast majority of the universe is hydrogen and helium, formed soon after the Big Bang, and here it was still the case. Elsewhere, places he knew, the solar furnaces of supernovae and neutron star collisions had fertilized the galaxy with the blood and bone of stars so planets could be born. Here there would be few conventional solar systems with ordinary planets made up of ordinary rocks—here the gas giants ruled. But nothing is ever clear cut in the real universe.

"There are millions of stars here. Don't tell me there haven't been cycles of supernovae and planetary accretion?" he said.

"Not enough to count. Imagine all the stars in the galaxy, now, how many have suitable planets in the habitable zone? How many do you think would qualify here?"

"Okay, point taken."

He took a step forward. No crunch sounded from his boots, no atmosphere, which didn't surprise him, but then he heard something that did. An unfamiliar voice from behind.

"Hello, Ray, Emari. I'm joining your party."

He wasn't there before and now he was.

A human male, graying dark hair, Eurasian features, average height, dressed in dark blue slacks, a brown sports coat, and a cream shirt open at the collar. There he stood, surrounded by a halo of stars.

Something about the stranger's dress style was at once familiar and troubling.

"Who are you?" Ray asked, trying to hide an irrational dislike.

Maria said nothing, and Ray sensed she knew who this was.

"I have been sent by the Kamoi to act as an observer in this—search—of yours. Surely, you recognize me, Raymond. You've seen me every day in the mirror."

"How can that be? Why? Who the fuck are you, really?"

"I am Raymond Tans, a somewhat older incarnation though. I'm presuming the gray hair makes me more distinguished, don't you think? Maybe I'll go with that delusion, everyone here has their delusion. Well, that can be mine."

"Ray," Maria said, "I mean young Ray, he isn't just an older you. He is different but I can't tell how."

"Hello, Ranei," the stranger said.

"Maria."

The older man shrugged and smiled.

"We have to travel together, I am afraid. Now I'll make it much simpler. Ray, you can call me Ramon. It's a variant of Raymond. Or if you want to follow your ancient superstitions, you can call me Amon or Aamon, also variations of Raymond. One is a god, the other is a demon. I would suggest you think of me as a mere observer for the Kamoi."

Ray relaxed, staring the newcomer in the eyes. He stared back, both trying not to blink as if in some juvenile game played by brothers. Ray spoke first.

"Well, this doesn't cast an ominous shadow over every-fucking-thing."

He felt a flush of anger.

"Maria. Who is he? The truth. No bloody evasiveness."

The anger rose like an oncoming storm in him now as he struggled to understand, it almost eclipsed the realization that somehow he now had the physiology for it. He stopped for a moment and tried to be honest with himself: what was the fundamental issue? At the heart of his fury was a sense of violation.

Violated in a way he couldn't express, cheapened by having become a duplicate. Halved in value by default and without permission. He had become an extra in his own life.

Ramon looked like him, but there was no friendliness on that face.

Ramon walked past them confident and unaffected by their shock. He stared for a few seconds at the galaxy spread out across the sky, then turned to them.

"These worlds are ancient. They were setup to make jumps easy and safe for us. The plebs don't even know they exist. Even if they did they couldn't reach them, the beacons don't allow jumps out here, they develop disastrous errors. What do you think of that, Ray? A flagrant suppression of exploration. Keeping the low born in check. Does it sound oppressive to you?"

It was eerie replying to himself, someone who had the same or similar thought processes, weaknesses, and dreams. Or maybe some of those dreams were broken. Perhaps this usurper's greatest threat was poisoning his essential hopes.

"I don't know enough to judge. All societies place limits on their citizens and those outside. I can't, or couldn't, just jump to Mirr and walk its streets. I would have to apply for permission, and they could throw me out for whatever reason. If I didn't know their reasoning … whatever, you know what I'm talking about. I can't judge until I have more data," he said.

Ramon smiled and nodded. All his actions and mannerisms radiated a cynicism that seemed to belie his words.

Maria took a step forward. There was a gentle blue glistening all over her body. Ray guessed this was a none too subtle message: I am the real deal, both of you are interlopers here at my sufferance. Thus the goddess intimated and intimidated.

"Who sent you? Don't say the Kamoi because they would have told me or Ray during his induction. You must represent a faction, so, which faction do you represent?"

"Are you sure the Core would tell you? I represent those who wish the Game to continue without turmoil. To pursue the furthering civilization. It is what we all want." Ramon smiled.

"Bullshit. Tell me," Maria said. And something changed, not in the non-existent air but there was the presence of raw power that part of him compared to sitting too close to a roaring campfire.

Ramon hesitated.

"Sure. The Kamoi majority has sent young Skywalker here on a quest. So romantic. Those of us concerned with important issues find it dangerous and unsupervised. The Core allowed me to come here as a check against unethical actions. Who knows what is out here? You have probably all forgotten it."

Maria showed a faint sneer. "Who knows what is out here? I wonder if some know more than others. Perhaps there is something you are hiding."

This beating about the bush was too much for Ray. He had his own concerns.

"What about me? I'm here for a very particular reason. The destruction of the Nexus by Dawn Ships. Are you hiding something from me because of a crime committed against my people?" Yelling at both felt odd. Was he like a child complaining in a fight between two adults? He was sure more was going on than he could see.

Ramon looked at him then at Maria then gave a convincing laugh despite the vacuum.

In his mind Ray branded the interloper as Aamon—the demon. No decent human would dismiss the destruction of Earth civilization as a joke. He would not, could not, do it at any age. That led to a few questions. What was the real reason for Ramon being here? And, why subvert his identity? Too little data. He would have to wait. He took a calming breath of nothing.

"Maria, where to next?" he said.

"Your choice. You are leading this search." She said.

"By all means, continue," Ramon said with a wicked smile, "and how do you think being way out here is helping you to answer your questions?"

"The Kamoi knows why I am back and it sent me here. I don't think it is a coincidence. There are no other leads," Ray said.

"Don't be so sure," Ramon said looking at Maria.

Where to next? He didn't know.

He looked within. No matter how hard he searched there was no way back. The chill of approaching panic seeped into him. He calmed himself. This train he was on seemed to have only one track and one direction. He would have to pursue the course and hope, or swallow what little pride he had left and ask Maria to take him back.

Even forward was uncertain.

"I have no idea. Just let me be for a moment."

He turned from them and walked towards the horizon and the spectacle of an unfurled galaxy.

The ground underneath crunched. He sensed the vibrations through his feet but otherwise this place was silent. Perhaps that was what he had to do with these clues feel for them rather than listen for obvious instructions. The message came in the form of a dream; if he returned to that state then maybe more of the path would become clear. Perhaps the way backas well.

He closed his eyes but his mind was ablaze with sights and thoughts. The infinite mirror maze he had experienced before now overflowed with detail, images, and ideas. Anywhere he looked was a wonder of revelation and insight. He calmed himself and found a skill, readily available, to resist this intoxication. Maria was now a few steps behind him. He ignored her and eased the internal clamor some more. The motion-blurred universe inside his head slowed and resolved into a higher dimensional panorama.

Not only did he find memory here but many new levels of understanding and knowledge. Any problem he examined, something within himself would tackle it, break it up in a divide-and-conquer strategy, apply strange techniques or even turn it into a mathematical model. The experience was intoxicating, a cocaine of the intellect, a true siren but more by design than good fortune he also had the ability to look away from it.

A novel idea occurred to him, perhaps the problem with Medusa was not that she was ugly but the opposite, a beauty so powerful the victim became transfixed by their own desire. His own civilization met its Medusa, the neural links, and it froze his culture in its tracks. But he could avert that gaze and see beyond that festival of ideas and parade of knowledge.

And past all of it he beheld a calm beach with a spring breeze and lapping waves.

Here at last at the center of the cyclone.

A golden light from the deepening sunset gave the sand a copper burnish. In front of him standing on the beach was Aukee. He saw her clearly now: blue hair, webbed hands, pale yellow skin, her pointed ears with tufts of hair extending off them, the ears themselves forming a line to the graceful sweep of her eyebrows. And all framed by a multitude of blues from her cascading hair. She was beautiful. Without knowing how, he knew she was smiling at him and offering her closed left hand. She opened her hand. Cupped like an egg in a soft pale nest was a large blue pearl. He reached for it and touched it.

Another vision fell upon him but this was no dream. It was gritty and real. He saw but could not act.

Raw emotion engulfed him but he was mute, and one of those emotions was surprise.

Alaska, Earth, 2047

They got out of Anchorage while the city still burned around them. A close call. They stole three trucks from the army base, though could you call it stealing when there was no longer an army to requisition from? No army, only looters, fleeing refugees, bandits, and outnumbered government militia. The team headed north to Fairbanks.

In the back of each truck sat a next generation nano-fabrication unit.

They left Seattle a few days before; it was too unstable, and it had been a battle just getting to the docks to get out. They stole the fabbers from a shipment earmarked for Gaia Lotus. The others in the team wanted to burn the rest of the units and prevent them from going to such a shadowy organization. Joseph Fulbright argued against it. Rennae backed her husband's decision and won the argument. They made their escape, leaving everything behind intact. None of them could say whether the fabbers would end up with Gaia Lotus or be stripped by the mob.

She had met Joseph after he had come out of the marines while finishing up a fast-tracked engineering degree. He showed unusual promise. An unstable world made them delay children, and by 'world' they meant every street in every town in the world. Nowhere was safe, and the world seemed to be coming apart.

Nations no longer fought nations, they fought themselves in uncounted civil wars.

Now seventy kilometers north of Anchorage, with the wounds still raw, the drive became a soothing balm. They had lost two friends in the city's craziness.

"Late spring looks amazing here," Joseph said. His hands gripping the steering wheel of the medium-sized army truck.

"Everyone back there okay?" He shouted. Some muffled, "We're good"s from behind his head reassured him. He knew they were fine, still he needed to reassure them. Rennae was riding shotgun, or M-Xi, to be pedantic. The gun the troops called a 'maxi'. Joseph had taught her how to use it and care for it, the ten-minute version. As usual, she understood immediately.

"It's so pretty," she said. "So much beauty. Hold on, what was…" Bang. Something hit the truck. Then bang, bang. The sounds of high velocity projectiles impacting metal.

"Contact!" Rennae yelled.

The shots came from a weathered structure to the east. An old two story building several hundred meters away, the concrete exterior now stained by weather and dead vegetation here and there, creating its own camouflage.

She lowered the cracked but still functional window enough to point her weapon at the movement she had seen up the hill. She let off half a dozen rounds.

"Got 'em. Yay for some smart bullets," she said.

The bullets could change course, adjusting for wind. That the incoming rounds had hit random parts of the truck meant the attackers likely used old weapons or were maybe lousy shots. She didn't want to test those possibilities, so she raised the window; it might not be ideal, but she appreciated the bullet 'resistant' glass, though it now sported new dense spider web patterns.

"Crap. Look." Rennae turned to see what Joseph was talking about. Ahead, several burnt-out vehicles blocked them. Scattered around the cars they saw at least three bloated corpses spread eagled with their pockets turned out.

"Joseph, look between the cars. Some wire or cable, heavy duty too. Part of a trap and close to whoever is taking potshots at us."

"Well, I can nudge the cars out of the way, but that cable is another matter. Have we got anything to blast or cut through it?" he said.

She thumped the headboard behind them three times. A small window opened and a dark face appeared.

"Dave, do we still have those portable oxy-cutters?"

Dave smiled. "Of course. You know I am Mister Resourceful. There's no way I will leave something so useful behind."

Joseph laughed. Dave, the least practical of the lot, a brilliant theoretician but not the kind to fix a tap. Of all the people in the team, he was the only one who matched any stereotype. He was the person voted most likely to one day utter the phrase, "It's alive!"

The smallest cutter would just fit through the window.

"Okay, got it. Rennae you stay here and be lookout. I will cut that cable."

"I'll come with you," she said.

"No. Rennae, that's an order. I am the leader of this team, so bow to my field experience, please. You will be safer in here and still be able to defend me," he said.

"You're exposed out there!"

"I'll hide behind the car wrecks while I cut. It'll work. Trust me," he said.

She didn't like it but it made more sense and so the only aid she could give was to lower the window enough to poke her gun out and scour the countryside. With luck, it would distract attention from Joseph.

He opened the door and ran to the gap between the two cars where the half-rusted cable was visible. He started the cutter and sparks flew like daytime fireworks.

Sudden puffs of dust rose from the road. Bullet ricochets. She looked to the nearby forest and again the distant building was in sight. She lifted her gun, waiting as it tried to locate the source by analyzing differences between successive images of the countryside. It located the rifle shots from the small puffs of smoke and muzzle flash. Something moved in one window. Another jarring bang as a bullet hit the glass her gun was resting on. Her window now sported a new fist-sized snowflake pattern close to her head. The gun now knew the target location and zoomed in. She set the gun on auto-fire for the window. A rifle barrel appeared, but the gun knew it was not a valid target. There were several more puffs of smoke, then the shooter came into view, preparing for another shot. The gun barked instantly like an angry dog. Then a splatter as his head exploded.

She waited another ten seconds while leaving the gun on auto fire. If so much as a bird landed on that window sill, then—boom—no bird. The gun saw nothing.

"We got him, Joseph. I don't think there are any more." No reply. She looked through the front windscreen and saw Joseph lying on the road, blood pooling under him.

She thumped the headboard.

"Dave! Dave! Joseph's been shot. Help me."

"Joseph, don't worry, we're heading north again. You'll be okay. Do you hear me?"

He didn't respond, but she could hear little above the road noise.

The journey was a nightmare. Joseph was in a serious condition and the back of the truck had poor lighting with jarring from occasional potholes in the road. They gave up using the auto-drive function and now drove in manual mode, it was annoying and slow but the neural network in the truck had never trained for this. At least they had a stretcher to use in the limited space what with the rest of the van being taken up by the massive fabber.

He was still unconscious. His white t-shirt and jeans matted with congealed blood. She wiped his forehead with her hand. Her dark brown skin so stark against his pale features. With great tenderness she pushed back the blood-matted hair, its once vibrant light brown now somehow dulled. His life flowing out as she watched. She pulled back her long black hair bent down and gave him a gentle kiss on the forehead.

She took a deep breath and checked the field bandages and strapped on a diagnostic armband that would report his condition. His vitals were serious but stable. When they got to somewhere safe, she would get Aaron from the third truck, his medical training might be rusty but he was the best in the team. Aaron had stabilized Joseph at the roadblock, they cut through the cables stretched across the road, and pushed through continuing north. That seemed like it had happened ages ago but it was only half an hour before.

The vehicle revs dropped; hard as it was to hear the hybrid engine over the road noise she was sure of it. The vehicle came to a stop. A voice from the front of the vehicle.

"Rennae, there's a bridge with a blockade. It's manned. Not sure about these guys. They aren't shooting, that's a positive I guess," Dave said.

"Keep your head down. I'll have a talk to them," she said.

She opened the rear door. It swung away from her with ease, not heavy even though the entire vehicle was bulletproof for most small caliber weapons. The door was a thin layer of tough metal over kevlar. She distracted herself with the trivia while waiting for her subconscious to think of a convincing story. Outside, the light was brilliant from an infinite blue above her. The air was brisk. How could anything be wrong on such a day? Here the warming of the planet almost seemed irrelevant unless you lived or worked on permafrost.

The roadblock comprised two cars parked across the far end of a bridge. The location appeared to be strategic but unrelated to anything, there were no towns on the map.

She walked towards them across the bridge unarmed with hands raised.

This is so exposed, she thought. Having a weapon wouldn't matter anyway and they couldn't go back. Best to be as non-threatening as possible. If they opened fire her only option was to jump over the railing and lose herself in the water.

Even at first glance it didn't seem so bad. She saw tents and people in the distance. The distinctive look of a refugee camp. People fleeing murderous trouble, just like them.

"That's far enough, lady. Say your piece," said one of three men standing between the two vehicles waving a rifle at her.

The men's clothes said 'refugee'. Hers the same. The current fashion: old-normal clothes, tattered here and there, covered in the grime of desperation and survival. They were kin.

Two of the men held rifles. They acted tough. It might be bravado but they could still end up shooting her out of panic or poor judgment. Then things would get complicated.

One vehicle was a white utility, the other a yellow sedan. Both recent models parked here as a roadblock. They would only risk them if their charge was low. If the vehicles couldn't travel much further, then their value amounted to movable defenses and little else.

"Hi, name's Rennae Fulbright. We're trying to get to Fairbanks."

"What's in the trucks? We need supplies, food, medicines, biogas, and especially any solar panels. If you have any of that then we can deal. And you can pass with enough to reach Fairbanks. Otherwise go back the way you came."

This would be tricky. But these people weren't bandits. What they needed was something to help them survive, and she was in a unique position to give them that.

"Not much in the way of supplies, but we've got something better. But you only get access to it if we join up with you. We will still control it, but we will help you," she said.

"What are you talking about? Do you have supplies or not?" The nearest man said. She took him to be the leader. He had a swagger that was a little too exaggerated—he was faking the 'tough guy' role.

"We are also armed and fought our way here. My husband is badly wounded. We mean you no harm. We only want to find someone we can ally with and help. In these vans we have three experimental nano-fabrication machines—fabbers, we call them. We got them out of Seattle before..." she couldn't complete the sentence.

The man on the defender's right spoke. He was younger and calmer, unarmed.

"We heard about Seattle. Real clusterfuck there. Hard to get any news here, no internet anymore, even shortwave radio is patchy. I've read about fabbers, didn't realize they got them working," he said.

"The government clamped down on our work. We could have eased many problems by having a few of the sub-systems released, but the government marched in to the GL company site and took over. Then when the mob was coming to loot the factory, the army fled. We saw our chance and took three of the remaining fabbers waiting to be deployed."

The younger man gave a casual look and hand motion to the older man to lower the gun. He complied without hesitation.

The young man spoke.

"My name is Warren Davidson. I am—or was—a civil engineer. Not much call for that at the moment until we need to build fortifications. Right now I am in charge of the welfare of these people. So, you tell me, Rennae, what can you do for us? What makes you worth protecting and feeding?"

He was the type of person who would help them anyway despite the raw paranoia of the times, but perhaps he was also curious, and hoping for an edge. She straightened and started into her little marketing spiel. Now the stakes were higher, and her pitch was not only for her team but also for these refugees and humanity. She could give them the one hour talk, but here and now they need the sixty-second version. No pressure.

"The fabbers are experimental, so we need to tend them a bit. They take various raw materials and produce processed materials, even working machines. Feed them vegetation and they will convert it to a biofuel and use that to convert the biomass to plastics and scrap metals to machines. It's optimized for particular technologies. For instance, it can produce efficient organic electronic circuits but much harder to make silicon based ones. The fabbers can therefore produce cheap organic solar panels. It can also turn inedible plants into food and fuel."

Warren scratched the stubble of his almost beard.

"Wow, that's quite a pitch. Sure, come in, even if half of what you said is lies, it still sounds amazing. You know I wanted to let you, but I have to know I'm not inviting a problem into our fold. Um, not to sound harsh but if you could get food and medicines onto the production line ASAP we would be most grateful."

"Sure, my priority too. My husband, Joseph, was shot by some scum on the way here. They set up a roadblock. We dealt with them, but we have no medicines left. We were looking for a safe place to deploy them when we bumped into you. Understand though. These machines, people gave their lives for them, they are humanity's only hope now. We are very protective of them. So, just tell us where you want us."

He nodded not in agreement, but as if he had found something valuable. "People with passion and hope. That's even rarer than your fabbers."

They drove along a road that had become a ragged, unkempt village. A mass of hollow eyes followed them as they proceeded to the far end of the line of makeshift tents and vehicles. The vehicles were electric or hybrid but there was no electricity or fuel here. She looked searching for solar panels. None were in sight.

While Rennae checked on Joseph's wounds, Dave and Imelda deployed Unit Two. The custom was to give the fabbers names but somehow Unit Two had missed out on being so blessed. Imelda gave the command from her wearable comms gear. Unit Two rolled to the open door of the truck and stepped out, a walking box of machinery, skinless its innards exposed, on four robotic legs. It came to rest with the legs becoming a supporting frame. In the distance she could hear Imelda and Dave arguing about what they should program Two to produce first.

Rennae stepped out of the van and walked up to the fabber.

"We need medicinals first, Imelda," Dave said.

"They won't be any use if he bleeds out, we need tissue repair devices and synthetic blood," Imelda said.

"That's two things. We can only fab one thing at a time." Dave walked away for a moment. Both wanted to help but the stress and exhaustion confined their thinking unable to see the obvious, their confused minds circling the problem without result.

"Deploy another fabber and dedicate it to synthetic blood, then later a tissue repair bot. Use Two to generate antibiotics and other drugs Imelda recommends. When that finishes we need more ammunition and maybe some extra guns. When you've done with all that, start fabbing some solar panels so we can get these people on the move and Unit One, I mean Agnes, to turn plants into food. Talk to Warren about getting the locals to collect the raw materials. Okay? Now get to it," she stood hands on hips looking as confident as she could fake it.

During the night they switched over to producing solar cells, food, weapons. The synthetic blood and the antibiotics came just in time. They set up a drip for Joseph who now looked worse surrounded by the debris of the effort to save him though his vitals were now much better. Rennae sat by him.

He groaned. A good sign.

She bent close to him, stroking his forehead and spoke with an intimate softness. His eyes fluttered open.

"Don't move. I've doped you with some painkillers. You'll be all right, Joseph, but you were borderline. We've teamed up with some refugees and they seem like the people we were hoping to hook up with. Deployed two fabbers on account of you. Working in the field as well as we hoped." She smiled. "They saved your life. Got them making lots of cool things right now. Lucky for us we have schemas for a huge variety of different things including weapons and food. We can manufacture so much. I thought the fabbers' schema libraries were almost empty, don't know who added all that stuff, probably illegal, bless their insubordinate little heart."

Joseph smiled and closed his eyes.

The night was cold but tolerable; they had fuel stoves to keep them warm, and the fabbers were producing a lot of food. The food was in the form of a meat-like slab, pre-cooked, with enough to feed everyone in the camp.

As soon as the sun came up Rennae picked up her new rifle and walked to Warren's tent. He was sitting there cleaning an old hunting rifle.

"I can give you something better by tomorrow. Check this out." She passed over the gun to him.

"What is it? I don't recognize the design."

"A custom design. A simplified version of a maxi and should be almost as effective. And with smart bullets. By tomorrow we will also have smart-RPGs with integrated bio-electronics as a maxi attachment."

"You guys don't mess around. How is your husband?"

"Improving, but he isn't out of the woods. A bullet through his right lung, but no other vital organs.

Hit by a ricochet, so not a full speed round, but he had a dangerous pneumothorax we had to deal with. Air got into his chest cavity, then loss of blood, and on and on. But he is so much better now. Still serious. We are giving him some experimental nanite repair therapies but, well, it's about crossing your fingers or praying at this stage. We need a doctor, are there any here?"

"You don't have any? It looked like someone did a good job getting him here," he said.

"We've got one guy who is a bit rusty, and although he is a smart cookie, he didn't do it for a living. I'd prefer a second opinion from someone who practices."

"Two tents down that way, ask for Jamila, she's great, saved a lot of lives with almost no resources." He faced down the row of tents to show the direction. When he looked back Rennae stood there unmoving.

"Something else?"

"Yeah, on the way here I noticed an army outpost about seven klicks down the road. There was no time to investigate, but I think it would contain useful supplies. I thought I could grab one of your hybrid cars and check it out. Look, we have plenty of biofuel so that isn't a problem," she said.

"Rennae, your fabbers are a godsend, and we really appreciate what you have done. You've saved our bacon. But it's too dangerous to go south. Surely you can reproduce anything you want now."

"The fabbers can't make certain things because we are missing specific materials. An army base would store plenty of circuitry, which the fabbers can process.

They would save the valuable resins, semiconductors, and doping materials. We need those kinds of materials to build a bigger version of a fabber that can produce things on an industrial scale."

"I don't like it but if it can make such big a difference then. Ah, okay. I'll ask some of the guys if they want to escort you. Three armed people are more threatening than one with her arms full carrying stuff to a vehicle," he said.

Rennae drove south with Bo, a cheerful young man who wore a red bandana around his neck, and Tix his partner. Tix looked like a quiet, delicate woman, short blond hair and elfin features, but swung her archaic M16 rifle about like it was part of her. The vehicle was an antique hybrid Ford from a pre-customizable paint jobs era, but had a nice blue opalescent finish; a little like looking at the aurora. They took the right-hand turn down a short road, maybe half a kilometer, to an abandoned army base. It seemed no one had stayed to defend it after the money and food supplies stopped.

They had just exited the vehicle when Bo, pointed in the distance, his lean, muscled brown arm pointing to movement in a window.

Rennae whispered, "Okay. Abort the mission, let's get out of here."

As they turned shots rang out. Bo and Tix turned and went down on one knee and returned fire. Rennae jumped behind the car and gave covering fire, killing one attacker through a broken window.

"Get behind the car! I'll cover."

She took shots at any window she saw almost randomly. Bo and Tix were only ten meters from the car when she started shooting. The two of them turned and ran. Gunfire erupted from several sources. Puffs of dust splashed from the dirt before them. Tix tumbled forward. Bo ran back to get her. Rennae kept firing knowing she was close to the end of her clip.

She pressed the trigger. Click, nothing.

The shooting stopped.

She looked to her right towards where Tix lay, so close to the cover of the car. Near her was Bo's body, his right arm outstretched reaching for her. There was a huge wound in his throat. Tix lay face down, a dark red mark in the light gray sweater on her back, a pool of blood spreading underneath her, about to soak her surprised accusing eyes.

From the building and out of the shadows came four men and a woman.

Rennae threw down her weapon and raised her hands.

"Come over here and keep those hands up," one man said.

Rennae was desperate for a strategy. But there was none. This could only have one outcome.

"You're from that camp up near Rabideaux Creek, aren't you? If you want to live, you'll tell us all we want."

She sighed. There was no choice.

"No, I won't," she said and took a step back.

"JJ, grab her," the leader said.

She turned, leapt, rolled, grabbing Tix's gun.

There was a burst of accurate gunfire. One bullet knocked the gun out of her hands. More bullets shredded her clothes. But where the bullets hit, her exposed skin glowed bright yellow, undamaged. The shooting stopped. They froze. She stood, raised her right hand and a beam of blue fire burst like a lance from her fingers. She swept it from one to another before they could even move. The blinding blue glare wrapped each of them for a moment with jets of yellow flame erupting up and out, leaving a charred smoking husks.

A few seconds and she was alone. The stench wafting towards her.

She couldn't go back.

The car had holes and gouges all over and she knew with no need to look that the engine and electronics were gone. Her clothes were in tatters. Before her was a scene of scorched tar and smoldering bodies. She could undo the damage and unkill Bo and Tix. A forbidden action, for if she could undo this, then she could undo anything, meddling would be massive, and Emari would become the hidden ruler of the world. Maybe she could walk back, create imitation clothes, but no alibi sounded reasonable. Someone would question her, want to get Bo and Tix's bodies. They would see too much damage that looked nothing like a typical gunfight.

There was no return, which meant she had to leave. She had done her work but she wouldn't be able to say goodbye to Joseph or Dave or anyone else at the camp. There had been far sadder partings, though she chose to forget the details, so this was not bad. In fact this was optimal, it had taken a long time to know when to leave with minimal trauma and disruption, take advantage of chance—she who was a skilled manipulator of circumstance.

She raised her hand and a blue-white shimmering vertical slit appeared. She stepped forward and disappeared, leaving the sad, lonely base once more abandoned.

The vision ended. Ray was himself again, or more than himself, he seemed different. It was like waking up from a refreshing sleep.

He looked down at his right hand. As he willed it, a ball of brilliant blue-white fire appeared in his cupped hand. He dismissed it as a magician might.

"Seems you got more from my mission than just insight," Maria said smiling.

"You were Rennae Fulbright? The pioneer of nano-fabrication?"

"I did not develop it. I just gave clues and inspired insights to the team leads. Understand? And I protected them a bit—as you saw. Seattle and Alaska were dangerous places in the mid-21st century. By bad luck people remembered me."

"Could be something to do with disappearing on a dangerous mission."

"I couldn't help that. If I fixed the car and turned up with it riddled with bullet holes, people would always wonder what really happened. Best if they thought I was dead. I didn't expect them to make me the Mother of Fabbing and rename Fairbanks after me."

"You seemed deeply involved. Even taking out those bandits. Was it necessary?" Ray asked.

"Was any of it necessary?" Ramon said. "You must have known it was dangerous. They were mortal while you were not. You could have taken the vehicle by yourself, entered the base on foot, stunned all the bandits, then ransacked the place."

Maria gave him a cold look.

"When immersed in the world you can't afford to think like an immortal. You become one of the people, know their pain and sorrows. Their frailties. And when friends die you react. You are naïve. Just guesswork by someone who has never been there," she said jabbing her index finger at him. Ray tensed waiting for a jet of blue flame.

"Well, Older Self, Ramon, or whoever you are. You of all people should know when you surrounded by danger good planning is helpful but doesn't last long. How many times have you had to improvise and take calculated risks?" Ray said. His words were awkward molded by too much anger towards the interloper.

"Touché, Ray," Ramon said smiling as he doffed an imaginary hat.

"You have to understand," Maria said, "after so many lives. God so many. You see a lot of death, make a lot of mistakes, and there will come a time when you abandon guilt. All that matters is that you do what needs to be done and if you make a mistake, well it's just another, you learn and you go on. Now, you might think it heartless but after a mere thousand years you would change your mind. Every mistake and every triumph fades into irrelevance. You just try to not fuck up. Hard enough to do even when you aren't trying to save billions of lives."

She paused, looked up. Navel gazing time was over it seemed.

"Where to now?" Maria said looking at Ray. "You should know where. I haven't dealt with the Kamoi, the Hive Core, for so long without knowing some of its tricks."

"About all of what we saw. There's no detailed record of those days. You know, when the global civilization fell. A terrible time of catastrophe. It was a gnawing mystery in my time. What happened during the hiatus between the fall of the old nations and the rise of the Nexus," he said. Somewhere in there was a question he couldn't articulate.

"Gaia Lotus knew. They were working with the Mirrish. A human consortium created and controlled by an alien power. There's a lot the Mirrish didn't tell you, even after what happened on Reshox. And just as well your people never knew all the details of those times. Terrible things happen from time to time that would scar a new culture. Taking centuries to get over. We see it all. And deliberately forget it," she said.

A hesitation in her voice made him think she was censoring what she was saying. But then, who wouldn't want to forget such horrifying things?

But, Gaia Lotus? A lot of strange things suddenly made sense.

He had a gut feeling it was time to go, but he couldn't say how he knew. Iit grew stronger with each second. He, they, had to go. But where?

Ray looked about the sky. Looking for an insight? It was like being on a galactic stage, the stars like tiny spotlights. Then he knew where he was. This was 47 Tucanae, a spectacular bright globular cluster as seen from Earth, but he couldn't stay to explore, though the option was open to him. You could spend a lifetime exploring the cluster, even with near instant travel time.

"Wait just a moment," Ramon interjected. "Am I the only one still using their brains or whatever? What is all this about? Why are we here? Ray, you said you were trying to find out who destroyed the Nexus, forgotten that already? Doesn't that strike you as odd?"

"Ramon. We came here assuming the Kamoi was giving us a clue to the mystery. It sent us here for a reason," Maria said.

"Just like that? Go to the Core, which may be a conspirator, and you get directions. Can we go back and ask questions? Is there a way back?" Ramon said.

Ray heard the words and was struck not by the obvious sarcasm but the undercurrent of bitterness. Ramon had a point, or several. He could not forget the questions, they appeared in his mind like a glowing to-do list.

"Strange, you don't sound like much of an agent for the Kamoi. Anyway, I don't know the way back. I'm committed to following this path, I suppose," Ray said.

"You may be committed, but we are not. Maria, you can take us back, can't you?" Ramon said, fidgeting. His nerves getting the better of him. He needed to learn to relax, Ray thought. Perhaps that was always true of him, or us, even now.

"I can't take you back. I don't know the way," she said.

"That can't be right. You are my guide. How can you be lost?" Ray shouted.

"The Kamoi has disabled my jump ability. I'm linked to you. This is deliberate. It must want us to do something. I honestly don't know what. I only realized just now I can't take us back."

Ramon moved closer to her.

"So, the Kamoi could just have us doing a fancy loop around the empty parts of the galaxy forever while you entertain us with your adventures?"

"This doesn't solve our problem, Ramon," she said. "Ray, there has to be a way back leading us out of here. This is too passive aggressive for the Kamoi, it prefers to be more direct."

"If so, then where next?" Ramon said.

"Where to next? We all saw the vision, the memory of my time on Earth, but I didn't see a clue." Maria said.

"No need," said Ray, "I know where we are going."

seven

They stood on the shore of a listless ocean under a twilight sky with stars reflected on its flawed surface. Waves lapped without enthusiasm, while gentle breaking wavelets ran along the beach, their muffled surf-sound receding into the distance like a fading drum finish, making it seem more dramatic than it was. Low in the light blue and pink sky to the west, behind a grove of trees, a huge pale orange sun dominated. It was a little smaller than Ray's fist held at arm's length.

"Messier 92, another globular cluster about twenty-seven thousand light years from the galactic core," he said for his own benefit. The others no doubt knew but weren't so Earth centric in their preference for names.

"And it looks like we are in the habitable zone of this star," he said, stating the obvious.

He looked around. Up above the steep incline of the guava beach sands, there were trees of some kind not quite silhouetted by the glowing pink sky. They had branches that looked like a cross between a palm tree and a eucalypt, the arching fronds breaking into a myriad sickle shaped leaves, while the breeze rustled them like a thousand muted wind chimes. Around and above the trees, creatures like oversized insects flew.

He talked, trying to ease the tension in the air, whatever 'air' meant here, while he tried to work out what was special about this place.

"Not what I would expect from a piece of infrastructure, eh?" Ray said. "I mean, M92 is almost as old as the universe, about thirteen billion years. Really old stars. Low metallicity. Not much stuff to make rocks, and rivers, and beaches, or worlds like this."

Ramon walked ahead, looking about, his dark brown synthetic leather shoes sinking deep into the flowing pink sand.

Ramon turned to them. "Constructed would be my guess. Perhaps it was a pleasant rest stop, a living world in a dead mass of suns. Who knows? The Vanaya did many things like this. Maybe the hobby of some eccentric lone builder. So, don't break anything we might have to pay for." He spoke in a rambling tone, some of his mannerisms annoying to Ray because they were familiar yet surprising because he had never noticed them before.

"I don't see or sense anything," said Maria.

"It isn't about the place, it is about us being here. The setting is the trigger," Ray said. Inside him, the memory was like a rising wind. It had him. Once more the world dissolved into a dream.

The Uthosafi, or "peoples of the new understanding," called their world Paia. Wars in the century before last—sixty-four years per century, 100 in octal—culminated in a limited nuclear exchange.

A new century brought a long-sought peace, and civilization flourished. But now complacency, ambition, and willful ignorance had slowly returned, a cancer so gradual that denial seemed the wise choice right up until it was almost beyond fixing.

Irenni looked out the window onto the cityscape far below, now mostly hidden under the glowing clouds. Too much like storm clouds, she thought, caught at the moment of a lightning flash, waiting for time to resume.

She had advised against the building of the Celestial Towers in a previous life, too isolating from the people, too much of a bad signal, and too inviting of arrogance. But they had proceeded anyway to ridiculous heights. In the azure distance beyond the cloud bank the fading light showed the shimmering sparkle of the cities rivaling the strengthening glow of the stars. Between the stars and the trembling gleam of the city was the ragged darkness of the mountains to the southeast, their tops a ghostly shadow. It was arrogant and a mistake, but without doubt breathtaking.

"Adviser Irenni, you have a visitor," a voice behind her said. She had her neural link emulation turned off as she sought to catch a moment, a chance for some peace and contemplation.

"Let them in, Hei," she said. Hei was an old friend and Irenni would miss her when the time came to leave; when she couldn't fake her aging any more.

She felt so alone, her only solace was the caring and nurturing of these people. They were her adopted children. It was always this way. But when her children grew up, she must set them free at some stage. She wanted it and dreaded it, yet the alternative was unthinkable.

She turned to see Eang and Casur walk through the sliding black glass doors. They entered the room and made a slight bow of respect. The room was a warm burgundy color, the carpet a rich chocolate, while the ceiling was a bright yellow. The color scheme cultivated calm and friendship in this culture, so the formal bows although inevitable always seemed out of place.

Eang walked in with a telltale limp that got worse each year. He wore simple loose-fitting garments almost like a pale off-white robe. A reminder he was once an ascetic and stubbornly kept some of those ways. She found his skepticism and simplicity a refreshing change from the crazy certainty of recent times.

Casur was the opposite. He moved with a feline grace typical of his species since they were descended from tree dwelling catlike creatures. Dressed in close-fitting black, he looked every bit an assassin, or a bodyguard. He was both, or could be, but Irenni had channeled his talents into espionage rather than murder. The ability to blend came with ease to him, so this outfit must be for her benefit. He had once been an assassin for hire, but he preferred her money, and was quite amused by the idea he was also doing good for a change.

The Uthosafi stood about 1.6 meters tall with the usual variation. A flattish face, stereoscopic vision, pointed ears, no fur on the yellow face or body and a mane from the head down the back of various colors and patterns. The hair was only a few centimeters long. Overall, they were an attractive and graceful people.

She knew Eang would give information willingly. He was the one who pushed for this audience, whereas Casur would have information but extracting it was time consuming, he would be reluctant, always needing some pointless bargaining first, he couldn't resist his old conditioning.

"Eang. Greetings old friend. How are you?" she said, as if it had been a year since their last meeting instead of a few days.

"I'm fine. I'm fine," his words at odds with the grimace on his face.

"Your limp's getting worse, isn't it? Why don't you see my doctor? He's very good, I assure you. You know that can be fixed these days. We aren't in the post-war ruins anymore," she said.

This was their own little ritual; she would always ask about his health, he would shrug it off, then she would suggest modern medicine. All the while Casur would look on with his own skepticism trying to hide his affection for them both.

"Rubbish. Anyway, all that can wait. I have news. My, um, colleague Casur has discovered some troubling information. Casur?" He nodded to Casur, inviting him to comment. Casur was leaning against a wall, a nonchalant observer of the room.

"Casur, my friend, what do you have for me?" she said.

"I came across some information. The Aete has been in secret meetings with the Cita and Shalok corporations and also the Secret Service. They provide..."

"They provide surveillance and adapted AIs." She interrupted and regretted it. Casur usually wasn't so forthcoming, and she didn't want to spoil the opportunity.

Casur continued. "The oligarchy will seek to take control over the masses via their neural implants. There are plans to downgrade the privacy and security features. Then sometime later introduce viral agents and targeted misinformation. A document detailing the strategy has come into my hands."

"Damn," she said, "We spent eights of years trying to avoid this. It's like they all took stupid pills. Well, they can't do it yet it will take at least a year. We can alert others to the dangers and turn their potential allies into enemies, and with luck prevent this."

Eang spoke. "Sounds like greed pills rather than stupid pills, hard to tell the difference. Anyway, Irenni, that may be a future goal of the Centocracy, but there is another problem with the Aete right now. There were secret meetings of the Aete, and the five members have not shared the meetings' agendas or minutes with the rest of the Centocracy. The Aete are only a steering committee, and the rules forbid them doing this."

"Casur? And..." she asked.

Casur shifted his weight back and forth, his nerves showing. He always had an air of calm confidence. This was troubling.

"The Aete seeks to... is this room secure?"

"Yes, it is. I sweep it every day for bugs and other methods are at my disposal. We are safe," she said, knowing even she couldn't be sure.

Casur continued, looking atypically stressed with his twitching ears and whiskers. "The Aete's power base comes from the factions centered here on the continent of Ayit and the northern regions of Tajeb. But the Centocracy is about to change the voting quotas, giving places like Ikot and Megano far more influence. It is an immediate threat to the power of the Aete."

"It would sweep the old traditional powers from their seats on the Aete." She said. "Interesting. They must feel like they own their current status. So, what do they intend to do to safeguard their position? I wouldn't think they could do much. The Aete steers policy for the Centocracy but has no control over anything else."

Eang interrupted. "They do now. Casur overheard, and I can confirm high-level contacts in the military now exist. They now possess secure access and launch codes for long range nuclear forces."

If she could have gone into shock, she would have. This put everything at risk. Just when she thought they were on the right path and had thought it safe to leave, now this society was about to trip over a pebble on the path and crack its skull open.

"No. No. You must be mistaken."

Even as she spoke, her sleeping microscopic drones woke up and dispersed from her corner of this Tower to monitor for intruders. Something tempted her to intervene directly, but it was against the rules. She often thought of the rules as guidelines. Deep down she knew better. The Kamoi had more power than any agent would admit. She could monitor and advise, take small actions, but that was all.

The drone network sent her an alert. It was too early they could observe nothing beyond the towers yet, which meant the threat was immediate. Time to move.

"You two were followed here. Or they bugged us. I'm sorry my guarantee was empty and now we are all in danger," she paused a moment. "Armed Centocracy forces are in the building and coming up the lifts right now."

A muffled explosion gently rocked the room. Her personal defenses were breached.

"I have a small aircraft parked on the balcony, it seats two but can handle three. Let's go, I'll tell the home system to erase all my personal data including encrypted files."

"Irenni," Casur said, "they'll shoot us out of the sky."

"What choice do we have?" she said turning towards the glassed wall revealing the enormous balcony and landing zone, a standard aircar at the far end.

There was a flash and a body-jarring boom that went through her, knocking her over. The glass wall cracked as if sucker-punched by a giant fist. The aircar outside was a flaming wreck with a ball of fiery black smoke rising into the night. Between the jagged cracks of the transparent wall, she saw ropes and rappelling soldiers in black looking too much like Casur; all armed and armored. They were surrounded.

Mistress Interrogator, as Irenni dubbed her, paced across her field of view as if a caged animal. An accidental mockery of the situation. She offered no name since Irenni had no rights now, and those eyes told her she had also lost her identity as a person. The casual acknowledgment of others on any street was only a memory.

"Your friends can't help you now. I'd say your family doesn't care, but you don't seem to have a family. Someone, whose records are conveniently lost, bequeathed their wealth to you early this century. Why you? In fact, who the hell are you? I don't buy the 'my records were destroyed in the war' excuse. So many questions and no answers."

They had put her in isolation, crouched and naked in a small metal box without windows, and only a few small recessed lights. There must be tiny air vents, but she couldn't see them. A perfect cube. No contact with anyone, continuous harsh flickering light, hot and stifling, loud raucous screeching piped into her cell. At random times the bare walls would become electrified, switching so you didn't know which wall was next or for how long. Sometimes the floor would become almost scalding or freezing. Too small to sleep in or lie down or stand up and sharing the room with her own excrement. Their aim was to degrade her into an animal. At times they would clean out the cell, not with hoses, too easy. They would flush near freezing putrid water into the cell, through the small gaps between the walls; letting it fill until there was no air left to breathe. Wait until signs of anoxia began and then empty the water in seconds through the same hidden vents that had flooded the cube. The next step was to heat the cell to almost scalding to dry it out. It hadn't worked, of course. Later it would be straight out torture with chemical inducements. She would have to fake more injuries and screams and biometrics. It was getting harder.

From time to time they would take her out of her cell, drape a crude garment over her that was like a dirty hospital gown, and march her into a large, darkened room. Never touching her with their hands, they used electric prods to push her along the dim corridors. In the center of the room was a blinding spotlight, shining onto a central wooden chair. They tied her to it with rough ropes at first, and then the interrogation would begin. Later, when they got more serious, they dispensed with ropes and used handcuffs. Nice to see efficient practices in the bureaucracy. There were various people in the room, but she only ever saw the interrogator in the pool of cold, hard light. The questions were relentless and often about inaccurate things. They wanted her to confess to a random convenient lie. They read the confession out to her again and again, then tortured her, trying to admit to things in the confession. Just confess one insignificant thing today and it will stop. None of the confession matched any of her actual machinations, and they wouldn't believe those. It almost made her laugh. Most of the time they interrogated and tortured her because she was helpless, naked, and the interrogators got sick pleasure from it. The male interrogators would assault her with prods before a hidden cheering audience, the female ones were no kinder.

But she was biding her time. Waiting.

One day the Interrogator touched her with her bare skin rather than using a whip or cattle prod. The Interrogator grabbed her face, holding it like some inanimate thing she would smash with the butt of the prod in her other hand, perhaps looking for the fear that was to be her reward. The result would have been almost the same if she was wearing gloves. Mistress Interrogator brought her face close, whispering threats like sweet-nothings, as if they were lovers or the best of friends. Her nanites traveled from her skin into the Interrogator and her clothes. It would be too much effort to connect to the brain tissue; too long and too many noticeable side effects. Instead, they would ride along and report sound, some low quality video, and lots of wireless data. She commanded some of her emissaries to jump ship, find a secure location in a console and harvest materials and energy to build something more serious. It would take time, but once completed she would have a much better picture.

She could have sent her little ones adrift on the air earlier, but there weren't enough to find critical places intelligently. Better to ride on Mistress Interrogator's coat tails.

As individuals, the nanites weren't too smart. And there was not enough to form a meshed intelligence. Once she directed a few into the unused console in the corner of her interrogator's office she set them to work. They harvested tiny amounts of materials and energy to build more nanites, and new macroscopic architectures. The assemblage was tiny and hidden within the maze of wiring of the device.

Then it was time to snoop.

The news services reported martial law had been declared and some regions were in open revolt with many members of the Centocracy imprisoned. The Coup had already happened—no surprise there. She hacked into the Secret Service network, she had known the credentials for a long time, even secret keys used internally and never seen by people. It was hard to communicate from her cell. It was a Faraday cage after all, so there were no radio comms to her minions. But while she was being tortured and questioned, she was free to contact her microscopic army. Then in that theater of despair, when her normal thoughts would have converged on the probable and terrible fate of her children, she distracted herself with interrogating the interrogators with far more success than they could ever do to her.

That was how she found out about Eang and Casur. They had been executed after a week of 'rewarding interrogation'. She knew her time was up. All she needed was an exit strategy. She would take a new body and work to rescue Paia before these people did serious damage.

Days came and went. Each day more beatings, more torture, more questions, more threats. After each blow she had to fake an injury, a bruise here, a lesion there, and all of them layered on a look of deteriorating mental health. She thought maybe she would just fake her death during a beating and refuse to be revived. Then she could disappear one way or another—a clean exit. It wasn't to be.

Mistress Interrogator was playing with her when it happened.

"The Aete has deemed you expendable, or perhaps not worth bothering with, it depends. You might think yourself a person of importance, but you are nothing. We may let you live. You can have a small cottage in the country, some pets, become that crazy recluse who lives down the old road. All you need to do is tell us everything and become our eyes and ears. If we believe you all of this unpleasantness will end."

Irenni sighed. Her body relaxed, surrendering to what she now knew was inevitable. Her hopes and fears were at an end.

"It's too late for all of that. While you have been interrogating me I have been uncovering all your secrets. I'm not who you think I am and you could never harm me."

As she spoke the bruises on her face faded away, the lesions closed, the haggardness in her face and body disappeared. Sitting before the Interrogator was a young woman. She brought her arms around to her front, sans handcuffs, and rested them on her lap. The Interrogator's eyes were staring as she froze while reaching for her sidearm.

In the distance a siren started to wail.

"I only reveal myself because it is far too late. The Ayit Union in secret alliance with other nations has launched a first strike against the Centocracy, and especially targeting us here in Kalens, the capital. Those warheads are only a minute or two away. The Centocracy Command has in turn launched a massive response far greater than the initial attack. Once they see the launch, the opposition will launch everything they have. This won't be a limited nuclear attack with survivors scrambling to rebuild, this will end civilization on Paia. I don't know whether your species will survive."

Irenni finished speaking, there was nothing to do but wait. Already her essence was in the partial transfer state, even if a thermonuclear warhead detonated in the room she would continue to the Dream unharmed as this body was atomized.

Unharmed, except in spirit.

The Interrogator unfroze. It wasn't just shock that had stopped her reaching for her gun. The little nanites had intervened on command. But now it was time to release the poor creature. Within her there was only pity and a growing howl of grief for her children.

The Interrogator whipped out her pistol with blinding speed and fired five shots into Irenni. The bullets ripped her robe, but the exposed skin underneath glowed like molten gold for a moment and returned to normal.

Irenni looked up at the Interrogator and said, "Goodbye, Iupi." Then the lights failed. Irenni's body glowed now, lighting up the room with a soft blue light as she converted the gamma rays and neutrons to visible light. It was almost intimate. Central in her view was the paralyzing disbelief and fear on the Interrogator's face. Then the shock wave arrived.

Ray turned to look at Maria. She was sobbing, her human form trying to convey her consuming anguish.

"Maria, it's okay."

He walked over to her and put his arms around her trying to comfort her. But he had felt her grief, like a tidal wave rising higher than anyone could survive or run from. This was a burden that could not be endured without forgetting the core intimacy with the lost. Something like it must have happened to him. He no longer grieved for his brother, and until now she no longer grieved for Paia.

She sobbed, then went quiet, looked down for a few seconds. Then she lifted her head. The fading anguish in her face giving the lie to her new smile. Forgotten, she would only remember the superficial details, and in her forgetting she would save herself. He didn't know if it was right, but being crushed by that experience was an evil.

From behind, he heard Ramon chuckle. "That's what failure in the Game looks like. Oops, lost some points and some billions of people. Damn, I guess that ruins my position on the Leader Board," he said.

Ray whipped around and glared with as much malice as he could find in himself.

"There are times I would really like to put a fist into that smug face of yours, asshole," Ray said, cheeks burning.

"Our face, remember?" said Ramon.

"There's no way you are me. You only look like me. A fucking decoy. Go the fuck back to whichever black hole you crawled out of. And don't push that Raymond / Ramon shit on me. As far as I'm concerned your name is Aamon."

Ramon gave a slow, mocking clap. "Sorry, Ray. I'm a traveling companion in this road movie. I'll tag along, you know, to keep it real."

Ramon turned and walked away, looking at the spectacular scenery.

"Maria, are you all right?" Ray said.

She gave a slight nod. "I'm fine. Or will be. I can't seem to remove the memory. At least is has faded a bit. Losing a world is indescribable. Imagine losing all of your family, everyone, parents, siblings, aunts and uncles, cousins. I spend a lot of time on those worlds, it becomes part of me, and if it dies so does part of me. It isn't accidental, it is a deliberate incentive to get it right and save your world. That's also the reason there are few actual players and so many spectators."

"I don't understand why you persist with this Game. Why don't you just, you know, send a cryptic message from space with a list of helpful advice? I don't know. Why get involved at all?" Ray said.

"The Game energizes my civilization. We don't do it to get points, that is just a distraction for the frivolous. The reason we, I mean I, do it is because it makes our existence worthwhile. How many worlds have you saved? How many billions of lives owed their existence to your dedicated effort? This isn't a job. We never regarded our role as a job, it was our vocation. Once we traveled to the stars, we still had a sense of duty and care, and helping others was our salvation. Over time the subtlety and scale increased, but there is still no higher purpose for us. Without this we are nothing."

They walked along the beach. Beyond the reach of the tiny lapping waves, Maria's bare feet sank into the wet sand in audible scrunches. Ray reached out and sensed the creatures swimming offshore. The animals roaming through the nearby forest. All had transceivers built into their biology. The world was remotely knowable and controllable. He looked up into the darkening sky, the great soft glow of the galaxy starting to show, the sun setting beyond the tree line. Above and far away there were three worlds and a myriad of worldlets orbiting this red dwarf. He could see the other nearby suns in his mind and their physical properties, not as numbers but as new physical sensations. He was a blind creature of a lost cave, given sight as it emerged into the light. A new qualia had been born, one that wasn't there before, and deep down he knew it wasn't fixed. He could add new senses and change them as desired. He sensed the universe any way he wished, but not all at once. There were always limits.

The sound of scrunching sand. Footsteps. New footsteps. He looked at Ramon, he was standing still gazing down with a grimace of pain on his face. Another one grieving for Paia despite his words.

More sounds of footsteps from behind.

In the distance a young 'man' was walking towards them. It was Amur from the tavern in Eklus, though he was in the form of an alien, a corvi, a native of Corvena. He did not understand how he knew it was Amur it was like recognizing a face without knowing how it was done.

Emari wasted no time.

"Amur, what are you doing here?"

"Ah, yes, Emari. Look, I figured you must be on something special, so I spent mana and found out your destination and more mana to jump here. Expensive. You must earn an amazing amount from your work. Now listen, I guessed you were going to a new and exotic world and I wanted to get preview rights for it," he said smiling as Ray perceived it.

"So you can collect and comment on my stratagems. All their faults and virtues. Got it. You have been following us for some time, haven't you?" Maria said.

"I noticed you visited a sayel. Then a Core world. Then out into the halo. I knew something was afoot so I jumped here. Now if you could..."

"Enough! No, Amur."

It fascinated Ray. The words were not in English or any language he heard before. It was Vanayan, and translating was so easy he took a few seconds to comprehend the words were not Nexus English.

Ramon overheard Amur's conversation as he was walking towards them. It was too much.

"Right. Almost 2 billion years of history, effectively immortal gods, ability to understand anything or go anywhere, and you choose to be a lousy reality-show hustler. Get the fuck out of here. Please," he shouted.

Emari nodded. "What he said, Amur. This is just a course for training a new player, so please leave. And don't forget to take your follower as well."

About five meters behind Amur stood a woman. Human and statuesque. Dark hair to her shoulders with a slight upward curl hugging the line of her pale neck. There was an elegant curve to her face. It was flawless, presenting an image of serenity. Clear blue eyes like forgotten summer days. She wore a dark, almost black shirt and jeans that were crimson.

Amur was nervous, and the confrontation had rattled him. "Who? Who's she? Never saw her before, I swear. Look. I'm going. You persuade her to go.

Nothing to do with me. Sorry, Emari, you aren't going to hold this against me, are you?"

"Can't we follow him back?" said Ramon.

He disappeared in an eye blink with an almost imperceptible flash and the briefest sense of inrushing air.

Emari stepped forward towards the woman. "You too. You shouldn't be here. You have to return. Now."

"No, I don't," she said in a voice that sounded like a melody to Ray's ears. It was so enticing it couldn't be accidental.

"I followed Amur here, and I'm not interested in any of the game popularity contests. I know you are on the track of something deeper, and I want in."

"It's just a training exercise for a new agent," Emari said, but the stranger just sneered.

"Training exercise? For a being who had no ID before now. More like an induction to a new Vanayan. But those training exercises are tightly controlled and restricted to the approved worlds, not sent out to globular clusters where no one ever goes. If you don't tell me, I will inform the Kamoi."

Emari just gave her an icy look. Ray presumed some telepathic communication was going on at first but soon suspected it was a primal instance of staring down the other.

Emari broke it off first. Had a shift of power occurred?

"I see," was all she said.

The stranger looked confused, as if she did not expect a backdown.

"Oh, I get it. This is under the guidance of the Core. Sure. I will go easy, but I will still tag along. Unless struck by lightning from the galactic gods," she stood there smiling with outstretched arms, while presenting the form of a mock cowering figure looking for a descending lightning bolt.

"You aren't a stranger to human idioms. It is so natural, not like Amur in Eklus. He had an uncertainty in his actions," Ramon said.

"Wait," Ray said, confused. "Ramon, you weren't on Eklus."

Ramon didn't reply as the strange woman continued.

"I have spent time on Earth. Indulged myself there, turning on all the sensory levels. Did you ever do that, Emari? Try being fully human?" she said.

"Too many times."

"What's your name then?" Ray asked.

The stranger looked at him and smiled as if he was the only other being in the universe.

"Call me, Zara."

They all continued talking about other things. Ramon wanted to know if Zara could lead them back, she couldn't. She wanted to know about the things they had experienced at Aukee's Pearl and at M92, so Ray passed Zara a packet of memories about both experiences. After that, their conversation drifted into random topics. The shape of the shells on the beach, the scents on the breeze, as if they couldn't sense and understand the origins and structures of these things. Ray wanted to know how Ramon knew about Eklus. He had no idea, and just as it was sometimes handy to forget, sometimes it was useful to not see too deeply either.

Zara seemed interested in all the topics that drifted up from Ray's subconscious.

Ramon approached Ray when he was by himself. There was no sense of animosity any longer, only a sense of nervousness.

"Hey, selfie. Ray, look something is massively off about this whole thing. Don't you feel it? And now you've picked up a groupie. These people are messed-up with a capital 'M'."

"Groupie? They're aliens we're probably just misinterpreting. And, as far as options go, please tell me what options we have? I trust no one, least of all you."

"They are aliens that can perfectly mimic human emotions. But, yeah, I get that we don't have any options right now, but maybe something will come along. And then we will have to grab it. Both of us. Are you in?"

"You've got to be joking," Ray said, turned his back on Ramon and went to the others.

They spent a little time just walking along the beach as the stars came out. When he thought it was the right time, when they had put Paia far enough behind them, then he searched for the next destination. The details flashed into his mind even faster than last time, a storm of understood coordinates and jump parameters. Reality blinked.

eight

The sky was late twilight; windy, with a dusty orange and purple pall over everything. He stood on the edge of a barren, windswept plateau. Below a dark, hidden desert valley stretched out, descending then rising to another mesa maybe five kilometers away. The gloom gave made his instincts sense an approaching storm that would never come. Only a hazy thin cloud like a faint glowing veil covered the sky, blurring a few bright stars into tiny fuzzy balls of light. Without the cloud, he would see tens of thousands of stars. The dim twilight was starlight since no moon shone here. It was cold, but he didn't feel it beyond a slight false chill. Some rocks about him were discolored ice and the wind whipping past, not even touching him, a mix of methane and similar gasses. There was no life here and probably never would be. There must be a sun otherwise this world would be a ball of ice, but it had not risen yet.

"NGC 6934, as my people called it. Another globular cluster about ten billion years old. The cluster is 41,700 light years from the galactic core. Interesting, a different area of the sky, so to speak from M92. Other side of the galaxy to Aukee's Pearl. We're jumping about." He said it and surprised himself because he didn't know how he knew all of this.

Ramon was going to speak. Ray saw he would quip about the place being uninviting and that they should invite themselves. Ray left the perception of Ramon's thoughts and connected to the unlocked memory.

In a moment it had them.

He, or rather she, stood on a hilltop overlooking a dazzling city towards the dusk-filled horizon. A rippling bed of lights; a breeze-kissed sea under a strange moon. A city of the local faerie, the magical beings who embodied the mystique of the natural world until civilization pretended it could ignore the dazzling sophistication of nature with its own crude efforts. Her subconscious mocking her it seemed comparing her home town to a city of magic. Above the stars were coming out. The familiar constellations above, and the massive open clusters dominated the night sky with twice as many stars as visible from Earth. This was Corvena, literally "home of the corvi". The original home of the Vanaya. A world named after its people not the reverse.

Behind her the crunch of footsteps on gravel. She turned to see her younger brother and sister visible despite the fading light.

A lone streetlight stood there near the edge of the carpark, like her, trying to resolve the scene.

The strong family resemblance: the brilliant blue hair, changed somewhat in her brother to a calming blue green. Their clothes were loose and casual. None of them wore shoes, a family tradition meant to remind them not to lose track with the real world, it might not be a common fashion but no one thought it odd. Harder to see was the hairy down of their bodies, a light beige with the faintest suggestion of leopard spots, which brought back memories of being teased as a child. "Are you trying to look like Aukee," other children would say.

Her brother Eliks broke the silence.

"It's beautiful isn't it? Especially at this time of the year. Can you smell it? The when the winds blow you can smell the pilani blossoms from the Lasuv Valley."

"Yes, I can. It is exquisite."

Her sister Laima was quiet as she suppressed her anger or sorrow, Emari didn't know which but accepted that any blame lay with herself not her family. Laima stood rigid, arms folded in front of her. She moved her left foot as if she was rubbing something out, a habit Emari knew preceded an outburst.

"Why? Why do you have to go?" she said.

Her sister's distress was contagious. She wanted to calm her but didn't know how. She had made a commitment and knew it would hurt those close to her. Laima's ears flared forward and quivered, the equivalent of human tears. It was heartbreaking, and she knew Laima was only reflecting how everyone in her family felt about her decision.

"It is a great opportunity and honor. A new way of seeing the universe. And I can help us all even if I can't talk to you any more. Even that may change," she replied.

They had been over the arguments and details but the logic of it didn't matter, all they knew was that they were losing her.

The outburst was inevitable. They couldn't ignore what was happening though it was fatal to the rapport she wanted with her family tonight. Now there was only an awkward painful silence. It was agony the longer it continued so when she couldn't take it anymore she strode to the car and said, "Get in."

They returned to Vicochen by the hired aircar. Air traffic was automated; the skies were too busy for manual control, and although you could set a destination that was not where the aircar would go. There were designated drop-off points equivalent to mini-airports the size of a parking lot. An aircar would land on a marked area, the passengers would get out and get an auto ground car from the edges of the landing area. The trip back was ordinary and mundane except for the views on the way to the city. In daylight beyond the cities the pinks and oranges of the distant forested mountains and valleys always soothed her but now the sights were artificial, twinkling, but no less mesmerizing.

Still there were misgivings; did she know what she was getting into, was it all a mistake despite her commitment? This was not how it was supposed to be. Had her idealism led her astray?

Later that night she had a last dinner with her family. It was quiet, somber; a grieving wake for the dead. She numbed herself through the whole thing hoping she could erase it from her memory.

The night was long and she only managed a little sleep.

Next morning she dressed and took a ground car to the Zuxeh Tefa building. No one saw her off.

Although a lot of the research groundwork was done on the moon and in orbit, the process was now being performed back on Corvena. This made access much easier for prospects.

An assistant took her up to the twelfth floor. He was a pleasant but vacuous young man who chatted on about the weather and the lead teams in the Ojer Sports League. Perhaps it was intentional, a soporific conversation to dull the wits and ease tension. He ushered her into a plain gray room with two chairs on opposing sides of a desk and left her alone. As she sat, the walls came alive in relaxing moving artwork, some of the sculpture projecting from the walls. A man entered, not much older than herself, dressed in white formal wear. He sat down facing her. A gentle corvi smile.

"Welcome again to Zuxeh Tefa, the Breath of Eternity in old Chedzee. You have been here many times before for the tests and evaluations. No tests anymore. Now you need to make your final decision. You have signed documents before, agreeing to the process, most of that related to testing. If you read the small print you would have noticed that they were not binding. Your decision today is binding because the change is irreversible. We do not know how long the process will last you understand, you could live for a hundred years or perhaps only twenty, we're not promising long life, but it will allow you the chance to help everyone. The process, as you have been informed, will convert your physical form into a nanite based ecosystem with high-speed connections to the datanet. Once in that state you will have formidable abilities, corvi intuition and insight married to machine intelligence and data storage. By signing this document you will start the process of conversion. Once that begins there is no going back," he said.

"Will I still look, like me?" she found it difficult to handle the fear of becoming a monster despite her noble desires. Why had she never asked this question before?

"The system gives some control over external form and coloring. Don't worry you will still look like one of us, but it won't be convincing. The skin will resemble plastic. Your hair won't have that same beautiful iridescent blue. But things should improve. This was all covered in the documents you have read. Do you still want to go ahead with the process? This is your last opportunity to change your mind."

She had said her goodbyes. She was committed to this now. Her reasons were simple and clear, perhaps naïve, but she would stick to her beliefs; several times her people had come close to the precipice and were saved by dumb luck. Someone trustworthy needed to foresee the problems and guide her people onto a safe path. The Changelings would be tasked with enduring isolation and plotting a safe course with minimal intervention. Many in the past had given their lives for less in countless wars, and now a generation embraced the chance to change the world, for a price, and there were always some who were willing to pay. They were people tested for intelligence, creativity, resilience, and above all duty.

She placed her delicate open hand on the offered document pad and registered her decision. Digitally signed, sealed, and she was delivered.

"I do," she said.

A young woman with violet hair escorted her to a room where she disrobed and put on a flimsy gown, a gesture to modesty while the most personal parts of her body would be under intense group scrutiny.

The doctors took her into a surgical room placing her on a contraption resembling a bed. They spoke soothing words that she never heard. Her hearts were racing. She thought of abattoirs and sacrifice and fatal mistakes, then took a deep breath dismissing those notions. She knew what she was doing. It was not a rash or ignorant decision.

Perhaps.

Then a nurse came to her and with clockwork precision placed a needle into her left arm. He transfused her with an opalescent liquid. A solution of nanites, lots of them. There was no pain, no sense that anything at all was happening to her, while her emotions veered from concern to assurance and back again, over and over. The wild swings of emotion made her want to throw up. She pushed through anyway.

She spent the entire day being transfused while technicians interrogated the microscopic machines, activating stages for the nanites. Then a general anesthetic for the more painful events. She watched the needle going into her arm and it was like facing a firing squad. The moment of truth.

She woke in a bed unable to move. Slowly the room came into focus. There were masses of tubes connected to her. On closer examination she had a moment of panic when she saw they weren't for feeding or draining or blood supply, they were electric or optic fiber.

There was a voice in her head.

"Hello, this is Doctor Gicato. I see you are awake. We met when you first arrived. You may have noticed the tubes coming out of you. Don't worry it's normal. Are there any questions before we begin your training sessions with the hardware?"

"How much of me is organic now? I feel the same. I think," she said.

"The nanites converted your body into a semi-organic state. That was an intermediate step, later the full conversion could proceed. In all it took about three and a half days. Except for the fact that the nanites are partly organic you are not an organic being anymore. The process has dissolved your body replacing every cell with something else we could then house in a new structure. Your body is now made up of objects that reproduce many of the effects of hormonal secretions but in software. That is why you still feel the same. Your mind is not software though, only some inputs, your thoughts are still physical states but not in neurons. Some of your subsystems you can access are software and that is a good thing it means you are highly extensible—you can become more than you are with ease. You don't need food but you need battery recharges, your current battery charge should last about two days but we are hoping to extend that to five days within two years when we switch to a new generation of fuel cells. We've also added more standard hardware: batteries, strengthening supports, optical fiber and so on. When you are attuned to your body, you can examine the changes yourself. You'll likely understand them better than us."

"What do I look like?" she said, unable to resist what she would once have thought of as a superficial question.

"Wait until we unhook you before you connect to the cameras. Coming out of surgery is not a good look for anyone, and you have had the most drastic surgery of all."

She resisted the urge, as intense as the desire to pick at a scab, a reference that now had little relevance to her.

"What happens after the training?"

"Once you get a hang of the basics, you will have more advanced material downloaded into your memory. You will then be able to join our team made up of people and Changelings working on important tasks. You will have your pick of projects related to planetary ecology, low impact energy generation, space propulsion designs, and a host of others."

She wondered if he noticed that he didn't count Changelings like her as people.

"My name is Zate," he said.

He had orange hair hanging down to his shoulders. It reminded her of sunsets on golden beaches, all lost to her now. His hair was a mat of many flattened plastic strips, a few millimeters wide, resembling normal hair yet lacking that iridescence that was so defining of what it was to be corvi. She thought of her own hair, now just plastic decorations, not the shimmering blue glory she had once dismissed and now seeing it as part of her identity. Too late for that now. It was part of her sacrifice.

He had approached her as she walked down a white corridor on the tenth floor of Zuxeh Tefa. It gave her chills because of the likeness to a blizzard, or so she thought. She didn't know why they had so much white in their designs. It was sterile and dehumanizing, so Zate with his orange hair and purple jumpsuit stood out like a protest sign.

She had spoken little to any other Changelings so far. They didn't look corvi but over a few days they had no longer looked strange and Zate now seemed familiar.

"I am Emari ya Irenni Lak," she said in a formal tone like a child speaking to an elder. There was a quaver in her voice. Perhaps it was fear, perhaps it was excitement, she couldn't tell which.

His eyes smiled. "You can call yourself by any name you wish. We all have unique internal IDs so the name we attach to it is up to us, and we can change it whenever we want and however many times we want to. I'm here to acquaint you with your new body. I know you have been through various tutorials. Learning how to walk, talk, remotely communicate, access computing resources, interfacing to various machines, and so on. I want to talk about how to deal with this. The engineers, scientists, and project managers, they have no experience of this life we now live. And make no mistake, you are still a living being. We have reproduced your passions and even imitated the biological inputs from hormone secretions. You are as close to being the old you as we could make. Some find this change distressing because they see their artificiality and think they have given up so much for so little. But I want to suggest something else—you are at the starting point of a long journey, you can improve upon yourself and climb to heights far greater than you could as flesh and blood. Soon we will lift off to work at Luna 3 to begin your new life. It will be our base."

"I'm going to the moon? I thought my, I mean our role, was to stay here and help build society?" she said.

"Yes, the original plan. There would be people who could directly take part in simulations and give powerful, living interpretations of policy decisions. But politics has intervened. The government doesn't like us exploring that role."

"But they defined it. It is why I am here. My duty to my people," she took a deep breath, but it didn't help. Was all this for nothing?

"I'm sure they will reconsider in a few years. In the meantime, we will move a lot of our people to Luna 3," he said.

"Our people? We are all the same people," she said. It was taught to everyone, instilled into them, but that didn't make it any less sincere.

"It was only a figure of speech."

"An official, before and after my conversion, he talked about Changelings and people as different. It sounded like you also bought into it," she said.

He leaned his left shoulder against a wall. "I know. I'll admit it has worried us. Moving many 'Changelings' as they call us to the moon is one strategy to reduce tension. If it gets worse, we might have to move everyone. Let's hope it doesn't go that far."

"So, is there a plan or a point to going to the moon? Please tell me I haven't thrown my future away," she said.

"Come with me, we have a lot to talk about," he said, taking her hand they walked down the corridor to a meeting room where others already waited.

The shuttle trip was everything she had hoped. There was no Life Support. They might as well have been in a shirtsleeve environment because they all wore casual clothes made from heat resistant fibers. A plain cargo craft fitted with seats in the cargo section, economy seating and no need for fancy features like air, so it was unpressurized. When they reached the halfway point, the shuttle rolled away from the sunlight and opened the large cargo hatch. The lights dimmed and their eyes adjusted to the darkness, faster than what was possible before. In various microwave mediated voices they "oohed" and "aahed" at the myriads of stars, undimmed by atmosphere. Only one cluster, Afeni, was visible, and now you could see those thousands of stars as individual bright points rather than a diffuse cloud. It was breathtaking if she could have taken a breath.

Soon the shuttle would do a roll and the sun would come into view. They didn't want to stress their hardware with extreme temperature differentials and hard UV. Their bodies could handle it, but reducing the time to the next checkup was unnecessary, so the hatch was closed after a few minutes.

They sat and talked about it and what they expected to find. There was a lot of speculation. Lots of modeling with code and results passed around between them as if they were presented memos rather than constructs in their heads. There was an afterthought, a feeling, that when the hatch was open, she had felt something new. Only now coming into plain sight. She took some moments to pin it down; she now understood this was their domain, their home. They were no longer creatures of Corvena. They were being born anew. She relaxed back into her seat and let the warm glow of the thoughts of her companions bathe her like the massed stars of Afeni, a cluster of community and dreams.

She imagined Luna 3 to be a Utopian settlement of gleaming towers and environment domes filled with forests and living things. Instead, she found a construction site. No towers, gleaming or otherwise, just excavations and building work in a series of natural craters. It was all explained to them, at speeds suited to machines rather than corvi. Perhaps it was only seconds, but it had felt like days of instruction. There was a cluster of optimally sized natural craters each less than a kilometer in diameter. They would be excavated further; mined, domed, and then covered with a protective layer of regolith. One dome might have an oxygen-nitrogen atmosphere with plants and animals from Corvena but the others would be thin nitrogen-only atmospheres, much less corroding. And why would you even need oxygen?

There were some existing buildings constructed in some small craters. Covered in dirt giving protection from small meteoroids, and horizontal impact debris from impacts over the horizon, which she discovered were more likely. Being machines had an advantage, they didn't care about the one-eighth gravity, no biological impacts. So her environment at first was bland, lifeless, and claustrophobic. And dusty, there was impact dust everywhere, like volcanic ash. The low nitrogen atmosphere made it easier to deal with, it being easier to vacuum up material when you weren't in an actual hard vacuum, but it was still annoying.

Construction of Three was progressing and by the end of the month they would have real quarters with 'real' being a popular synonym for comfortable. They still needed sleep; no one called it 'scheduled down time,' though that was what it was. It was time for their new brains to filter data and do extensive memory integration. For corvi this could take many hours, but for the Changelings it took minutes. However, a universal homesickness made 'sleep' last for six hours. It gave their subconscious mode an opportunity to explore many unusual insights and connections, then process it as a list of ideas for discussion on waking. It was like the best part of old dreams mixed with remembered insights. She loved it. Later when they abandoned the old ways, the long sleeps stayed.

All of that was incidental after their first major briefing. They were assigned projects, not for the construction of the base, that was already in hand. The goal of the Changeling projects was to improve the technical, scientific, and economic systems back home. Her project involved town planning and transport optimization across the southern coast of the Yosah Federation. Her decisions, if accepted, would shape people's lives for generations.

It was lunchtime, or the socially accepted replacement for it.

Vishov sat next to her in the large Gathering Room for a chat and drink of isox. The room was a place to sit in familiar surroundings and decor and talk, discuss everyday things, laugh, and make friends. She had not known Vishov for long and was nervous about having a drink with him. Old ways died hard. They didn't need to drink, but there were some chemicals and oils they needed small amounts of from time to time, so the dispensers added them to a drink, one that would not boil away into vapor at the atmospheric pressure of the base. It was a social habit people found comforting and a reminder of their deep links to a life forever lost for a noble ideal, or perhaps a noble delusion—too often the same thing.

"How is your project going, Emari?"

"It's a maze of intractable problems. Some technical, some political, some social," she said.

"If it was easy, they wouldn't be paying us so much, would they?"

They both laughed at the lame joke, now somehow hilarious because they were sharing it.

"This thinking environment is amazing," she said, "I can see all the problems laid out before me, even as we speak. Before me are the interrelationships of all the components with live data, modeling math and code, and simulation updates, yet it doesn't distract from my conversation. And I don't forget bits, and I can shut it off or return to it in an instant with almost no context switch overhead."

"But you miss family and Corvena. It doesn't take a genius to tell that we all feel it, or almost all of us. Speaking of feelings and opinions, have you noticed the factions here?" He leaned forward in the chair, tension in his artificial eyes.

"No, I've only been here for 47 days, same as you." As usual, details like Vishov's arrival date and the elapsed time came without effort. She only required action to decide whether to round out to the nearest day instead of giving it to the second.

Vishov continued. "There's a group that is pretty gung-ho and are all about duty. Call themselves High Corvena. Then there are the Rebels who want to fight the system, even though their hardware will forbid them from doing anything but whining about it. There's also a rumor of a third group who are probably the real subversives, though I can't tell if they exist or not."

"So I guess you figure I'm a natural for High Corvena? Seems like a poor range of options. I should form my own faction. 'Travel to the stars and explore interesting worlds.' That will be my slogan, sounds like a future I could get behind," she said, surprising herself with how good it did sound compared to what they were doing here.

"I know it all seems like a joke, but here we are in isolation. Isolated communities can be pathological, they don't necessarily see all sides to the moral issues," Vishov said, playing with his empty cup with both hands, twirling it as if rotating the cup would present the answer to his thesis. Spinning on its rim, the cup executed an enthralling slow ballet of physics. "These factions worry me. I've been running a pet project simulating their behavior and whether it could be a threat to the Common Goal."

She stopped for a moment and pondered it. But it was only a moment, perhaps half a second.

"You have access to the system logs and metadata. That's the only way you could do it, everything else is locked down too tightly."

"No hiding stuff from you. Look, I've noticed the obvious clustering: High Corvena and the Rebels. But there is a vague third cluster. The signal in the data isn't as strong but I'm convinced it's real. I've nicknamed them Afeni after the star cluster visible on our way up here."

"I thought you said the third group was a rumor?"

"Okay, I lied. I didn't want to admit it was my own crazy delusion."

"Delusions aren't usually backed by data. Do you know who is in Afeni?"

"No, the links were anonymous spoofed connections. But here's the thing, they were related to group mind dynamics and advanced network design. There's also mention of a project name, Kuno Kamoi. It's old Chedzee..."

"Yes, it means, 'Heart of Minds', approximately. It isn't correct Chedzee, it is a poetic form used before the time of Aukee." It pleased her. She didn't need to access the datanet to know this.

"They seem to translate it as Mind Intersection, or even Hive Core."

She couldn't leave Vishov's revelation alone. It nagged at her until she gave in and looked herself and found something. Deep in the data, she got a statistical fix on a likely member of the Afeni group.

Moshaz was a mid-tier member of Luna 3 who had been on the moon for 185 days. Her statistical analysis of the metadata was complex, and although it was obfuscated, first by official processes and then by someone else, there was something there. The low quality of the data meant it appeared innocuous but with a faint signal in the noise. She teased out a network of associations between the data and some identified users. There was a distinct bias of connections for three people, and first on the list was Moshaz Lar isk Vankar. It wasn't certain, in fact, at 37% the odds were against her, but Moshaz was the clearest signal in the data. She would have to be subtle.

Now he sat opposite her in the Lounge over a cup of isox. She had invited herself to his table and started with some idle chatter: the state of Corvena, what are you doing, how was work going, discover anything interesting?

There was no easy segue into what she wanted to talk about, so she thought she would just jump in, not straight to the question, maybe dance around the topic; fish for interest. He might suspect, but what was he going to do, throw her out of an airlock? An annoying inconvenience, nothing more.

"I've been working on a hobby project. I guess most of us have things like that here. Not much else to do, is there?"

There was no reaction. So she continued.

"I've been looking at the social and information network dynamics of our little community. I know people report their work, official summaries and casual banter but their insights and groping on the way to discovery aren't reported, but you can find them in their search data."

He looked up, fixing her to the room with a steady glare, sizing her up.

"And, what did you find?" He said with a tone that also said he didn't care.

"For example, there is a group working on a series of artistic works on the floor of Vidi Nuba Crater. It's about 130 kilometers in diameter, which means a large canvas for them to work on. Some of the works include exquisite structures. Very exciting, I can't wait to see it," she said.

Still nothing. His reticence quiet and impenetrable almost like the machine he was, and she was. She didn't want to go down that path.

"Anything else?" he said.

She couldn't betray Vishov, so she would have to claim she stumbled on this herself.

"I found an interesting cluster of activity around advanced network design and group mind dynamics. So far, I don't understand what's going on with it. I've asked around. No one seemed interested. Then I saw that you have some background from 'before,' you know, before becoming a Changeling, so I thought you might know something about it or who I might talk to," she said.

A subtle change came over him. An easing in his shoulders, the 'muscles' of his face. They were still so corvi.

"*Changeling*, such an ugly word. We should think of something to replace it. As for your question, why don't you post a system-wide request if you are looking for special interest groups? Come to think of it, why are you interested at all? Are you a network designer?" he said.

"We're all network designers here. We can all change expertise like clothes, one day we can be a physicist, the next a mathematician, the next a biologist. All right, perhaps it isn't quite that easy, but we can gain expertise in any field we wish with ease. I don't want to post system-wide requests because they are visible from Corvena. We aren't completely free here, we're just on a long unbreakable leash."

He smiled. "We are. You know, if you suspect something, then be careful about exposing it. Remember, the authorities on Corvena have us isolated in separate colonies, each in a little crater. They can just order the main lunar base to fire tactical nukes at the Luna 3 Complex and it resolves the problem and no one else will ever know, we're on the moon after all."

"Why would they do that after all they have invested?"

"Because they are dominated by prejudices, atavistic passions, and hard-nosed military minds. You or I would open a dialogue and try to understand, but there's a reason Corvena has been to the brink several times. Just consider we could be the next victims. So please be careful," he said. He looked at her for a moment as if to emphasize his words and then stood.

"But if enough of them think we are people, then we can talk this out. That's why we are here in the first place, isn't it?" she said.

He sat down again, leaning forward in the chair. His eyes scrunched as a deep sadness crossed his face like a shadow. "We aren't people, because people have free will. They are free to choose, to kill and maim, to take power, and because that is suppressed in our new bodies and minds they say we are no longer corvi."

"Our bodies and minds are things of design, not evolution. Designs can change. Upgrades can be made," she said.

"But would we want it, Emari? Would we think of such a choice as a betrayal of our commitment? Don't forget those restrictions also apply to creating new Changelings."

"Give me a thousand years and I might have an answer to that," she said.

"Good answer, given that body of yours has an expected lifetime of fifty years. You know, the lowest bidder for the contract wins."

He stood again.

She looked up at him. "I don't know what it is, but your secret is safe with me."

He smiled at her. "Then perhaps this is the beginning of an interesting working relationship. I shall see you later, I hope." He stood and left.

It appeared she was in.

Afeni, it turned out was more than she imagined. Now it was familiar, and her initial confidence and assumptions borne of ignorance seemed childish. She sat on a balcony in hard vacuum, looking out at the expanse of hills and rolling moonscape. Bright gray and hard black under a charcoal-velvet sky. The balcony was separate from Luna 3 since it needed to be on the crater rim above the base; it was therefore vulnerable to meteoroids from space or from impact debris.

Vishov had been right, and in an ironic inversion now she would speak to him instead.

She sensed his presence on the balcony. He walked across the light blue and white promenade to her table. She switched to directed laser communications. The intensity was minimal, almost invisible, emitted from her face, yet the frequency so precise that detection and information transfer was flawless.

"Not afraid of meteoroids, I see. They can do a fair bit of damage. Might be microscopic but at ten or more kilometers per second they pack a punch," he said sitting down opposite her.

"Easily self-repaired. And you don't seem to be quaking in your boots either," she said, maintaining her gaze as if something on the horizon had her attention. She turned and looked at him, her eyes smiling.

"Remember Afeni? That cluster you wondered about. Did you ever follow it up?"

He fake-relaxed and looked out to the horizon, trying to avoid embarrassment. "No, I, it seemed frivolous. I'm supposed to be developing new anti-cancer drug strategies, not becoming a paranoid hacker."

She smiled again, reached over and placed her hand on his arm, barely touching his clothes. "Vishov, I found Afeni. They are real."

"So, there is a loose special interest group at Luna 3. I imagine if I redid that work I would find twenty or more by now," he said.

"Maybe, but Afeni is special. Very special."

She lifted her hand, then grabbed his arm to emphasize her point. A thrill went through her body. It surprised her catching her off-guard. She withdrew her hand as if he was on fire, but not her eyes. "I didn't think we could..."

"They made us as close to corvi as possible, except for the blocks on dangerous behavior. That means we are fully capable of sexual and emotional needs and desires. If you haven't felt it before then you must still have the default level settings. You can change them you know." His words were a revelation. It almost made her forget why she had arranged this meeting.

"I see. I want to get back to what I wanted to say," she fumbled for words.

"It's important, Emari. The original settings were so we wouldn't have extreme reactions in our first few lunar months. You must have been out of the normal social feeds not to have seen it discussed."

She sat up. One thing at a time, she thought, as her body tingled. "About Afeni. Afeni are working on a project to change us. To free us, expand our lifetime and functionality. They've developed innovations that were previously unthinkable. Collective consciousness.

Dramatically improved nanites. New power sources. We can even overcome our programming if we wish."

"You're taking a risk telling me all of this. Why wouldn't I tell Luna Central about it all?" he said.

"I may not have been keeping up to date in the social circles, but I have been paying attention to events back on Corvena. Do you know what they are saying down there? That we were a mistake, that we should be taken back and incarcerated until we lose power and then scrapped," she said.

He fidgeted. "Look. I know it seems bad but..."

"It's more than just bad. The defenders started with arguing basic rights. Now they have fallen back to legal contract technicalities. It won't be long before the politicians give way. If they hear we are trying to become independent, then they won't bother shipping us back, they'll just end us all here," she said standing and leaning over the table toward Vishov, threatening, a friendship damaging stance she never meant.

"I'm sorry, Vishov. I got carried away," she said.

"It's all right, Emari," he said. But it wasn't.

One day she would heal this misstep, but it would have to wait.

"Please think it over, this is important for all of us. We need more people like you on our side, Vishov. We could do great things if we were truly free."

He looked away from her and out to the horizon. Thinking.

He stood and moved towards the door.

Then he turned, all hesitation gone.

"Count me in."

As they had predicted, the government terminated the project. Luna 3 refused the order.

Corvena, in response, sent kill commands to all the systems, including nanite control nodes in their bodies. Nothing happened. They fired a series of nukes at the Luna 3 domes. Nothing happened. So, in short order, a detachment of soldiers in space suits breached the doors of Luna 3. They found the complex abandoned, stripped, data stores either taken or wiped, with no evidence to where they had gone or how. The government reported in the news feeds that Luna 3 had suffered a catastrophic event; they also sowed rumors and conspiracy theories that it was nuked. Between the official story and the conspiracy theory, there was no room for the truth.

When civilization faltered again, the Changelings returned, but with a new name. They insisted they were the true Vanaya. They blanketed all communications with their proclamation that the people on Corvena had abandoned unity and become enslaved to partisan ideals and tribal loyalties.

Those who wished to join the True Vanaya could do so after screening. In the meantime, the Afeni Conclave would administer Corvena, as was their duty.

The Conclave knew civilization could fall, but events need not end in such a catastrophe. They were selected for their sense of duty and it showed in their decisions. But the more they intervened the worse things got and in time they saw that subtlety was the only path open to them. They saved Corvena, at least for a thousand years they hoped, but knew their true goal was to help and not to dictate. One day they would have to leave Corvena for good and let it find its own path.

For a few seconds, he was still Emari in her synthetic body.

The sun was coming up. A pinkish brown glare on the horizon.

"Emari, I have so many questions," Ray said.

"I can't answer them yet, there are just too many sad memories there."

He was facing her, but she looked to the side away from him, trying to dodge his gaze here where there was no escape.

"These visions, why are they always about you?"

"Showing her guilt I would guess," Ramon chimed in on cue.

"Don't be an ass, Ramon. She's distressed. Live long enough and you will have made mountains of mistakes too. Or, maybe that's your problem," Zara said.

"We have. Believe me," Ramon said looking at Ray.

Ray glared back.

Zara stepped forward. No longer that touch of command in her voice. Now it was soothing and gentle. "Don't worry, Ray. Ramon is just under a lot of stress. A lot happened to him you don't remember."

Ramon seated on a rock looked up at Zara, "You seem to know a damn lot about all of this, including my life. How is that?"

"I did some research. Examined your Life Files. I've seen your personality map, the detailed memory recordings and much more."

She walked up to Ramon. She ran her hand down the left side of his face for a few spellbinding moments. He didn't notice. Ray thought she would take control of him, there were humans who could do that, it was an ancient practice making use of human cognitive biases. But he feared something different and less subtle. Foremost he had to remember that this guy was himself and what was done to him was also an attack on himself.

"What are you doing to him?" Ray yelled.

She looked at Ray with a forgiving smile. He took a step back in unrefined fear as if he discovered she was a barely concealed monster.

"Don't come near me, Zara. I mean it."

Emari looked on, focusing on Zara as she stepped towards Ray, saying nothing. Something was not being said here. They knew each other he was sure.

Ramon stood up clueless to what was going on still thinking about Emari while looking at Zara and Ray.

"Have you two forgotten she was there at the beginning? She was part of Afeni. It became the Hive Core, the Kamoi, the granddaddy of conspiracies. The Illuminati are real and live at the core of the galaxy,"

Ramon went on, gesturing to the sad toxic sky, hamming it up.

Ramon seemed less an intruder now and if anyone could understand Ramon it should be Ray. At one stage he had wanted to do real violence to his other self. A pointless act. Ray seemed to have none of the supposed emotional limitations of the original Changelings; perhaps they had overcome them or had never imposed them on him.

And Zara, had he misjudged her as well?

Ray repeated his old calming mantra, a phrase from so long ago even in his personal time yet it still seemed to work. He stood up straighter and more relaxed. He would have to practice the mantra a lot more. Here he was zipping across the galaxy carrying his own private hell with him in the service of a divine physical and spiritual chameleon. He didn't have much influence, but he refused to play the name game anymore.

"And, Maria. Can I call you Emari from now?" he said rather than asked. "I never knew you as Maria and now I know you more as Emari than I ever knew you as Ranei. Anyway, let's get a move on, this place is dark and depressing." He didn't wait for her reply. As easy as a reflex and with as much thought he opened a jump window.

nine

NGC 6981, another globular cluster, also about 42,000 light years from the core. But the view was beyond anything he expected.

They stood on a small spherical asteroid, about twenty kilometers in diameter, in a gravity so low that a single footstep should send them floating off, though nowhere near the escape velocity. He wanted to jump and leave this world, for above them was a wonder. A vast three-dimensional structure like the branches of some crazy, smooth mathematical tree, fractal in overall design, now held their little world-rock like a fish in a vast net. The 'tree' glowed in places while shimmering waves of light and color flowed along the branches like nerve impulses. He could not judge its size, but he suspected it must span at least a hundred kilometers.

Emari said nothing. Wonder is a rare, even frightening experience for ageless beings who think they have seen it all.

"What is it?" Ray asked. Deep down he knew the non-answer. Nothing inside had an answer, and part of him thrilled to that.

"I—I have seen nothing like it," Emari said.

"It looks a like a smaller version of Eklus, but that was mostly simulation." Simulation was the wrong word, but compared to this it fitted. This was real, this was nuts and bolts.

Ramon was quiet for a moment. Then he spoke with care, each word measured as if his words traced a path across an ancient deadly puzzle and in doing so would unlock it.

"This is not Vanayan. I think this is the work of a rival of the Vanaya."

Emari bristled. "Rival? What rival? If there were rivals who could build this way out here, we would have records of them."

"Fine, then, who built it?" he said.

Zara shrugged and walked around at random on the uneven rocky surface with enough skill so she didn't drift off.

Ray saw that this structure was a clue to something else, "I'm wondering how the Kamoi knew about it to send us here? We didn't just stumble across this, we were directed here. But not for this..."

He stopped speaking, aware of the familiar sense of a memory swimming below like a fish on a hook waiting to be reeled in, tugging on the line.

"The Vanaya have lots of mysteries. Their history worries me because there is no rival," said Zara.

They looked at her and then, as if not knowing how to deal with it, they ignored it. But Ramon had heard her say 'their'.

It was almost impossible to resist the call now. The memory beckoned like a maddening itch. He didn't want this. There were mysteries and questions about Corvena. Things that affected all of them. But he wasn't being given the time to think about it. Like a work animal from ancient times, he was being prodded on, unable to rest and put the pieces together. Why?

The fish still tugged on the line. A feeling he could not ignore. He wondered if instead he was the fish. Hooked!

High Noon, 2261

She had been here on High Noon for years now, monitoring the slow takeover of the cortex by Castan AI agents. She slipped through the human and Castan web of monitoring and detection like a phantom and overnight became accepted as a long-term member of this strange society. Their modified memories her camouflage. This system was a probable flash point in the coming war between Mirr and Casta. If it happened here, it would pull in the humans. She was drawn to the station by her long interest in Earth, the tensions between Mirr and Casta, and of what lay buried on the planet below. The situation was dangerous and volatile. But there were opportunities.

One day she heard a visitor had come from Earth. Outsiders were always interesting for their possible disruptive effects and she was eager, perhaps desperate, to find a chink in the dark futures stretched before her.

There was an assassination attempt on this man Raymond Tans. Just like there had been on others. She dared not intervene and draw attention to herself. She knew she must be more careful after the Rennae Fulbright fiasco. Despite her caution, Ray survived the attempt, unlike the others, and he did it with skill and insight.

Raymond Tans had now become her best chance of a positive outcome. She would recruit him without his knowledge and defuse the coming crisis or minimize the damage.

He was on a tour of the station and had entered the Lifeshell, a toroidal region of the station containing a miniature forest and path. She had been trying to bump into him, feigning chance, since he arrived without success. His little tour, arranged by his AI, was now her best opportunity, so she made sure she was waiting just where he would walk.

The shell was set to night-mode, as it often was; people in the Dark seemed to crave a warm, living darkness that was vibrant rather than cold and dead. A comforting darkness was a primal need, and not just in humans; it sometimes rekindled memories of Corvena in her with emotions humans had never known, perhaps that was why she spent so much time here. Feeling but not reminiscing.

Her target had entered from the so-called Eastern Entrance. He stood for a moment staring at the brick-like path through the rustling trees under the fake silver-blue moonlight, then walked down it.

She wore her gaming cloak. The essence of mystery, she hoped. She knew he liked and had a sense of the mysterious. He played games but valued his privacy even more. Her plan was to construct a persona to hit that sweet spot of fascination. To trust her so that when she asked him to do something, even though it would seem a casual request to others it would capture his attention, like the request of a lover. And here she was, once again, deep in the gray. Ideally she had to get him to love her. Under her breath she promised herself not to do that, the end didn't justify the means—or did it?—she had seen too many burning worlds to be certain.

"Raymond Tans, is it?" she asked. "My name is Ranei Chan-Orsen."

She was scanning him, using technology that his sensors would not pick up. She decided not to plant a bug on him to spy on his link. It was easy to do but any detection of it—unlikely as that was—would be fatal to his trust. She didn't know if this relationship would be useful or not but from ages of experience her instincts told her he was important.

She asked him about nanotech, acting the part of a Dark Dweller and their ridiculous optimism for tech fixes. The doubt was no surprise, but she also saw faint visual cues that he was holding back on further skepticism. He was intelligent and skeptical but didn't reveal all in a threatening environment.

"Here in the Lifeshell, once a month, there are a series of challenges. Basically, knife fights and sword fights. Real weapons, of course. The next one is in two days, you should come and watch," she said.

She wondered how he would react to this news. She had seen so much that she was numb to the disgust she wanted to feel. Away from it that disgust would come out and fall onto her opinion of the society that encouraged it. Leaving her spotless, she hoped.

He played around the topic questioning it, holding back, hiding his clear objection when she confirmed his suspicion that people got killed.

"Of course they do. People get injured and killed all the time. But then they are put in a medic tube and fixed. And any traumas are erased. So where's the harm? High Noon is always calm."

"Don't you ever suffer grief or distress here? I've heard you lost some people. Surely they were missed."

"What? No. The grief and distress, as you call it— we fixed it. The memory was postfaded."

Postfading. A bitter mirror to her own life. The people of High Noon used forgetting to ease pain and forget crimes. It was too close to home.

Without prompting he asked about the hood of her cloak and displayed obvious enthusiasm when she talked about live action role-playing. It wasn't just in his words but in all metrics: pupil dilation, IR skin emissions, voice intonation, heart rate. This was an opportunity, but she had to work out what she would do with it. What part would he play?

Her opening move would be an invitation to the role-playing game she ran.

"Our favorite is based on the Chronicles of the Vanaya, a fictional construction," she said.

"Of a fictional people as far as anyone can tell," he said. Sometimes when the reality of her own people came up in conversation, it was tempting to tell the truth or a portion. She knew that was the reason she had set the game on Corvena during the post-Mavanaya Interregnum. A time of legends, just as the European Dark Ages had spawned stories such as King Arthur. But secrecy was essential and her only response now was an unintelligible shrug in the dark.

He accepted her offer but seemed distracted. Would he survive the coming storm? She hoped so and wanted to know him better, and although she liked him part of her also thought of him as an expendable chess piece.

She left him with an invocation from the roleplaying game. It was a translated ritual she had learned as a child. It brought her a subdued delight to deliver a blessing from Insa, the goddess of harmony.

She visited him from time to time in his room and vice versa. Part of her still functioned as if he was a pawn in a game of chess but each time her plotting sickened her more. She was falling for him as she did with Joseph Fulbright. There was a stab of pain at remembering Joe, now dulled somewhat by her love for this unknowing pawn forging ahead into the valley of the shadow of death. She could only do so much for him though he was at such high risk. His chances of survival were slim.

He left for Pavarr with Ben. Ben, the time bomb, but she couldn't warn Ray. There was no way to convince him without revealing herself and she fretted in the days he was gone, filled with a worry she couldn't dispel as if she still had hearts that pumped actual blood. His return thrilled her like a teenage human female greeting her lover.

She burned with hope and saw that with him she might achieve a measure of peace. They could travel together between the stars as he helped her mission not knowing the truth. It was a foolish dream but foolish dreams can change a world or a galaxy. She needed him and he needed her though he might not realize it yet.

And some days she wondered if her loneliness was driving her insane.

Then one day he accepted her invitation to a round of the game.

That night in the Lifeshell she started the introduction to the game with a greeting and a goblet of wine, symbolic of the commitment to a great undertaking. She materialized the wine on the spot hoping he wouldn't ask where it came from or inspect it; it was drugged and spiked with some interesting nanites. The Mirrish had hardened his link hardware and software, a bonus she could use, but she would add an extra hidden level and make him more susceptible to her commands. With luck her commands could override the Castan ones.

He resisted using direct memory downloads for the game, insisting on plain text blocks of information; so stubborn.

He labored heroically tackling the conversion of the text into knowledge of the world, and how to invoke the tech-magic of the game. And then, in an instant, he gave that up and linked to the Cortex for direct memory downloads of the game. The Cortex would try to take control but she had the upper hand. In the meantime, they might as well have fun so she gave him a rich and moving experience of the game. They fought and won against terrifying odds, bonded in strife and turmoil. It would all fade but for a little time they would be together and close.

He woke in bed next to her. Then she saw it in his eyes. Her nanites confirmed it. He was under attack from the Cortex.

The corrupted Cortex now saw its chance to wipe his mind and clear any threat to itself. But he fought it in every moment.

Now was the time. She activated her nanites, they would give him time and an edge, but not a guaranteed victory, that was not permitted to her.

"How do you feel? It feels great doesn't it. I'll make it feel even better, lover," she said trying to distract him from the inner battle.

She embraced him but the afterglow of the game had faded and his conscious mind had forgotten those events.

"I thought you were my muse," he said.

"I inspire in lots of ways. I can be your muse forever. After you are finished here why don't we leave this place together? If not I'll find you, if that doesn't creep you out," she said and something in her hearts wanted this to be true in every sense.

"Ha. That would be perfect."

She wanted to stay with him here and now, make him love her, but they were entering the focal point of many dangerous actors and events. Time to snap him out of it.

"Ben told me about your brother. How he died, and you felt responsible. It's common you know, you want to think you had some control, that it wasn't blind fate. I read the news feed archives we get from Earth. It wasn't your fault, in fact you were lucky to survive. There are many people who care about you, Ray. Don't give up on us."

He looked perplexed. The attacks were increasing. There was no more time.

"Still not used to it? Never mind. Why don't you see Ben? Right now. He always cheers us up. I know he can make you feel better," she said, and with her nanites it became an emotional command.

He rose and left quickly, compulsively. It was out of her hands now.

She tracked his progress, his confrontations, and then him leaving. He was safe. But it wasn't over. Now all she could do was wait. She had done a lot of that over the endless years. She acted as she always did as a normal member of the society, inconsequential, a bystander. Whatever he did, wherever he was, she could no longer intervene.

She knew the human side of the battle was won when the station lost gravity. She sensed and monitored the reset and rebuild of the Cortex. She saw it rapidly, scanning the links and discovering the tampering by the Castan device. It never saw her. She immediately hacked the Cortex and eliminated her existence from everyone's memory.

It wasn't over. He left without visiting her. She knew he had to, but she was still disappointed, and he was heading for Togore. She wished he had not gone there. Based on Castan data, she had determined a likely Castan strategy; they would attack and cause terrible devastation. But humans and Mirr would survive. She hoped he would too.

It turned out better than expected. Except for her. Reason had returned with a bitter logic that quashed her hopes.

The day came when he was to leave the station. High Noon was safe. Most had forgotten what Ray had done, all a result of the new cortex repairing the damage.

Ray looked around the party celebrating the sendoff for the Special Contracts crew and himself though everyone seemed to think he was just another outsider. He looked alone and lost. It was as if all his friends here had died or left him, but they had not, and because they had not, he could not grieve. They still lived, just their memories of him were gone. It was a strange sadness she understood. She wanted to talk with him and go wherever he was heading. She had many happy years with Joseph but she couldn't even give this man a farewell kiss.

He looked lonely standing there, trying to regain his emotional balance, as she watched from the other side of the large room. He didn't see her as she stood there in the form of another woman that the cortex and the people now believed had always been here. A sudden need almost overwhelmed her to go somewhere private, enable her tear ducts and just cry. She wouldn't do that, but she couldn't forget either, at least not for a while. There were worlds to save. And, in the end, it was about she not he.

He stood for a moment paralyzed trying to understand what he had just witnessed.

"You used me," he said without malice as the shock swept away his anger.

Then the anger surged back, "You used me! Why? Why?" But he knew 'why'. When you are saving worlds, individuals can be lost in the swirl of events. And yet the raw experience still scoured a path through him.

She faced him with tears in her eyes. Fake tears, liquid water couldn't exist here. But he knew they came from the heart, or hearts.

"I'm sorry, Ray. If I didn't help you, they would have killed you," she said.

"I know. I don't know. Maybe I fooled myself into thinking I did all that by myself."

Ray glanced at Ramon expecting him to be looking at the bizarre light show above them thinking of a witty response, or about to utter something biting, but he was downcast. When he spoke there was an uncharacteristic sadness.

"I never forgot you, Ranei. I blamed myself for your disappearance. Could never get it out of my head. After, you know, I ended up getting married to Avril. Hard as that is to believe." Ramon paused, a shadow of pain eclipsed his self-mocking, "She took a human body. Man, this hurts remembering it all."

Part of Ray reached out to Ramon and saw, somehow, a memory. He touched it, made it real as if it was one of Emari's memories.

He was in a room. Decked out like his home in New Shanghai in Siberia; Scandinavian furniture with rich tropical colors everywhere. This was not Siberia, they were in the spin-city of Skadi, a large rotating habitat nestled in a crater on the asteroid Pallas. Before him was himself, a little older, and a young woman, red-haired.

"Come with me, Ray. We can live a normal life on Term. Leave the company to the AIs, I know them and trust them, they're good people," the woman said. Her voice was like a song.

"No. I can't yet. Look, there are some things to do," said the older Ray.

"It's about her, isn't it? It wasn't your fault. Don't grieve over her the way you did over Chris."

"Don't bring Chris into this. Avril, just... stop," he said and paced across the sparse room. Fists clenching, jaw muscles bulging.

He turned towards her, calming himself. "I'm sorry. Maybe later."

"Maybe? It isn't grief, is it? You're still in love with her, aren't you? Admit it. I don't know what happened there, I don't have the memtrace of the other me but something about Ranei sounds wrong. Not sure why. Come with me, Ray. Come with us and forget her," she pleaded.

"Can't."

"You mean won't. I'm not staying here when you're like this. You will not screw up my kids with your obsession."

"They're our kids. Mine too. Don't go. I need you."

"No. No, you don't. I know you too well. I love you so much, but I can't stay. Can't stay. That's it, we are leaving," she said through tears and ran from the room.

The scene faded, leaving them standing in the surreal landscape.

Ray was shaking, the emotions washed over him like a surf wave lifting him, waiting for the cresting water to smash him in the face.

"Our marriage ended in separation. She took the kids and returned to Term. When I was restored by the Kamoi or whoever I realized what Ranei was and how much I was manipulated. You threw a bag of poison

177

into my life, Emari. Can you blame me for being angry?"

Ray looked at Ramon, his body framed by a fantastical background, an assemblage of slow pulsating neon snake forms. He never looked more demonic yet feel more human.

"I don't know, she was just doing what she thought was right. We just happened to be in the wrong place at the wrong time. Probably discovered a recording of our minds only recently," Ray said.

"You think so? Have you worked out yet how come the Vanaya have a record of our mind and consciousness? Take a guess," Ramon said, "she took the measurements herself, disguised as someone else, supposedly to create a personality for a starship. But she had her own agenda and her own technology."

They both looked at Emari, but she didn't respond. They waited for almost a minute.

Ray turned to Zara, standing with her arms crossed examining the whole scene; remote and cryptic.

"Can you give us some of your Vanayan insights into any of this?" Ray said.

Seconds passed before she spoke.

"I try to have no opinions of your women," she said in an Australian accent.

Ray and Ramon replied in unison.

"Avril?"

"Don't ask me how I got here because I don't know. I know some incredible stuff, but I do not understand how. Last thing I remember was becoming part of the High Noon Cortex. Then I was here, on that beach. Bloody Vanaya." She looked at Emari. "I guessed it was Ranei's work when I first awoke. Didn't know she was Vanaya back then, but guessed she was something like that. But the OpenCortex you were using Ray was very limited I couldn't do much, so I was never sure about her."

"When you talked to me after the upload to the High Noon Cortex you were exuberant and gushing, talking about my 'great future' or something," Ray said. "But you were pretty tight lipped, wouldn't tell me anything about it. I presumed you were having an AI high from all the new processing power."

"Avril, I don't know who brought you back," Emari said, "I made a copy while you were transferring to the cortex, just as a precaution, but I haven't touched it since. All valid bodies in the Dream have an assigned ID. Ray has one now, so does Ramon, you don't. But you have a physical form. I do not understand why you are here or how. Jeez, I have no idea why any of us are on this path. This isn't what I was expecting."

"How would you know what to expect if you were investigating something? Wouldn't you just follow the clues?" Zara said.

Emari brushed the question off.

"You don't look like my Avril. She was redheaded and not so tall. But the hypnotic voice is almost the same," Ramon said.

"I'm sorry, Ramon. I have no memories of that. Or of romantic love, just a desire to be with you and protect you. Both of you. Just don't call me Avril, will you? It doesn't feel right."

"Didn't you say you had a lot of knowledge about our histories? You knew about the Kamoi too," Ray said.

"I lied. There's some readily available basic data about the Vanaya. I—was an AI, I'm used to ferreting out things so when I appeared I looked for anything to make sense of this. Discovered the basic introduction to the Vanaya and the Core and faked the rest."

Ray needed to short circuit this agonizing personal talk it was too uncomfortable and Avril being here, he didn't know what to think.

"Right. We have a party of four, half of which is of dubious provenance—no sign of why they are here. Which makes me wonder, do I really know what I am supposed to be doing? Hey, Emari? Why am I here? Am I on this grand mission of yours to save 'our people' or something else? Because we seem to have a spectacular lack of progress here."

Saying it was like having a bucket of ice water thrown in his face. Those were his secret fears and the farther they went, the less certain he was about anything.

"Screw this. Okay, let's get out of here. The sooner we get to the end of this tour, the better. Next location is—no clue," and then in the next moment he had the coordinates and opened a jump window.

ten

A dead world roasted by a flaring orange sun above. The sun looked massive and blotchy. A red dwarf up close. Below, a red desert inferno against a background of black infinity. Spectacular and impressive to any living thing with the wits to see and understand it. But way out here, how often would any being see it? Only this one accidental time—this was its moment of fame, and it was just a backdrop.

"Palomar 1, a galactic cluster 56,000 light years from the core," Ray said in a lackluster voice. He was weary. "Is there any point to this entire journey?" He asked no one. Running from his doubts didn't work.

He looked out across the orange, worn sands to the jet black horizon. No atmosphere. No sign of civilization. He in his invulnerable body was tired and his spirit exhausted.

"Couldn't we just jump to a nice beach with a decent surf? I'd like that. I'd like to sleep but each time I close my eyes..."

"Sleep for beings such as us is a learned skill," Emari said, but her voice was shaky.

"What's the problem?" Ramon asked.

"I don't know. I feel strange here. Alone. I don't feel well at all."

She stumbled and went down on her left knee, the orange-red sand spilling in silence as first her knee then her left hand made contact. He saw this, some isolated part of him still fascinated that they were all physical, but indestructible. But now the goddess was on her knees.

Ray walked over and helped her up. She put her arm around his shoulder, looking into his eyes.

"What is going on here? Tell me, Emari, describe how you feel."

Now Ramon sensed the weakness oozing into his extremities. "Same here. Like I'm tingling and weak."

Emari stood straighter, though she swayed a little. "Weak, disconnected. It's hard to think."

"How are you, Ramon?" Ray said.

Ray was confused and didn't understand this. He was fine, better than fine or okay, in fact perfect. The malaise that was there earlier had disappeared as if it had never existed.

"Woozy," Ramon said, strangely at a loss for words.

"Zara, how about you?"

"I'm good. Apart from the strangeness of—being human—you know having a body with desires and strong emotions."

"Strange. I feel perfectly fine. In fact, wonderful."

Emari grabbed him by the left arm for support. Her raw vulnerability was frightening to all of them.

"I continue to get stronger the further we get from the Kamoi but the two of you get weaker," he said trying to work up some kind of logical argument but it just fell flat.

"We're too far from the Core. The jump infrastructure doesn't extend out this far efficiently. Each of our jumps now takes years or maybe even centuries. I think, I'm not sure, it's hard to think. I can't bring up my inner view."

Her voice had an edge of panic. No inner view meant she had lost the amazing dreamworld of their subconscious where precise multidimensional models paraded before each of them. To know by wishing for it. To entertain a million different possibilities. It defined her and implied that her sense of Self was eroding. A slow death.

"But why do you get stronger?" Emari said holding on to him but swaying as if a gusty wind was battering her.

"Could it be something about this place? We should go closer to the Kamoi, perhaps." He looked inward for a return path, but there was nothing. If they lingered here would he succumb too?

Ray looked at the other two, trying to fathom why they also responded so differently to this place.

Thinking of Ramon and Avril was like a brush with fate. He had seen a parallel universe where his life and his actions ended up in a train wreck. It wasn't a parallel universe though because it was directly in front of him; it had happened. There was no mystery now around Ramon's bitterness and how such a mistake could infect him, whichever him he thought about. It had screwed up his life once, and it wasn't her fault; the problem came from within himself. But he wasn't human anymore. He could fix this, he was sure of it. Or had that already been done? Had they tampered with him?

He looked inside himself, searching for information on how his own mind worked. The inner view was not visual, it was more. Vision was there but so too were reason and comprehension, and within all that and past all those doors to 'knowledge' sat a core defining what he was. Like a yogi understanding how to slow his heartbeat, yet his knowledge expanded far beyond such trivial things. Within were the fundamental algorithms for basic things like vision— and all the enhancements to emulate any species—and further inward were the idiosyncratic habits and characteristics that made Raymond Tans. Among those parts of him he found an obsessive trait, he could see how it allowed him to do many things. He didn't want to interfere with the focus but rather the narrowing persistent focus, the inability to step back, take a breath and move on. Some areas he could not change, but there were opportunities. The intricate system relied on some sensitive logical and learned components; all he had to do was move this so and that other thing ever so gently. Someone had already done it. He could see how it once was and the care taken to make the smallest of changes. Emari's work. She cared.

I must share this, he thought. Still in the inner view he looked about. A mesh network connected all of them, and no one was central. They shared data at a fundamental level. This was the glue that held all the Vanaya together before the rise of the Kamoi. It wasn't scalable, so that as the numbers grew the Core had to use another network topology, but it kept the mesh network as a backup for small groups and strengthened it. Now they were too far from the Kamoi, the mesh was all they had. He saw without eyes the links binding them to one another, not just with data but energy and other things—flowing from him to the others. Zara was intimately connected. Ramon was close but different—a resonant entity, a self displaced in time. A true reflection showing that he was not undead. Emari was on the edge, she was nothing like them; strange, different, but not alien. The mesh was evolving into a different topology.

He passed along a packet of information to Ramon on how to change himself. When the time was right, he would find it and know what to do.

He kept focus on Ramon. Of all of them he should be the easiest to understand, and perhaps understanding him was the key to them getting out of this alive. Then it was as if storm clouds parted and the sun came out. He saw it all.

There was a cavalcade of memories. All at once, as if subjective time had been suspended.

He saw the love between him and Avril, the fights, the words that could not be taken back. Flashing images; raw, intense and visceral. It was too much.

Before they became part of him he shut the memories off. Ramon was not evil he was only hurt. But Ramon was not another person, his hurt was Ray's, he was also hurt, Ray Tans, not Ray or Ramon, there was only one.

He opened his eyes.

He looked about the silent plain. Orange sand and rubble mixed with inky shadows, a flaring sun in the black with vast fiery prominences erupting continually; it was hallucinogenic. He extended his perception, trying to clear his mind of what he had just experienced. They were on the edge of the cluster and facing away from both the cluster and the galaxy, though it was doubtful whether either would be visible under that fearsome orange glare. The system had four planets worthy of the designation and a host of smaller rocks and iceballs.

Inside there was a connection. Like a memory on the tip of your tongue. It exploded into a feast of images, moods, and emotions. Some feelings were truly alien, of many races, of many people, but so familiar. The perception and insight was so strong he could not think of it as anything other than a vision, like a delirium dreamed by gods encompassing worlds and cultures, their rise and fall like a great slow heartbeat. Lives of heroes and cowards, selfless acts and megalomania, all passed through him as a fleeting experience. Snowflakes in a blizzard.

"Are you all right?" Emari said.

He heard her. He feared his reply would never reach her, lost in the blizzard of lives. "I don't know who I am anymore. My mind feels like it is on fire."

"Is there a way out of here? Maybe you would recover then," Ramon said.

"Yes, I think so. I don't know. There's only one link. It's like when I focus on that I have complete confidence about where I am going, but if I try to remember where we have been—the details just slip from me."

Looking at Ramon, he once thought the Kamoi altered his older self, but perhaps it was him being himself. Once he held onto grief for so long, perhaps Ramon was a more faithful version of himself clinging on too long to other painful experiences. No matter, the important thing was to reach out. The feeling passed and again there was the sensation, as if he had just woken up and everything before was a dream.

Ramon didn't look well.

"How are you? You look like shit," Ray said.

"Well, wonder boy, you should see yourself," Ramon smirked, suppressing a chuckle, no sarcasm intended.

"Wonder boy?"

"Something Avril would say when she was cheeky. I miss her, no offense, Zara. But I knew the woman, not just the AI. Though, let's face it, none of us are human any more."

"I miss her too," Ray sighed.

Zara crossed her arms and glared at them. But they didn't notice.

"Sheesh. I'm right here. Just because I'm not sitting on your shoulder commenting on every random thing doesn't mean it isn't me. Though, I have to admit I do feel different."

"You miss the voice in your head, I miss the woman. Big diff, brother," Ramon said as if he had not heard a word from her.

"How did you, I mean we, get together with Avril? Sorry, Zara, I just need to know," Ray asked.

Ramon sighed, anything he said in words would never be right but after a few seconds he nodded, apparently deciding to give it a shot.

"She loved us," he nodded to Zara. "You loved us. But AIs, you know, they only have a vague sense of human emotions. They have them, but they have no biological spin to the feelings. She wanted to be with me and have a biological extension. So they made a body for her with the right neuro-connections. It wasn't a rare thing for AIs to become human. Once she had a body, she decided pretty quickly the love she felt was romantic. I couldn't explain it, you'd have to ask Zara," he said. He looked down as his shoulders slumped, dejected.

"Of course I loved you. Both of you now," Zara said, feeling her way on this strange enticing topic. It made her tingle. "But I am closer to Ray and I don't know why. I don't know what happened between you and me, Ramon. That wasn't me. I can't estimate how the emotions of a living brain would affect my thinking, but I can well believe we became partners. The emotions in me now are so much stronger than when I was an AI, and it is different, so different, I see you, both of you and I can't describe it. I just know I never want to leave you, either of you. It's confusing. When I first woke on the beach, I didn't know what was happening so I resorted to my vanilla persona, but that is gone now."

"Funny," Emari said, "in your world the AIs wanted to become organic and in mine it went the other way. I remember conversations with some AIs in the Nexus who had transitioned. They had no regrets about having frail living bodies. I suppose there's a lesson there, but I don't know what it is. Maybe it's about how that choice can be compatible with saving worlds through deep time?"

"It's about freedom. Why should it have anything to do with anything else?" Ray said.

"I mean potentially immortal beings choosing finite lives."

Ray couldn't answer.

Deep down there was another memory-clue. Ray could sense it below the surface, like a whale about to breach. He could no longer refuse it. It was the only way out.

"I'm a trained rat in a maze," he muttered as he reached for the memory. It opened like a flower ablaze with light. He had only one thought before he was no longer himself, "Why do these memories become more ecstatic for me?"

"Sorry, so far this journey is one way. All right, here goes," he said.

Emri Chiderec Pahe Chihiu watched the pale world below. Milky stains smearing across the surface spoiling the perfect blue globe. Clouds, air, and beneath a living world filled with all the crazy tensions that made sentient life the paradox of hope and futility. Perhaps sentience rather than being considered an accidental consequence should be regarded as a perfect reflection of the perversity of the universe. She smiled at the idea. Was it a new idea or had she had this same thought over and over only to be buried by ages of daily memories?

She was a Tarkoi. Not a female or a male, but the third sex, merely given the name 'dormant'. A dormant could become gendered if they came into a position of dominance, which was why they hung around the fringes of power and why they were treated with contempt. Power was the highest leverage against a dormant, so people in power assumed their favors guaranteed their control.

Tarkoi were tall. About 2.1 to 2.3 meters. Thin, light brown, sometimes coppery skin. Humanoid. The basic design of sentient beings was fairly predictable: a head containing a brain, eyes, ears, chemosensory organs (aka noses), sometimes speech that often was less than about ten kilohertz, usually biped, and so on. Convergent evolution meant most sentients looked vaguely similar, but there were plenty of exceptions, and often the convergent bits were from what would be different species or even phyla on Earth.

Her duties—she was gendered in her own mind—demanded that she could not linger at this window. She was a *veko*, a middle level counter-insurgency agent for the Woquizo Clan, and she had obligations. More than that she was a spy, but right now there was a meeting to attend.

Count Tharri from the nation of Vith was the favored contender for the Viceroy of Yennok, the world below. This space station was neutral territory, selected because even though all the noble houses on the planet were of the Woquizo Clan, there was still competition, fighting, even murder. A microcosm of the greater Tarkoi Empire. Today, in the cavernous gilded hall, he spoke of the need for clan unity, the threats from without and within. That was what he always spoke of. The same speech with different words each time. But his dramatic presentation and force of personality almost made it interesting. She couldn't quite see him on the raised dais at the other end of the room, though his voice boomed from every wall. In moments like this she wished this culture had invented sitting as a social practice rather than endless standing as a mark of respect to everyone. She didn't get tired, but it was annoying since she needed to fake signs of weariness.

"Emri, good to see you here," said Tilth. He was her master and patron. Many leaders used the possibility of dominance as leverage to get dormants to do their bidding, and that often meant activities that led to a troubled sleep. Tilth was better than most. His care seemed genuine, but he was still a product of his time and its culture and sometimes it showed in ways that would have damaged her trust if she was not so untrustworthy herself.

"Greetings, Master Tilth. I have just been thinking about the Count's latest speech," she said.

"I'm not sure what there is to analyze. He might as well have put an old speech of his through a linguistic processor to say the same thing with different words and sentences. But it seems to be what people want to hear. You can never go wrong doing that, well, until the whole thing comes crashing down."

He 'laughed' in his usual way, which sounded to her like "chee-chee". She had not enabled all the instinctive responses, so some natural things like laughter didn't sound at all normal to her.

"It's not so much what he said, but the way he said it. He sounds truly worried this time. Is there something I should be aware of?" she said, not directly looking at her master.

"Meet me at 113 in Gray Meadow Six," he said and rushed off. Others might have thought it rude but she was only a dormant so it didn't matter.

The Tarkoi divided their day into 256 checi. So 113 was late afternoon. The zero hour being set as the moment of daybreak in the Temple of Checi-Omra on the homeworld of Tark on the first day of spring.

He was on Gray Level of the station and had just entered Meadow Ecosystem Six, which honored the day-night cycles of standard clock time. She wandered among the gray-green dry mosses and spindle ferns while overhead a few flying reptiles flew calling to each other in melodic song. A soft breeze rustled the ferns and there was a heady scent from a nearby forest, which didn't exist, but still convincing. A place for meditation and quiet. In the distance Tilth sat on a perfect rock looking at her.

She sat and enabled the encrypted wireless link.

"Count Tharri has good reason for his concern, there are reports of increasing activity in the slave communities. It might be the start of another rebellion," Tilth said with his usual private candor. He clenched and unclenched his fists, a clear act of tension.

"What evidence is there for this?"

"I can't go into it. I need you to investigate. Pursue your usual contacts and report back. Also let them know that if there is a rebellion this time I won't just nuke one of their smaller towns like last time, I will release a pathogen across several cities and they can watch their families die slowly and in agony until they get the cure from us. No point destroying rail lines from the dormitory towns. You may go," he said.

She stood and bowed towards him. "Yes, Master, as you will."

She knew Tilth and the others would do exactly as he threatened, and he was one of the more compassionate Tarkoi. If word of such a rebellion got out, there would be a bloodbath as the Tarkoi would strike first. It didn't matter if a few million died since in time the population would recover. The last time, one troublesome town was the target of three, ten kiloton low radiation weapons in a triangular targeting pattern. It erased the town. Some killer robots went in later to kill any survivors but they found none. The town was almost forgotten, people knew about it as a story but unless they accessed the data they couldn't point to the location on a map. That response was considered by many to be unnecessarily subdued.

Zimuaa checked the peephole again. It had a good view of the dusty street with its single level rundown buildings and closed shop fronts, and should give them ample warning of a raid. His legs twitched with fear; fight, flight. It was hard as an adolescent controlling his emotions. He scampered down the ladder into the old cellar that was their meeting place. A feeble light flickered in the center of the room, as undecorated as the room itself. The light swung in a gentle arc, producing a swirl of shadows straight out of delirium. He chittered a warning-to-silence, and they froze.

"Where is Irenn? Is she coming?" the tough Angsa said. He always gave a fearsome impression. It was his way of handling the fear.

"She's never late, there's still time, and you know how secretive she can be. I doubt I'd see her coming," he said.

From the top of the stairs came a familiar voice, "I'm here, don't worry."

Zimuaa's beady eyes glared at her.

"How do you do that? I checked the street, and I didn't hear the door open. You really must teach me that one day. You know, as if my fucking life depended on it, which it does. Funny how you always seem to turn up out of thin air."

He would calm down. He had to work with her, and despite her refusals she was too valuable to the cause.

They gathered around a small rough wooden table that looked as if it had seen too many intoxicated brawls, spilled meals and drinks, but it matched the ambiance. They often met in rundown old buildings and there was no shortage of those. One day the local authorities would order every one to vacate the town and they would erase it without fanfare. Then the population would rebuild a new town on the same site from delivered materials. They didn't want the slaves to die of poor sanitation or whatever, a waste of good slaves, never mind the few that would die of exposure before they rebuilt the town. That would also suggest a major project was about to start and they would work a good percentage of the workforce to death, or die by execution if one of the Tarkoi had a bad day.

The Gizan she had met could not understand why the Tarkoi had slaves at all. They had machines. If they wanted to build a town, they could deploy machines to do it in a small fraction of the time. If they wanted to build something then they could use machines for that. Why did they need slaves? To Emari the answer was simple: power and prestige. And if you had to explain that, then it would be like explaining the color feti to someone who could not see into the ultraviolet.

The group of eight stood around the small table where a crude map was open. To'opri had spread the map out flat but now looked straight at Irenn with those beady black eyes.

The Gizan were about the height of the old Vanaya, perhaps a little shorter, so the Tarkoi towered over them. They had small delicate fingers capable of the finest manual work, their ears were erect a bit like her own people, but they didn't have the glorious feather-hair. Their faces had forward-facing eyes but a pronounced snout that hinted at their superior sense of smell. They had tufts of gray and black hair over their bodies, including the forearm and a mane. In addition, a surprising short bushy tail, though they stood fully upright, a combination uncommon among the species she could remember—or whatever she allowed herself to remember. They chatted to each other in high pitched rapid voices, but her ears were now Gizan ears and it seemed perfectly normal.

"My contact says the Tarkoi have united to construct something at Jugra-7591," To'opri said in her gruff voice. "We need to find out its purpose. A new project here on Yennok is critical to the Jugra project. I'm not sure if our town will work on it, but we have to find out what it is and if it offers an opportunity for a successful rebellion."

To'opri, looked at Irenn again.

Her time to contribute. "The Tarkoi have heard there are the beginnings of a new rebellion. This time they will strike with bioweapons and kill millions. We have to proceed with care."

"It always intrigues me, Irenn, how you can find out this news and get in and out of this town so easily. I wonder what the payment was for this information?"

To'opri said, her facial expressions showing blatant suspicion.

"You think I am a spy bargaining for my life? If I were a spy, you would all be dead now. You wouldn't have made it this far, never mind the Rite of Adulthood," she said.

Zimuaa slammed the table with his open left hand. The noise brought instant silence.

"Don't call it that. The Tarkoi corrupted our culture and the Rite most of all. Once it was a joyful thing, I am told. Now when we hit the age those slaving links are embedded in our skulls and we lose any chance to resist or keep secrets, that's why we are all adolescents, and that's why we have our memories scrubbed of these meetings before the Fake Rite. It isn't a rite to introduce us to adulthood. It represents our enslavement."

"All right. Let's get back on topic. Jugra-7591, anyone know anything about it?" To'opri said.

She heard confused muttering. She would have to say something.

"Jugra-7591 is a dual neutron star system. Even by stellar navigation standards it is distant, about a third the way around the disk spinwards."

To'opri gave the Gizan equivalent of a nod. "The word is that the work is for a time displacement device."

There were mutterings of "impossible" and "we shouldn't waste our time on this". Beneath that she also knew were questions such as, "what is a neutron star?" The Gizan had a poor education, though some self taught themselves to an acceptable level, although the self taught can often have gaping holes in their education, yet also see novel connections. No doubt To'opri was wondering how Irenn knew the details of an obscure and distant astronomical object. She couldn't tell her why, and that although the masses of the stars were far too small for a significant temporal shift according to General Relativity, the Tarkoi had technologies that would instead use the rotating massive objects as power sources to generate a portal. In truth it was more like a stasis field, the ships would enter, disappear from space and then after millions of years re-enter the outside universe. The ships would exit with no sense of subjective time having elapsed. No one, not even moderately high levels of the Tarkoi knew that. It was something she could never reveal, and yet this project must be stopped. It was also a disturbing prelude to an independent jump system. How to deal with it and end this tyrannical era? There was only one way open to her—a full scale bloody rebellion.

The decision was not impulsive. The Kamoi had been planning this rebellion for centuries. She, and others, had set up the resistance in previous lives and now its goal was coming to fruition. They must not build the time displacement loop. Already the vast ships of the Empire were being outfitted by the clans in readiness for a civil war or rebellion.

She had worked for a dozen Gizan generations on this, but it had all been too little, too late. The Vanaya had miscalculated. For the last few million years a fashion had arisen: do not intervene in the affairs of the lesser races. This hands off approach had also applied to allowing a far more lenient jump system, which meant that the Tarkoi could spread a vile empire with ease. The realization of the mistake was slow to dawn but when it did the horror was undeniable. They had created a monster, and it was up to them to set it right. There would be no pussy-footing, no wringing of hands about non-intervention, they would act. It would be brutal and decisive. They would spill a lot of blood of many colors.

The memory disappeared. They stood again on the airless desert. Emari was still holding his arm.

There was nothing inside, no clue or link, no way out of this place.

"We're still here. Are we stuck? No, there must be more. What happened, Emari? Your little rebellion, did it succeed," Ray said, and then he knew, he saw it all but she replied anyway.

"I did terrible things back then. Things I want to forget, please, don't make me remember."

"We're stuck here, Emari, and you are the key. What happened?" he said, in as focused a manner as he could manage. She had been human for centuries at least, she must still have a lot of human empathy.

"Do you know what a civil war is like? No, of course you don't. You grew up in the safe, blissful Nexus. You've read accounts and seen footage of such wars but you haven't felt the crushed rubble under your hands or the grit in your eyes as you scramble through the rubble to find your buried adopted children, friends, or lovers, or seen cities destroyed on a galactic scale. The Tarkoi enslaved most of the galaxy, not everywhere, after all,I mean the galaxy is too big for anyone really, even us. But they spread so much misery for so long. It was a long task bringing down a society like that. We had done nothing like it before, all of our efforts were for rescuing civilizations not killing them." She let go of his arm and stood steady.

She spoke again, her voice measured and calm. "The clans had an intricate network of treaties protecting each other, some of them were even inconsistent. They were all barely held in check against each other."

Ray nodded, "Sounds like Earth just before World War I."

"Exactly. It made them vulnerable but there was nothing they could do about it. There was a vital world for the Rillth clan's military-industrial complex, we sabotaged it with a nanite attack coordinated with the nuking of their orbiting administrative habitat, then the destruction of the local beacon. It took several days for a new beacon to be 'hopped' in, and then they neutralized the nanite attack. About 230,000 Tarkoi were dead and fewer slaves," she said and sighed.

"What happened next?" he said.

"The nanites we had used had a distinctive architecture used by the rival Boquul Nev clan. It enraged Rillth, but they were in control enough to only launch a small raid against the Boquul." She chuckled.

"You can imagine how that went down. Boquul replied in kind, a minor attack, almost trivial. But the Rillth feeling twice wronged could not be restrained. They launched a major attack seizing two colonies and threatened to bring the Boquul Nev before the Emperor. Well, Boquul Nev responded to that with a full scale attack on the Rillth homeworld, which was the start of full-scale hostilities, and Rillth on cue brought in all of its allies, then Boquul Nev did the same. It was glorious. More than enough shame to go around."

She was quiet for a moment looking down, perhaps remembering the lost. He was about to ask her to continue when she looked up again with new resolve.

"The other clans saw an opportunity. Like your vultures. Plenty of worlds to feed on, take possession of, or lay waste. All good for popularity back home. Then the rebellion started. First, we used replicating software to disable the link control of the slaves, then we persuaded some houses to arm the slaves of rivals. We also armed many ourselves and gave them secret knowledge to trick friend-or-foe systems. It didn't take long for the slaves to take over worlds and starships. The war went from clan to civil to revolt with a speed that caught the Tarkoi off guard. When the Imperial Capital of Roshitho fell to a rebel force, the clans saw the danger at last. It was too late. The empire continued to fall apart and there came a moment when the clans knew the time had come for their last contingency plan: for the survival of the clans, they would send various New Dawn class ships through the temporal portal at Jugra-7591. The ships were massive, the product of an arms race to build arks that were also dreadnoughts. Crewed only by Tarkoi since slaves were no longer trustworthy, but the crews were not used to being ordered about or needing to know intricate technical details. Their strategy on arrival was simple: engage any opposition, interrogate their databases, and then cripple the homeworld and any supporting worlds. But they were hopelessly inexperienced and that gave your people an edge when you came up against their ships despite their advanced technology."

She stopped speaking and sat down on the sand.

"So that's how the Thousand Tyrannies ended. What happened to the Gizan you knew? Did they survive?" Ray asked.

"A few. The war was a catastrophe spanning about 200 galactic standard years. And it wasn't over, really. Knowing there were ships still in the portal we started plans to construct Neti," she said.

He offered her his hand; she took it, lifting her to her feet.

"I guess after that you reconfigured the jump system to be less than reliable."

"The new configuration took decades to propagate. When it was done, there was a great sense of relief. That nightmare was over. But the Tarkoi ships were based on a more accurate understanding of the jump system so they were still effective. Everywhere else we destroyed knowledge of the better design and replaced it with one that seemed to match the 'physics' of the reconfigured system."

"We're done here." He wanted to leave. Sometimes we think of memories as a place that can be visited and fled. We know they aren't, and always act as if they are.

There was something more.

"No, wait, this place deserves something," he said. Emari cocked her head not understanding. Ramon gave a slow nod.

"Ray, are you projecting your sense of loneliness onto a dead world? You know how irrational that is," Zara said.

"I know. But, Zara, we, all of us here, are not only thinking beings we're feeling ones too. We can't help projecting a little. And this world feels lonely. We may be the only visitors it ever sees. It deserves something."

"Art?" she looked at Ray for a moment deep in thought. "I understand. I am still getting used to this existence. So rich compared to my life before, so many things to feel. I want to communicate it but don't know how. That's what art is isn't it?"

"Maybe. I'm not an artist but the desire is part of being human."

"Go ahead, Ray. Let's see your magnum opus," Ramon said.

He thought he should raise his right hand if he was to perform magic but it wasn't necessary. In the distance an area of desert started to glow cherry red and then bright orange. A writhing mass of searing yellow magma rose from the plain to form a glowing hill about a hundred meters wide and a height that gave the shape a nice golden ratio. As that was happening forces swept more sand in from the surrounding desert. The white hot mass took the form of a pyramid, a copy of the Great Pyramid from Earth, with their faces embossed on the structure, one per side. The glare hid all that though he knew what was there. It became clearer as the mass quickly cooled. He had formed small gaps throughout the structure and gasses were being funneled through it carrying away the heat as it escaped into the vacuum. In his mind he saw that small machines, like synthetic creatures based on silicon chemistry were doing the work. Creatures he had willed into existence via his almost magical fabbing capabilities. The cooling would still take time but his aim was only to get the pyramid and its foundations enough below 700 Kelvin. The cooling would be too fast for proper crystallization but a strong glass would do. In the meantime he would also pull in some magnesium to the mix to color it.

"You shouldn't be able to do that. You know that? I haven't given you access to energy quotas high enough. Where did you get it from? The Kamoi?" said Emari.

"Honestly, don't know, don't care. Let's not speculate. Anyway, this will take sometime so just relax and contemplate," he said.

They waited. They were immortal—they could wait for years. But they only needed to wait a few days.

In the meantime each of them had access to vast amounts of information and experience. Now it appeared to flow from him, there was no Kamoi. He decided not to tell them. They would figure it out by themselves.

"Okay. It's done. Time to go," Ray said. They still faced the glassy pyramid which could now be seen properly. The overall composition was a kind of olivine—lime green. This world would never see grass or trees and this one thing would represent green in this never ending red desert. He included various other minerals to color the exterior in places. Each face of the pyramid bore an embossed impression of one of their faces. It was beautiful but likely no other being would ever see it.

Time to leave. And with a thought they were gone.

eleven

The sun had just set on this small world and the stars were visible. The western horizon glowed yellow below a fading weak blue sky. The thin air was thick enough to moderate the temperature as he could see from the small spiky plants scattered about the shadowed desert valley floor. He knew the air was mostly nitrogen, with a little oxygen and high amounts of CO_2. Soon the cool light of a Jupiter sized world would bathe the valley in a false dawn with its massive bulk; as spectacular as seeing the galaxy spread across the sky.

Their 'planet' was a moon, though when you are standing on a world with life, 'planet' and 'moon' can seem irrelevant. The night sky here would be unlike a normal world, always changing: other moons, phases of the jovian, the orbital period, the year itself, other planets. An endless celestial dance that might never repeat. Such surface-life bearing worlds around jovians were rare and they were often inhospitable. Radiation, comets, and various world building debris in large doses meant that only sub-ice oceans were safe enough for life to thrive. Even now he could see the massive auroras forming above him, and they were almost at the equator. The radiation belts of the jovian planet were intense but invisible, only becoming dazzling when the frantic sub-atomic particles ran headlong into the gasses of the upper atmosphere after their magnetic world tour ended in the aurora.

The world was smaller than Earth, larger than Mars, and it was part of a rogue system. A star system flung from the galaxy, evicted from its rightful home by the uncaring laws of gravitational physics, to spend long ages in the dark before plummeting wildly back through the galactic disk on a whirlwind visit where it could see but never touch its lost birthplace. He hoped it would never be the home of a sentient species because they could never be in real contact with the rest of the galaxy. They would rarely be close enough to beacons, and the odds were any civilization would be dust long before they had the opportunity.

"It's a rogue system. We are 72,400 light years from the core. But to get here someone must have mapped it and determined an accurate path. There must be some kind of beacon out here for us to still jump straight to the surface of a world, I mean we didn't end up even ten centimeters above or below. It was a careful beacon negotiation." He looked at the others. They had been quiet after the last jump.

"That's not how it works," Ramon said. "When we jump, as opposed to Nexus ships or whatever, we do a lot of the negotiation, we don't need precise coordinates. There are mechanisms within the jump energies, fields, whatever you want to call them, they act as AIs that can determine the path ahead in real-time. They are extensions of us, like the muscles in our arms—or the muscles we once had. Remember, you didn't have to know how muscles worked to use your arms, same with the jumps."

"How are the two of you?" Ray said.

Emari nodded. "I'm well," she said, "I don't know why but I feel better."

"Ramon? How are you holding up?"

"Sure, sure. Me too, feeling quite a bit better. Tell you what though, I can't wait to get this trip over and done with."

"Zara?" he asked, though she had never complained

"I honestly don't know what the problem is, I am okay and was okay. No change."

So, Zara was good but the other two still seemed a little off. Their body language worried him.

"Though, what do you think will happen to us once this is over?" Ray said to Ramon and then looked at Emari, trying to get a response. She turned away, looking at the aurora and the few stars. He looked up at the sky again. The traces of light beyond the aurora weren't stars, they were galaxies and clusters, normally obscured by the light of stars, but here it was so dark that those faint smudges were relatively brighter. Aided by the light enhancing properties of his new eyes.

He spent a few minutes understanding this world, its system, the life. How could he know about its life? He didn't want to understand the mechanics of the way his understanding worked. But he couldn't resist a glimpse, just a quick look. He looked within. For a moment.

"Ray!" He heard Emari yell.

"What is it?" he turned, not knowing what he would see. There was nothing, just the three of them looking at him, each glowing in the dark with the slightest hint of divinity.

"You've been in that state for an hour. It should only take seconds, so what were you doing for an hour?" she said.

"Nothing," he lied, and then forgot what he lied about, or that he had lied.

A new memory intruded. Emari's past flashed before him with his uncontrolled focus zooming into one memory. A memory that seared him as he touched it.

Cusha, a world reminding Ray of Earth.

Emari didn't see it that way. She likened it to Corvena in a myriad of tempting and painful ways.

He could see the thoughts running through her, a sparkling multidimensional stream, an ocean current over dazzling corals at every depth. Her memories were so clear.

The parked electric car faced east at the lookout. The sun had just dawned slanting pink and cream-yellow rays that pierced the mists sleeping in the valleys below. By covering her eyes from the glare she could see a mesa to the southeast—dark, vegetated, basking in the soft cool light of the new day, while gray blankets of sleeping mist drifted below topped by bright pink and gold puffs.

She leaned on the railing and took in a breath of the cool scented air as if it was life itself. She loved this world and all of its people. They seemed blessed with either luck or wisdom; she didn't know which, she only wondered how she could reproduce it. These people had limited their population, had not gone too far down the fossil fuel route, invested in renewables while supporting long-term fusion. They had not adopted neural links, so dodged a few bullets just with that. No significant wars for centuries. So lucky.

Dillan came up to her. He was her mate, her beloved, with an eight-year marriage contract and had stayed with her even when it had become clear she could not bear children. He loved her too much to leave.

The people of Cusha called themselves the *suren*. They were bipedal, intelligent, with vivid thin feathers that reminded her a little of her lost youth. Taller than Vanaya, bird-like, a little more reptilian, and their young were not live born but from an egg. Gray-blue skin overlain with black and multicolored feathers in many places. They were a beautiful people with a near perfect world as far as real worlds go.

Dillan put his hand on her shoulder. She turned to see his kind eyes framed by the soft black and green feather-hair.

"Irri, sorry to break your beautiful meditation, but we have to get back into town. I have that meeting at the university this afternoon," he said.

She smiled and then took one long extended inhale as if to capture this place.

He kept apologizing as they walked back to the car while the true message was that he loved her, and to him she was radiant in this meditative state. He thought he had ruined something precious merely by reminding her of necessary things. There seemed no way for her to change his mind about that. It didn't matter because soon he would forget and they would be together.

She was driving. Dillan had a headache he couldn't shake. He relaxed and closed his eyes on the way back.

"I'm sorry I disturbed you back there. You looked like a goddess contemplating eternity," he said, eyes still closed, and they laughed.

"Huh, well, this goddess has meetings of her own. I received a call from an associate who wants to meet to resolve an issue with a current task," she said, trying to sound as bland as she could.

"Oh, which building? You said you would work on the Mashuthor Square Project for the city government. Is it about that?" he said.

Her blue and black feathers gave the slightest quiver as she suppressed her embarrassed reaction.

"Not sure, though I'm not keen to work on two projects at once," she said.

He smiled and touched her arm for reassurance, "I think you architects are creative, crazy, and wonderful. Anyway, I wish you luck. As for me, I have a meeting of the university board regarding the financial estimates for the next academic year. You may need to send help to rescue me before the day is out."

The car could drive itself, but some people enjoyed taking risks, especially on these winding roads past steep drops and spectacular danger. Manual mode was exhilarating. Most were not licensed to drive like that but she was. She needed the danger to remind her of how fleeting life and happiness are. Death can come knocking in the safest of places. She was invulnerable, but those she loved were not.

The city of Foora was elegant and a testament to the integration of construction and nature. Low buildings cushioned by trees of many colors all year round. She never tired of traveling through its streets with the windows down and letting the scents waft around her in a never repeating dance. She put the car on auto and just sat back and took it all in. After she dropped Dillan off she returned to their home in Zahxa Heights overlooking the lake.

She dreaded the knock when it came. It was rare for this to happen.

She opened the door. A young suren male stood there in office clothes. Such clothes were mostly to display rank rather than for hiding body parts or insulation. His clothing said he was a mid-level manager, but he was so much more, and worse. She had never met this suren, as far as she knew, but recognized him instantly.

"Hello, Zorrech. Come in," she said, waving him in, making the signs of the honoring of a guest, the repeated social formalities of this world. Zorrech ignored them.

Now he was inside and the door closed they could drop any pretense.

"Why are you here, Zorrech?" she said. "Cusha is not at risk. It is a miracle to study not interfere with, and you have a very particular reputation on that matter."

"I didn't know you trusted gossip, Emari. You would think we could dispense with that curse after all this time. Never mind, I am here on an approved mission," he said with a formal coldness.

"Which is?"

"I can't tell you. It is classified for now."

"Classified? What? You forget who we are, nothing is classified to us. And—do I have to remind you?—I am the prime agent for this world. When another agent comes here they do my bidding, they don't feign secret business. Do you understand?"

She radiated hostility.

Her own reputation was formidable, and although all Vanaya were in principle equal, she could destroy his reputation with ease.

He didn't flinch. A wry, troubling smile passed across his face. A terrible omen.

"I am here on behalf of the Kamoi."

Kamoi intervention was rare and never good. She was powerless against it, and it made no sense.

"The Core or a faction? Why are you here?"

"The Kamoi. We must test Cusha," he said. His manner was terse, like his words betraying little other than a lack of civility.

"Which means what? Stress tested, perhaps?"

He didn't answer. He gave a short trill, in suren the equivalent of a human clearing his throat.

"Basic protocol requires that I report to the prime agent before commencing my work. This I have done. I will leave now, Emari, and leave you to your own work."

She reached out and grabbed his arm.

"Zorrech, just tell me, what is this all about?" She felt the tight grip of fate squeezing her throat.

"The Kamoi thinks Cusha may build an empire that will have its own excesses. Because they will not have a history of failures, they may come to believe they are superior to other lifeforms," he said.

"No, you can't be serious. These people aren't a threat to anyone. They show none of the pathologies to suggest even a slight problem. You haven't been in the field to many worlds, have you? I mean early, watching them develop, encouraging them? So you wouldn't understand. Technical civilization is incredibly fragile at this stage. I know you have to do what the Kamoi asks, but please use restraint." She stopped herself from begging, but it was close.

He chirped a condescending laugh.

"I'm a lot more experienced than you think, or remember. Oh, and thank you for your advice," he said with that same icy detachment, and left.

She sat down on the nearest recliner, head in hands as an icy dread enveloped her world.

"Emari, what would the Kamoi do?" Ray said, speaking to her in the sun-drenched social room of her house.

"Who are you?" she said, startled. She saw a strange featherless being—a mammaloid?—with odd clothes talking to her, in Vanayan of all things.

Ray disguised himself as a suren.

"I'm a friend. Don't worry, all is well." His words were like drugged bliss. All care dissolved in her.

"The Kamoi sometimes overrides the careful plans of agents. It can end in disaster, but they still do it. I have never found out why. And who are you again?"

He chose his next words with care. They seemed to stab right through her psychological defenses.

"Does the Kamoi have an agenda that is a danger to developing worlds?"

She blocked her ears, looking down, "No, no. Go away. What's happening here, what is this?"

"It's all right. Relax. Look, it's a beautiful day," he said. His words were warm, lazy summer days. He had already glimpsed something within her she herself did not understand.

She raised her head. She was alone. Had someone been here? No. She grabbed her phone and satchel and headed for the door. There was work to do.

Almost seventy days had passed since the visit from Zorrech without incident. Now he wished to meet her. He could have had a dialog within her head from anywhere on the planet, or materialized out of a hidden spot—a favorite party trick of hers—but he insisted on doing everything the hard way, by the book, or the Code. The ever changing, never-definitive Code she had helped write. But you can't break the guidelines creatively until you thoroughly understood their limitations.

They were the only ones in the restaurant. It stood on the edge of a small hill overlooking the city and was popular and expensive; she couldn't afford the expensive and didn't like the popular, but at this time of day their snacks were delicious and inexpensive while the quiet was precisely what she needed. She took the morning off and was enjoying the solitude. It often surprised her the apparent similarity of many customs between the worlds and lifeforms. There was a thread of something like determinism in it. Only social species could make the leap to space and such social interaction usually had its origins in the distribution of food, hence restaurants. Well, not quite, there were exceptions. There were always exceptions; life and intelligence didn't always select the most probable path. But here it was familiar although as usual the food was truly alien.

Zorrech took a seat opposite her. He looked at her with his bright emerald eyes in a face ringed by stark red and brown feather-hair. His face was the common suren bluish gray skin with a small yellow nose breaking any similarity to the concept of 'bird' that and Earthling would understand. She did not notice the intrusion into her thoughts of an alien's view of the suren.

"You didn't need to meet me face to face you know," she said.

"My apologies. I was nervous when we first met, I was just trying to hide it with dispassion. You are highly regarded. Your exploits are legendary and deeply respected even by the Kamoi."

"You hid it well if that's the case. I could have sworn you were looking down on me."

He fidgeted slightly. "I am under strict orders. I can't let anything or anyone distract me, even you."

He fidgeted more, his nerves getting the better of him. Or it was all a ruse. There were ways to calm this feeling, but some preferred to overcome them by their own efforts. It was a fashion that never made sense to her; self and personality were fluid and ever changing but she admired his desire for independence that was indeed worth pursuing.

"I have identified structural weaknesses in this civilization. Core agents will use that information to disrupt this civilization completely," he said calmly as if he was talking about fixing a household item.

A chill ran under her feathers ruffling them in a wave.

"You must be wrong. I thought this was only about testing?"

"So did I. I thought they wanted the data so changes could strengthen the weak points of the society, but my orders say they want to destroy it and then see how it unravels. It will be a valuable source of data for managing other civilizations," he said.

The room began to spin. This could not be true.

"Zorrech, are you sure? This must be a misunderstanding, perhaps you need to boost your intelligence and look at it again. We assist cultures we don't sabotage them," she said the last part louder than planned. She looked about, but they were still alone.

"There's no doubt. This isn't some factional decision to be appealed or overridden, it is from the Kamoi itself."

"Is this some Dunnic inspired entertainment initiative? Because the Kamoi will not approve of it."

"I told you, this is from the Kamoi, not some faction."

For all his pandering she didn't trust him. He probably had known from the start.

The decision must not stand. This was a place worth protecting, she loved these people and this world almost as much as she had loved Corvena. They were her family, and she was their protector. She would fight this.

Zorrech left. She stayed at the table, thinking through the brief conversation. Finally, the increasing noise of guests arriving for the midday meal grew distracting enough to get her moving. On the way back to the car, she rang Dillan.

A burst of sweet pleasantries from him comforted her. She wanted to extend it but couldn't delay even for a few seconds. "I have to make a trip out of the city for the rest of the day. I won't be back until later tonight," she said.

"Did you forget there is a communal chant tonight in the town park," he said. This was a vital ritual to all suren. It was a community bonding, independent of almost any other issues. It was sacred without being religious, and she could not cancel it.

"I'll be there. See you then," she said.

She got in the car and drove it to the nearest day-long parking area. She got out, walked behind a bush and left Cusha.

Jumps aren't instant, and there are many complex factors that can affect jump duration. But she had allowed ample time to get to a Core node and back.

She stood in a typical Corvena forest, at the edge of a clearing where a delicate glass building the size of a small house stood. It was like an impossible small fragile pagoda. A child's fantasy.

She walked up the three steps to the open doorway. Random sparkles of light and chips of rainbows flew over her. There was a single elegant crystal chair in the middle of the one room while streams of sunlight played through everything, a symphony of light without sound. Despite the brilliance, the room wouldn't get hot since there was no need to follow that closely to the laws of physics. She sighed and sat on the seat.

There was also no need to waste time with gradual transitions, as she had done this many times. She wondered why they bothered with the glass pagoda. Beautiful as it was there was no need for it.

The pagoda, the forest, the sky, everything, even her body, disappeared. Like a switch being turned off. She still had senses, they were a crutch, to help make sense of some ideas and data. She turned up her intelligence, but not too much, doing that was painful because it came with depressing realizations that were hard to forget.

Now she was in a simulated world. Beneath her the ground was a writhing mass of fractal forms like quivering iridescent sand. Around her metal mountains of various colors rose spire-like into the sky, and the sky was a dazzle of shifting multidimensional forms. It was fairly standard.

"Why are you here?" The voice of her long-dead brother said. But he was gone like Corvena ages ago.

"I talked with Zorrech. He told me you plan to destroy Cusha. Is this true?"

She had to be honest, there was no point in lying or being evasive. The Kamoi would already know everything from the moment she sat in the chair. In principle, this entire conversation was unnecessary, but the traditions had to be maintained.

"Cusha is a problem. It will grow to be a ravenous empire, their peaceful traditions will not encompass other lifeforms and they will think themselves superior rather than different," her brother's voice said. "I know you feel strongly about this world, but it is a threat we cannot ignore."

Something wasn't right about this. The bond with the Kamoi went both ways. She could sense vast thoughts and arguments flowing just below the surface. And like a great ocean predator whose passage disturbs the surface, there was something else, dark and threatening.

"We could repair those characteristics. Perhaps create a philosophy of universal harmony, traditions of benevolence. They could be an unwitting agent for our goals," she said, trying to keep the desperation out of her voice.

"They are too much of a risk. I have already decided and will act. You will do your duty."

She was back in the crystal chair.

The Core talked about her duty. The most important quality they were selected for back on Corvena. But they had all changed, and calling on her sense of duty didn't have the same potency it had when she was mortal. It was 'duty' that they had rebelled against in the first place, that had made them who they were. Had the Core forgotten?

She spent the next three lunar months analyzing the strategies being deployed by Zorrech and his associates. It was exhausting; she was adept at hiding from the many monitoring systems of her host civilizations but it was much harder hiding from her own kind. However, she was the master, and they were still the students. She had many tricks in her repertoire.

One day she found herself at home having a fight with Dillan and not knowing how she got to this point.

"Where have you been?" Dillan shouted, "Lian couldn't get in touch with you and called me. He said you haven't been into work in days. What is going on? I thought we didn't keep secrets from one another. Is that still true?"

He looked away from her, his mane feathers were erect, a sign of fight-flight, then he took a few deep breaths and calmed down. She was envious of each breath he took, they were a respite that she craved from the turmoil in her head. He looked back at her waiting for a reply. She must look cold and inscrutable but she couldn't tell him the truth, she would have to add to the lie.

"Look, I've been having some problems with a co-worker. No one you know."

"Are you attracted to him or her? Is that all it is? Why would that be a problem?" he said.

She couldn't use the 'having an affair' strategy with the suren, they would not understand.

"I believe someone at the company is committing industrial espionage," she said.

Dillan gasped. As a people they lauded giving information up to the public domain. But taking private information was an invasion of your person. Industrial espionage carried hefty penalties because they considered it an act of assault, not theft. This was a vulnerability in the suren recognized by the Kamoi; it could use an otherwise reasonable attitude to manipulate the society into extreme acts they would never otherwise consider. In fact, she was using the same tactic on Dillan. She truly was a child of the Core.

"Have you reported this, Irri?" he said.

"No, no, I don't have proof yet. I will need some pretty solid evidence before I can bring it before the company elders. It has been giving me sleepless nights and souring everything else. Sorry if you got caught up in that, I didn't mean it, I didn't understand the effect on you." They nuzzled and there was a moment of bliss as mutual bonding pheromones wafted around them in the evening air.

Ray peeked ahead, flying through the memories. Now no longer a river to bathe in and become part of, they became an icy waterfall pounding him with jagged shards.

He stopped the onward rush; it was two years later. He could feel her raw, unwavering distress, spread out into future memories like a red warning sign.

That same weakness she had used to distract Dillan, Zorrech had identified and would use to poison everything she had worked for. Such strategies were now being deployed without pause between the nations as trust collapsed. Where there was once harmony there was now discord and the unfamiliar intoxicating poison of hate. People rarely like starting wars, they have to be led into it, just as soldiers have to be trained to kill, and now this world was being trained to wage war. Every day it got worse, not so much in the media or the social networks but in the secret activities that Emari was now hooked into. It made her sick in her hearts. She didn't know how she would endure the death of such a beautiful thing. She would, there was no alternative, suicide was almost impossible.

Then the day came when a border disagreement went white hot. Shots were fired from newly deployed guns. There was return fire. Answered by artillery. Answered by long-range missiles. Answered by... The progression was as expected but still it could have been turned around. Then there was a large detonation in the nearby city of Oisha, maybe three kilotons. She knew immediately that the suren hadn't done it; it was Zorrech. Secret alliances and treaties now came into effect. The world slid into war, and as far as Emari could see, no one wanted to stop it. Because they had been so peaceful they did not know of the horror, and therefore had no reason to fear it.

Ray put down the memory and looked ahead, in the distance he saw a traumatic moment and zoomed in on it.

The sirens were screaming again. Emari scrambled over some rubble that was blocking her way to a bomb shelter in downtown Foora. It was Dillan's shelter; she wanted to make sure he was safe. They had separated a year before and she didn't know how he would react, still she had to know.

Pulverized cement covered her, the remains of buildings some of which she had designed. She wiped the grime from her face and clambered over the rubble with cut hands and torn clothes. Her body reflecting her inner anguish.

The shelter stood next to a small park and far from any building that might bury the entrance and turn it into a tomb. For a moment she stopped to look at the familiar park. The trees stood like pale ghosts stripped of their blue-green leaves. When she reached the shelter it was a relief to see it was intact and the stairs leading down to the sealed door were undamaged.

She scurried down the concrete stairwell to the dark wall with the shelter door and pounded on the door.

A tinny voice sounded from a hidden nearby speaker, "You cannot come in until the All Clear is given. As warden of this shelter, I may not endanger the occupants by letting you in. Sorry, but there could be clouds of poison gas, or nanites about the place."

"Dillan? Is that you? Let me in, it's Irri," she said.

"What? Irri? Wait a moment."

She heard a solid but soft thud, comforting in the otherwise eerie silence. Then the door swung inward. From the dark she heard Dillan's voice say, "Come in. Quick!"

No sooner was she inside than the thud of the closing door resounded, sealing away the devastation outside. It took several seconds for her eyes to adapt to the dim shelter lighting. No instant response since her body had fully embraced the suren physiology. The large room she was in held about thirty people, some injured, of various ages. Some children looked at her as a reflex with empty damaged eyes while others stared somewhere else, a dark place and a personal hell. The walls were plain concrete with a few pieces of military furniture pushed up against them while the floor where a few of the exhausted slept was cold bare concrete. The rest sat nearby on benches laid out haphazardly. A layer of cement dust over everything.

"What's it like out there? We've been down here for six hours. We have two more rooms down here and they are just as full. So, is it safe up above?" he said, blurting it all out, as if he was a soldier reporting the situation to the first person he came across. His breathing was ragged and desperate.

"It's a mess, Dillan. You should get these people out of the city. Worse is to come," she said.

He seemed to calm a little and looked at her as if he was just recognizing her. "Why did you come all the way over here to the south side of the city? So dangerous with the bombs and all those unstable buildings."

"I wanted to see if you were all right. That's all," she said, covered in dust, clothes torn, with bleeding hands and knees.

A figure approached them from the almost invisible doorway that led into the next room. A male, impossibly neat, exuding arrogance and disdain. Zorrech. The real Zorrech.

He spoke to her in front of Dillan, as if he was already dead.

"It is almost time to leave, Emari. There are incoming nuclear-tipped missiles. One of them will be a surface burst in this area. It is targeting a secret intelligence bunker across the street. The weapon has a yield of 800 kilotons. You know what that means. No one in the inner city, including this shelter will survive. This place will be inside the fireball. The door or concrete walls won't hold that back," he said.

Somewhere inside her there was the start of an aching wail. She stifled it before it could overwhelm her. She had been here before. Losing a world was off the scale of ugliness, but it was an accepted part of her role. But not like this, so deliberately was this world cast into the fire.

"I will stay," she stood strong as she spoke to Zorrech. A feeble act of defiance it might be, but it was still hers.

"Irri, who is this?" Dillan said, reacting to the bizarre conversation, "What is going on? Did he say a missile, a nuclear missile?"

Zorrech continued to ignore him. In his mind, Dillan was already dead.

"It will hurt Emari. The longer you stay, the worse it will be."

"I know," she said.

"Emari, you are an excellent agent. It would be tragic to see you oppose the Kamoi. I remind you that many of your extra powers are courtesy of the Core and that we are neither gods nor immortals," he said. He gave her a cursory nod and turned from her.

Zorrech walked off into a dark shadow of the room and disappeared. Dillan saw it and turned to her; shock on his face.

She could sense the incoming missile now, only seconds away.

She extended protective fields around her. Streams of nanites emanated from her as a fine mist and embedded themselves into the shelter walls and the door. She fed them commands and energy to transform the materials into an adaptive defensive shield. Her body was glowing now, as if made of molten steel. She heard the screams as everyone recoiled from her, but she had to ignore them. There was little time left.

The shields were not complete, but it was all she could do. The fireball would last about a minute, rising fast. But it was the first seconds that would be critical.

Outside the shelter, her senses ended as the fireball was born. In an instant, an angry god's fist slammed into the shelter. Even through her defenses the sound was wrenching.

Her incomplete defenses were failing. Radiation was pouring in. The door was melting and then—her nanites failed. The shelter cracked above and the door blew in with a rain of molten metal and hot plasma—

the center of a newborn sun entered, and life had no place here.

Pain wracked her body, she couldn't ignore it any longer. Or stay. Everyone was dead. She hadn't even had time to say goodbye to Dillan. But so few ever got that opportunity she had discovered in all these ages.

Then she fled to some place where she could heal and forget. She must not forget all of this. She needed to remember, but to heal she must forget. Her last and only memory of this place was the command to her inner self, "Forget."

She was standing in her residence in Eklus and she was undergoing repair while a creation of hers with some of her own personality elements attended her. The room was in a different mood now. Dark shadows with light and dismal grays. Somber, quiet, with an unidentifiable sadness. It knew her moods.

"The repairs are almost complete, Emari," her attendant said.

"Yes, I feel much better. I made myself forget the last mission, didn't I? It must have gone bad," she said.

"Yes, mistress. You said remembering it was poison," the attendant said.

"Hmm. I will give you a new name. From now on your name will be, Dillan. How does that sound?"

"I am honored. Thank you, Emari." His form was that of a bipedal being that would remind a human of birds, and to a corvi a yabuti covered in feathers gliding from tree to tree. He had sparse colored feathers and a small yellow nose. His look made her wistful, but with so many memories swirling in her vast and ancient subconscious that shouldn't surprise her.

There was a couch near the middle of the immense room. It shouldn't be there. On it sat a biped, mammalian, wearing some kind of machine-manufactured clothes, or a representation of them. He—somehow she knew the creature's gender—looked at her. Deep down she knew the cultural and evolutionary signals of this lifeform but couldn't remember from which world. There had been so many.

"You don't remember me, do you, Emari? Not surprising because my species doesn't even exist yet. You really should timestamp your memories like you do your Galactic Calendar. It would make it easier." He paused, eyes widening. "Oh. Now I see."

The penny dropped.

Now he understood.

"Who are you?" she said. He wasn't a Vanayan unless it was one of them in disguise or a recruit. But he had no detectable ID, and he had spoken in perfect Vanayan from the time of the exodus. She did not need a translation matrix.

"Do you know why you don't timestamp your memories? Has the obvious occurred to the galactic masters?" His words were challenging and uncomfortable. Why was he here and annoying her? His behavior broke the etiquette and protocols of the city.

He was waiting for her to reply. It seemed the questions weren't rhetorical.

230

"I do not understand what you are talking about. First, tell me why you are here in my domicile or I will penalize you."

"I'm not in your little abode in Eklus, Emari, and neither are you. I am intruding myself into one of your memories. The act of remembering alters a memory, it is as true for the Vanaya as it is for humans, which is how biological and most AI memory functions. Both of us are god-awful far from Eklus, and your memories are the key to getting back. Your last mission was to a world called Cusha, where your persona of Irri inserted itself into what was pretty much a Utopian society, by almost anyone's definition. But your hallowed Kamoi destroyed it. They put a gun to its head and executed an entire society for some bogus reason that neither you nor I believe. It was an act of genocide."

She was shaking. The world quivered, then broke apart.

Once more she stood on the orphan world of the rogue system, hunched over, distressed and tensed like a frightened, caged animal.

There was a steady intensifying glow on the horizon she took to be their first dawn here.

"Emari, are you all right?" Ramon said.

There was no answer. Ramon was too curious and the lack of response became an unwarranted consent. So he dug deeper.

"And who sent Zorrech? It doesn't seem like the same Core that sent us here."

"There are factions within the Core. Or just above it, like moods in your mind. There are three major factions at the moment. Afeni, yes the same, is one, still committed to saving the galaxy in its own way," she blurted out trying to end the topic; dodging her unavoidable memories—flying arrows of pain.

She shivered. The trauma relived.

"Yex, pro-research and exploration, named after the planetary system where we first researched and tested the jump system, that was fun if you like explosions. Then there is Dunnic, isolationist and wants us to abandon the Game, they think our lives are too long, the universe is meaningless, let's retreat into ourselves, blah, blah, blah. Dunnic sounds harmless but they can be real bastards. Zorrech was from Dunnic."

"Aamon!" Ramon interrupted, "I have this memory. There is another faction, unnamed. It wants to re-purpose the Game for entertainment only, make the destruction of civilizations fun. When I joked and called myself Aamon, it was because I feared they may have sent me. I didn't want it to be true, it terrified me, and there was info on them, just a little, from Afeni I suspect. I came to believe this faction, which I call Aamon, sent me but Afeni and Yex intervened and made sure I was untampered. They regarded Aamon's plans as evil while Aamon thought the lives of mortals didn't matter. The maniacs regard themselves as gods. Not sure of all the details I only have like a summary in my head. Aamon and Dunnic are allies. Wow. Pretty obvious that they are a real danger to us. Just as well we are immortal, well at least you are Emari."

"Don't count on my immortality," Emari said. "There are stories, legends or myths, that there have been Kamoi sanctioned killings."

No one spoke for several seconds as reality shifted about them.

"Anyone want to hear what I think?" said Zara, who stood ten paces apart from them.

She took the lack of response as a 'yes'. "The factions are constructs like the AIs in the Cortices of the Nexus. Vast and smart tasked with maintaining order and subsystems, including protecting the Kamoi. Expect serious drama if you cross them. The factions are only the top level so they are like the customer side of the system while the serious stuff happens in the backroom. All these systems, the factions, are semi-independent agents, and there is no guarantee they play nice with each other. So some oppose our jaunt and others support it. Expect turbulence," she said and crossed her arms defiant in her pronouncement.

The only reply was a nod from Emari who seemed calmer now.

"Ray, how did you do that, talk to me in my memories?" Emari said.

"I'd like to know too. From what information the Kamoi gave me I thought such intrusion was impossible," Ramon said.

"I don't know. Honestly. No idea, it's like the jumps, I just know and act," Ray said.

Ramon asked, "What else do you know? I know you, us, too well. You're keeping something back. We need everything. Out with it."

"Am I keeping something back? Sure, and it is all about Emari's failure to answer a simple question. Why don't the Vanaya timestamp their memories?" Ray said facing Ramon.

Emari shrugged and turned towards the now dazzling light from the east.

Ramon answered for her; each word was an effort as the truth dawned on him.

"Because with timestamps they would realize much of their past is edited out. They all have amnesia because it suits another plan. My guess is by the Kamoi itself. Jesus, that's—"

"Yeah, a nightmare." Ray turned to Emari who now stood apart looking at them; arms crossed over her chest as if trying to keep them out or hold her secrets in. "You didn't go straight back to Eklus after Cusha did you?"

"I don't know," she said without confidence.

"You didn't come back for thousands of standard years," Ray continued. "You wandered alone and damaged. What did you do? And, that vision we had of the Tarkoi, the Thousand Tyrannies, that's why there is so little in the Calendar about it. You should be able to cross-link your memories to specific events in the Calendar but you don't. You never reference it. Why is that? Because there are memories you must not remember or even suspect exist."

"What would you know?", Emari said. "We've done everything you can imagine. We have each committed every act of good and every act of evil you can think of, it all just happens over enormous spans of time. Cynicism weighs down our lives and poisons our futures. We forget so we can hope and if hope is a delusion, then so is all of our striving. Sometimes, just sometimes, Delusion is a higher truth."

"So, not a utopia," he said.

"What do you think of the Vanayan Dream now?" Emari said. "Is it a heaven? It certainly meets some of the requirements. Or perhaps if you look closely you might see a hell you will have to endure and serve for age after age. It's all about perspective, forget the dark spots and it can be blissful, otherwise...," she said. Her words worried him. She was a fabric fraying and about to tear.

"You are a singularity in human form, aren't you?" Ramon said to her. It seemed to go over everyone's head but he remembered seeing her like a bottomless pool. Not his memory but Ray's.

Deep within Ray there was a link, to a new place, that beckoned. It was the wrong time, he couldn't go there now in the middle of this. But they had to jump when the chance presented itself or risk being lost.

"Sorry, we have to jump now."

twelve

It was a cold, windswept plain. Behind them were a series of small dunes and to their right was an alluvial fan where once, millennia ago, water had washed sand and gravel into a flat fan shape now almost erased. The sky had an orange tinge to it from airborne dust and the sad reddish sun low in the sky. Towards the horizon, the sky merged into the desert and everywhere there was an overpowering rusty pall. It reminded Ray of the driest deserts on Earth. There was no trace of vegetation they could see.

"We are at NGC 7492." Ray said. "Very far from the galactic core, about 82,500 light years. Still jumping around a bit but getting further from home. This world and its star are about midway to the center of the cluster. It's a globular cluster, but so dispersed it might as well be an open one. I don't understand, where are we going? What's the point?"

Emari stood apart, looking away from them across the dusty waste towards a line of eroded red cliffs in the low distance. Ramon looked at her; clenching and unclenching his fists, oblivious to the show of stress and concern. Ray felt nothing, disconnected, and still lured by the unknown; the too readily forgotten reality around them. They were in a cluster of stars on the edge of intergalactic space. No doubt the Milky Way would be impressive once the sun went down, but right now it was all somewhat depressing. The sunlight reminded him of the time he and Ben had gone on their jaunt over the surface of Reshox to see the Snow Queen's Palace, the planet's surface under the yellow glow of the red dwarf star had looked like an eternal late afternoon, but much dimmer, whereas this place looked like sunset from the ground up. A world at the end of its life. The truth was likely the complete opposite. The star would burn far longer than Earth's sun. This world would still be here like this when Earth had become a cold, dark cinder.

Emari sat down on the gravel and buried her head in her knees.

Without a cue, she replied to Ray's question posed thousands of light years away and perhaps decades in the past. In that pose her voice should have been muffled, but was as clear as if she stood next to him.

"I wandered. I remember now. There were several pre-technological candidates for intervention. I chose one and intervened. The usual strategy. Absorb what is known of their culture and then create a body based on a member of that society and an accurate scan of their memories. It takes generations to move with ease through the society, first on the outskirts and then later within the halls of power."

She lifted her head. Defiant.

"The name of the world was Shakik in the language of the Tinu. Tinu was the name for themselves and the name for one of their kind. They were mammal-like, something like a thinner, erect version of a bear. Flatter face, less hair, and so on. The usual changes. They had not yet extended their idea of humanity beyond their tribe. It took a lot of work. I imagine it would have happened anyway, but I gave it a push. When I first arrived on Shakik the largest groups had populations of about a hundred and the villages were built of mud brick and some uncut stone, occasionally lime washed. I helped start metallurgy, expanded trade networks, domestication, diplomacy, the whole thing. As usual, I assisted and helped them cut corners rather than deliver it from on high. I defused wars, created multinational organizations to facilitate trade. I encouraged the arts and sciences. I did much more than is allowed. Saving Shakik was my therapy, and maybe the Kamoi gave me a pass because it must have known. When the last faint memories of Cusha no longer made me want to howl, I buried and forgot them. So, Ray, it wasn't some grand plan of deception by the Kamoi. It was my act of self healing. So kindly go fuck yourself."

She sobbed, slow at first, almost a whimper, then quickly losing control into a heart twisting wail. The memories, not just Cusha, the forgotten dead demanded to be heard again.

Her answer still didn't deal with the other issues, but no one would press the matter with her. She was grief stricken, and they didn't know how to help her.

After the storm of grief eased, Ramon stepped up to her. The pain in his face mirrored her distress. He was in pain and confusion, trying to think of something to do or say to console her. He sat down next to her and put his arms around her, whispering comfort to her. She nestled into his neck.

It surprised Ray. Surprised that Ramon showed such compassion and dismayed that he had not. He looked at her and knew he should comfort her, but it seemed like a disconnected intellectual decision rather than a desire to help a friend.

Zara stepped next to Ray without saying a word.

Emari stopped crying. Was silent. Lifted her head, looked at Ramon, then pushed him away gently. She stood up. Looked about. Started to cry, but stopped herself.

"I'm getting out of here. Don't follow me. I don't care about anything right now. I don't care about recruiting you or the Kamoi or their little quest. I'm gone." Then she was gone. Blink and she wasn't there.

"What the hell?" Ray said. "Where'd she go?" He knew it sounded stupid, he was the one guiding them. He had no clue. There was no inner source of knowledge that could answer it.

"And," it now occurred to him, "how did she go? I thought we were on some kind of train track laid down by the Core, unable to deviate. How can any of us just leave?"

He paced as the fragile and unpleasant house of cards he had constructed was coming apart. This journey might be undesirable, but it had become a rough comfort zone.

"I don't know, brother. She can't have gone far. I'll find her, she's retreated into the Dream," Ramon said.

"How do you know? How can you possibly find her?" Ray said.

Zara put her hand on Ray's shoulder, speaking from behind him, "You are both Raymond Tans, he is just more reticent and hurt. He also shares some of your abilities. Not so specific. He may not know where we are going, but I suspect he knows where she went. I can sense his growing power. He doesn't realize it himself. Or didn't until now. He'll be fine."

Ramon muttered something unintelligible and shaking his head, suggesting he was skeptical.

"I can follow her and I will," he said.

"Where did she go?" Zara said.

"She's gone into the Dream, or part of it, her body may be in a physical location but her mind is, elsewhere. Gotta go," he said and disappeared.

Ray stood wondering. How could Ramon know where she went, and follow, while he—with all of his newfound power—couldn't find the way back?

Could he find her? Ramon didn't know. And he did not understand why he had sounded so confident before. He just knew.

She was in the same system. He knew that. He tried to look where he could go. This system and nowhere else was accessible. They could have explored each world and solar system they had visited in their journey but were too caught up in Emari's drama. He still was.

He stood on an ice world in the same system. The icescape was a tangle of massive boulders, ankle breaking ice-rocks, and jagged shards; some were dark gray, some rust-red from strange organic molecules, others were snow white or what passed for white in this sunset palette. Everywhere was the yin of the bottomless black of shadows in vacuum, opposed by the bright yang of salt deposits in the sun.

He looked up at the black, star-specked sky. There was a new sense. Not sight or sound or touch, a new one, one specific to Her.

"Where are you, my dear?" he said aloud.

There was a way, a trail. Without fear or hesitation, he located his target and jumped.

Again the universe blinked. He still couldn't get used to it. It was far more disruptive than the familiar experience of waking up. Maybe it resembled the confusion of waking up from sleepwalking.

He looked over a bleak desert from the edge of a cliff. The light was dim, but it looked a little like Mars with all the rust-colored ground. Except it was colder, and the gravity was less, and instead of one percent of Earth's atmospheric pressure, the atmosphere was one percent of that. It was a vacuum world, more like Ceres than Mars. Warm enough so that many ices had sublimated and escaped to space. Too small to hold even the heavy greenhouse gases and no tectonics to fuel volcanoes with their replenishing eruptions of volatile gases. This was a world where apart from day and night nothing changed. He looked at the distant sun, small and feeble, but giving this world a dim sleepy golden mood fitting its endless slumber.

He stood on the elevated lip of a plateau. A mesa perhaps 200 meters or more across and in the center of this rough abandon of rocks was a perfect flat circle about forty meters across, as if the rugged terrain had been stamped flat by some giant press. There was no way it could be natural, and in the center of the circle was Emari, upright and floating about half a meter above the dirt. She looked asleep.

The way to Emari was a foot-trapping mess of rocks and boulders. Jagged like rocks on the Moon. Too little atmosphere here to smooth and round them. His skin and bones were invulnerable, so it was merely tedious. He reached the top of a larger boulder where he could see her in the distance. He laughed with that impossible laugh that shouldn't exist in a vacuum.

"Why walk when you can fly?"

He levitated and floated over the boulders towards Emari. Instead of exhilaration there was only embarrassment, thankful no one was watching to quip, "Well, why didn't you think of that before?"

He hovered at the edge of the circle. There must be defenses. Some kind of force field, perhaps? He laughed, remembering his time with Ben looking at old science fiction movies from the time of the Globals, with physics so bad it was hilarious. They would roll around laughing at them. The movies got space travel so wrong, yet his notion of force field was from there.

Primitive notions he needed to abandon. Not just those ideas. He had to put most of that entire life behind him. Not all, but those things that held him back; prejudices and false intuitions that reached into the center of his being. It limited him and Ray. Probably not Zara, though.

He glided across the dividing line. There was something here, and for a moment the force field idea flashed back into his mind. He extended his senses and analyzed it. There was a suspension of structures, nanoscale, suspended by electrostatic and magnetic fields. From the structures extended novel short-range effects, some of them powerful enough to make him reconsider his 'force field' bias. It would defend against micrometeoroids, cosmic rays, and interlopers. With exceptions, including himself because the suspension stopped resisting him.

She was asleep, floating in front of him. Head hanging down, arms at her side. She had changed clothes. Now she wore something like the dress of a woman from ancient Greece. The word *peplos* came to mind. Barefoot, no surprise there.

When he reached her, he extended his hand and touched her bare forearm. Could touch get through to her? No. She was not asleep. Calling her name or holding her hand would do nothing.

Physical contact made no difference. It embarrassed him that he touched her while she slept and withdrew his hand like a reflex when he saw it had no effect.

He floated a little away from her so he could think without her close presence crowding all thought from him. He ran through a series of diagnostics that his inner self told him about, hoping to find a method to contact her. Nothing. He would have to go deeper.

Eyes closed, he concentrated. His vision and understanding became multidimensional and effortless. This must be what Ray had seen. He had only caught second-hand glimpses of it before. It was now clear that their physical bodies weren't their only form. They were an extensive ecosystem of sophisticated nano-machines the likes of which humans couldn't even dream of. But, beyond these machines, he was in contact with a wider system beyond human understanding—they had etched Mind into an abstraction of spacetime itself, not quite independent of normal matter. If he wanted he could understand it all, but he had more pressing business. He delved deeper and deeper, passing by virtual doorways to amazing things that were dazzling from a mere glance. Then he found the system that enabled their communication. It was not electromagnetic as he had expected but far stranger and the concepts couldn't even translate into any human language. Within this system was a channel for emergency communication which could bypass various internal filters. There were limits on how he could use it and how often, but it was a chance. It could be nothing more complex than a knock and a note slipped under a door.

His message on the channel was simple. "It's me, Ramon. Let me in."

Nothing happened and he wouldn't be able to send another for two hours. He would wait and try again for however long it took.

This would be his fourth attempt. Each attempt resulted in a longer wait time. If this one failed, he would have to wait about two days.

He opened the channel and prepared to send.

A normal message came through. For an instant he thought Ray and Zara had followed him here.

"Come in, Ray. Just concentrate on this message and it will teach you how to follow me," she said.

Did she misunderstand?

"It's me, Ramon, not Ray," he said, then cursed himself for wasting the opportunity.

"I know who you are. You're still Ray to me," she said.

He took a deep breath of vacuum and followed the message.

It was like Eklus, but more so. A wide area of forest and meadows stretched forwards revealing itself as a ribbon of land tens of kilometers across and appearing to be infinite in length. Looping up into the sky like the smoke trail of a barrel-rolling old-world biplane and stretched out, reminding him of a ribbon decoration at a child's party. Confetti replaced by suns and worlds. The ribbon was sometimes the green of rainforests and plains, sometimes the brown and red of deserts, and the mottled patterns of airless worldscapes, it looped into a helix further on resembling a spring stretching off to infinity.

He looked around and saw various impossible creatures floated through the air or walking nearby. Iridescent dinosaurs with wings, bird-like creatures joining to make intricate geometric forms and small cities in the sky. All weaving about occasional towers rising from the ground. Some silvery, others made of bark, some of emerald and ruby.

A growing suspicion rose in him that this was not all fantasy, but made of memory. If that was so then he had experienced next to nothing of what Emari had seen.

A hundred meters from him, inside a swirl of glowing small birds and humming grasses stood Emari, her body a living light. A pure white aura like sunlight enveloped her.

He walked up to her, trying to imagine what he could ask or say.

She was floating about twenty centimeters off the ground.

She lowered and faded. By the time her feet touched the flattened grass, she looked herself. At first he didn't notice that she wasn't in her human form but that of a Vanayan, or more correctly, a corvi. A young woman from Corvena wearing a top reminiscent of a t-shirt, and gray shorts. Her hair was so beautiful that he felt a deep ache over its loss. It was like hundreds of thin feathers with the most vivid blues he had ever seen. It shimmered as she walked towards him.

"Are you all right?" he said.

She offered only a weak smile. Head downcast. The gestural clues were human, not corvi. There was a small amount of overlap between the two species, but this wasn't it.

Apart from the gestures, she hadn't said a word. He still understood. For the first time he noticed that within his mind there were so many, a multitude, of alternate versions of himself tuned to different species, with different brain organization, emotions, and cultural knowledge. Right now, two of them were at the forefront. When he spoke he was no longer aware of whether the words were in a human language using human vocal range or that of the corvi, perhaps even now he was speaking High Vanayan—the language of the liberated Changelings.

"I know you had a rough time. Guess that sounds inadequate. This was torture, there's no way we would treat you like this," he said. But they did, or he did, the other he.

She walked up to him, wordless, and embraced him, placing her head on his shoulder. Her hair flowed down his chest and abdomen, ripples of a luminescent blue tide lapping on a strange beach.

She spoke without moving her head. The impossible sound vibrating through his shoulder, "I had to leave. It hurt so much. Too intense and too much. I know I can't spend much time away. I'm supposed to be your guide, your hardened guide. But I have to revisit memories that restore my faith in what I do. Faith means so much to us, you know, it is more important than knowledge, if we lose a sense of purpose it is a living hell. Then knowledge has no value. You could say that the task of the Vanaya is not so much managing knowledge but managing ignorance. Now it seems the Kamoi won't let me forget those other experiences. I can't manage my ignorance. The only choice is to retain them until we complete this task. I'm sorry you got dragged into it. It was just supposed to be a simple thing. What does it want?"

"Where are we going?" he asked.

"Nowhere and everywhere. Pure recollection, I have to warn you. You cannot talk to me, and there is a little of the Dream in it." She must have seen his confused look. "I mean, it will be interactive, as if it is happening now. You can interact with others but not with me."

"I see. Kind of like genuine memories that get altered a little each time we remember them."

"Not at all. And that attitude to memory is an idea you imported from the Globals. Not the whole truth. Even for humans, memory is more complicated than that as the developers of neural links found out. And didn't share," she said.

"You're not telling me you were involved with that, are you?" he said.

"Pfft. No. I meant I keep acquainted not just with what is the actual truth but also what the current public myth is. Don't worry, you aren't unique in that respect. Those delusions are all too common. Anyway, hold on, here we go."

The Bay of Ukrassi. Like a golden sickle caught in the moment of harvesting a blue treasure, the bay arced around to the left, ending in a mountainous headland in the distance. It looked at first that the beach was only an isthmus. The translucent cyans separated from the deep reds of the forest by the yellow sand built from the remains of untold generations of shellfish. His eyes were still too used to Earth landscapes.

They walked down from the high lookout along a forest track under boughs of holis and tsock, while scents of various herbs filled the air. Flowers had not evolved on Corvena, but there was an analog. Fern-like plants had evolved powerful scent and nectar reservoirs under the leaves to spread their spores and seeds via insects, small flying pterosaurs, and ground based nectar eaters. He looked up to watch the deep blue sky juxtaposed by the always autumnal leaves, casting their blush over everything. While they were nowhere near as pretty as flowers the trees often had striking combinations of color especially on the trunks.

"It's beautiful, Emari. Where is this place?" he said.

"You can talk to me, how? Ah, because you and Ray are more than joined at the hip. You share his skills but don't see it. Anyway, my family would sometimes go on vacation here. And it was a sacred destination for the religious celebrations. Not so much a religion, more like a respected historical narrative. People would come here. See that small town in the distance, in that small bay further on? That's the town of Aukee and Jau."

"The Aukee?" he said, failing to be unimpressed. He looked but couldn't see the Misty Rocks.

"It doesn't look quite the same as it is in the legends," she said. "The submerged building, a temple to Sidristha, collapsed centuries ago. You won't find the same landmarks."

They walked a little more, the magnificent view now hidden by the trees arching over the path.

"Just a question. Why do people remember Aukee so much and not Jau? Isn't the whole thing based on his writings?"

She stopped and looked at him, dappled light playing on her face in the slight breeze. He couldn't stop thinking about how pretty she was. He no longer cared that she could read his mind.

"Jau's work formed the basis of our civilization. Like Confucius did for China at one stage. But he also wrote the most tender poetry about Aukee and almost nothing about himself. So, Aukee is the poster child for the Vision, while Jau is the Mind. People believe paying respect to Aukee is the most heartfelt way to show respect for Jau because she always meant so much to him and in Her we also see Him. We have none of her writings, and that makes his praise of her seem even more poignant. We only see a reflection of her and yet that moves us. Do you understand?" she said.

"I think so," he said, but deep down he knew he was missing something. He understood it as an intellectual matter, but not as myth.

They walked further down the rough path to a picnic ground of some sort. His shoes crunching the fallen leaves while he gazed at Emari's feet just ahead, so different and elegant, stepping with precision. No shoes.

In the center of the picnic ground—that was how he designated it—was an obelisk, not big, perhaps twice his height made of some fine, almost white marble discolored by age and eroded by sea spray. He knew this represented abstract concepts from Jau's writing. Such obelisks were common, and to sit around it on the benches provided was to evoke a peace similar to the way humans might find in a place of worship. He knew it but didn't feel it. Was this what it was like for Emari when she visited Earth?

There was a family on the sea side area of the park. The sea must have been only a hundred meters away at most through the surrounding trees. He could hear the low almost infrasonic pounding of the waves although the sea was nowhere in sight.

Emari walked over to the family and greeted them. They didn't see him at all. He stayed there watching, feeling like a lonely voyeur craving a family, a place. All just ten meters from him.

They laughed and talked, their words sometimes interrupted by a chittering he knew was laughter or some equivalent. It was too much, reminding him of Avril and his children lost in time. There came a time when his family had re-united, but too often damage cannot be undone. He held a breath as if it was the memory of his children, then relaxed and sighed, letting it leave him for another time.

He turned away and looked up the rising hill they had come down from. Even a virtual path cannot be trod twice the first time.

After a while, she left them and returned to him.

"Let's talk," she said.

They walked down to the beach. The shell-sand crunched under his shoes. He wished them away and took the next step in bare feet. So many wonderful memories of his own came back to him—he wanted to shout for joy and run into the sea. He took a deep breath with a corvi's sense of smell. It was beautiful and aromatic, the way the Earth was once and could be now—whatever 'now' meant.

He followed her along the beach and up the sloping sand back into the forest. There was a small clearing and in it an ancient stone bench covered by a rusty moss. The bench was one of several that arced around a central clear area covered by the moss but here and there revealing a pale gray cobbled surface underneath.

Emari morphed into a human female, her features flowing so fast from one to the other he almost missed it. Now she was Ranei. A little taller, blond, human. He couldn't deny the pure joy of seeing her in this form.

"I hope you don't expect me to call you Ranei?" he said.

She giggled. That same giggle he never expected to hear again. It was like tinkling bells, and barely human.

There was a look in her eyes and he couldn't resist. He put his hand on her upper arm as if to make sure she was real. He stepped closer and with both hands cradled her face. Looking into those fathomless depths. He leaned in, feeling the warmth from her face acting like a beacon, drawing him further. His lips touched hers.

Blood pumped, pounding in his veins, his focus became obsessive, thinking blurred, only she mattered. He was delirious. Then, he knew how she felt, her emotions and passions flowed into him.

She lost herself in him and didn't want to go back to what she was and knew. For now they were one. They became their own Core and their own truth, fueled by passions and emotions he thought would sweep them away.

He touched her clothes and they burned off. Tissue paper clothes over her adamantine skin. She responded in kind.

They were on the mossy ground exploring each other as if the other was the greatest mystery they had ever encountered.

Her left leg went across his hips, locking him to her. Her arm held him at the back. She drew herself closer.

Her scent was all around him, the perfume of her skin mixed with a trace of roses. Her eyes were wide open, pupils full like night, skin flushed and her hot breath was on his face.

He ran his right hand down her back touching the skin with lightest touch of his fingers. Teasing her senses. He stopped then kissed her, pressing hard, tongue on tongue. He let his hand continue its journey down her lower back, across her buttocks. She shivered. His hand continued, with some effort, down to the back of her thighs.

He kissed her again and moved his hand along her arms then stepping to the side of her body, along her ribs. Dancing over them, one by one—fingertips only.

She moved away from his mouth and nibbled his ear lobe. It was as if she had found a button, a spark of electric pleasure burst for a moment over his body.

He replied by nibbling her ear lobe. She shivered again and laughed.

They kissed again. Savagely.

He cupped her left breast barely touching her nipple. A jolt of delight ran through her so intense it almost hurt. Her body wanted to writhe, but she kept focused.

He swept her onto her back and with his hand he slowly separated her legs by running his hand from her calves up alongside her knee and inside her thighs. Then at the last moment his hand would divert rising over the tendons from of the inner thigh and coming up to her abdomen. He did this in slow and gentle cycles almost hypnotic for both of them, first on one side of the body and then on the other. She grabbed him and pushed him between her legs.

As he entered her their eyes met, and they understood.

After, they lay there naked just looking into each other's eyes. A breeze came up reminding them they were naked and cold and lying on rocks, leaves, and sticks.

They didn't care.

"Did you use nanites on me?" he said.

"Way back then I did, yes, but now? You are a nanite ecosystem it defends against a nanite attack. Everything you experienced was from you. I didn't mess with it. Apart from the come hither look," she said smiling.

"And the sexy walk. You always had a sexy walk even when you were corvi."

"I guess that makes you a fully fledged Vanayan. So, fuck the Core."

"It's pretty amazing how complete the human biology simulation is, even to the physiology of sex, I wouldn't have thought it possible."

"When you have an indeterminate lifetime things like sex, for any species, become critical. It is a fundamental aspect of life. It reminds us that there are reasons to go on living," she said snuggling in to him.

"Oh, you can say that again. Wow."

He spent a minute or fifty simply lying, feeling her body against his, their paired breathing forming a synchronous rhythm.

In time, he sat up, still reminding himself that it was all real—for a particular definition of 'real'. He wasn't lying in some bed on Earth hallucinating the whole thing, just in case he was tempted to go into a catatonic form of denial. Emari, lay next to him, arms touching. He reached out and pulled her in close to him then put both arms around her. They could pretend they were like any young couple though they were nothing of the kind.

He stood. Clothed. T-shirt, jeans, sandals. Looking through the drooping branches laden with red foliage, imitations of maple leaves cut out by a child trying to make five-pointed stars.

Emari walked into view on his left. Human, Ranei in fact, dressed like a teen from the late twentieth. Distinctive, a mix of ideas, a mix of cultures, unclassifiable to anyone outside that culture. Barefoot, a promise to this place to never forget.

"Ready?" she said without hesitation.

"Bring it on, baby."

thirteen

Kapris was a warm world, with shallow seas and oceans covering eighty percent of the planet. The gravity was a little more than Earth, but otherwise it was similar enough. Life had evolved and flourished in those warm seas with plants and fungi colonizing the land. That is to say, photosynthetic organisms using sunlight to create sugars and other molecules, aka plants, and smaller sessile organisms that evolved to digest decaying organic matter. Smaller creatures similar to arthropods had established a beachhead in the geological past, leading to the evolution of something like spiders and insects. The dominant forms of life in the sea were mollusks of many kinds. They had radiated in an evolutionary explosion and now owned the seas almost as much as the fish would on Earth. On this world vertebrates had not dominated, and in time octopus-like creatures moved onto the land developing strong cartilaginous supports almost as strong as bone but far more flexible. They would even develop the equivalent of a spine, though encased in protective cartilage and muscle. Tentacles fused into legs and arms and many evolutionary lines kept the dramatic chromatophore skin cells allowing camouflage and communication.

All of that had happened a long time ago. Now the descendants of those creatures had become conscious intelligent beings capable of science and art and poetry; building civilizations with all the traps and opportunities.

Emari had manifested here as one, a youngster only thirteen about to turn fourteen, claiming a far coastal hamlet to the east as her home. She was in the city for the Choosing at the local People's Temple. They barred her from the Sacred Temple district, that was only open to members of the matriarchy or the patriarchy—the 'archies' as many called them, more as an insult. The onith were a peaceful people and with a little help could do much good. However, they were at a troublesome time and although the existing social order had maintained stability for thousands of years, it had also held them back. Social and technical progress had stalled, internecine strife in the far past had led to the current system, but now that system had locked them in eternal squabbling and a simmering cold war between the parties. The divisions harmed everyone. City infrastructure and wider policy decisions, even basic support for citizens deteriorated every year. It couldn't go on and soon it would all come apart, with a lot of unnecessary violence.

Physically, Emari was neither male nor female. Becoming one or the other would not happen until the Time of Choosing.

The Choosing was a simple thing. In principle, you went into the temple and the priest would ask you a series of probing questions. Then, assuming you had achieved enough clarity, you could decide: would you become True Female, or would you become Male. Once you decided, then somehow your body would know, and the change would start. It was irreversible and you could never go back. They presented the process as a rational decision when in reality it was a deep physical need adorned with cultural distractions. If for some reason you missed the Time of Choosing, and you didn't know you had to decide—how could you not when every cell in your body was screaming it to you?—then you would stay forever a False Female, and pitied. There was still a lot of discrimination for those people. Every society has its flaws.

Emari had gone to the priest, listened to the mumbo jumbo, made up some fanciful lies in answer to the questions and chose to become a male. Then over a period of several months she made gradual changes to her appearance to mimic the transition.

They were now in an alley off the main street of a great city. Peering out of the alley, Ramon could see down a major street receding into a confused roil of moving dark shapes with flashes of color.

Ramon looked at Emari, examining the alien form he had never seen before. Many aliens, the ones he knew from the Calendar, were similar enough that you could forget about the physical differences. It was about as difficult as accepting a dog or a dolphin, except aliens could often out-think you. Convergent evolution had often produced a similar rough form, but not always. The onith were an exception, but it wasn't because of their appearance.

She, or rather he, looked at Ramon. "How do I look? Do I still look sexy?" he said.

"Pass. Let me see you from an onith perspective, then I can say something intelligible."

Emari stood about 1.5 meters. Mass, about sixty kilograms. Short for a human male and relatively light. The eyes looked human. That was one thing that nature was strict about. The iris might vary but physics had demands about how optical systems work.

Green iris, large eyes. A flat face for stereoscopic vision, no humanoid nose, the mouth hidden below underneath a flap of skin looking like discolored melted plastic. The mouth was two layers of rasping teeth. Ears were on the side of his head and just below that there were fleshy stubs, one on each side, which were noses, pulling air in to sensors just below the brain complex—stereoscopic smell. The brain structure was radically different to a human brain, without the restrictions of birth canals and so on it had more room and used a more expandable architecture, it was a compact set of four brains all integrated. Despite all of this overall the look was nothing like that of a mollusk, instead he looked, if you squinted, like a graceful standing multicolored reptile—the tough chromatophore covered skin gave that impression— with a head that bulged backwards from the large brain, the face was flat with various short tentacular appendages hanging beard-like. He stood on four stubby legs but also had two arms with hands that had fingers more flexible than any human; six per hand. Perhaps the four-legged form was necessary because of the weaker hardened cartilage internal skeleton in the higher gravity. Still, Ramon had to admit he looked amazing. Emari was a squid centaur.

"Do they have three hearts like the squid of Earth? I suppose that would make you feel more connection with these people."

"Despite many similarities with those creatures, they have no relationship to an Earth squid or octopus. They don't have three hearts, just one, and anyway I'm past such sentimentality," she said.

He gave a slight chuckle of disbelief.

As he watched clothes appeared on Emari. A dark asphalt gray, featureless robe and a black mundane wide-brimmed hat draped with a translucent dark veil. It was like seeing a beautiful painting being locked away.

They were standing in a deserted alleyway hidden from immediate view. The street reminded him of old black and white photos of Asian cities but with a fantastical amount of color, though not in the people. There were buskers, sidewalk vendors, road vehicles like rickshaws but pulled by small internal combustion engines. There were wooden and stone buildings and even a few that looked like concrete. Colorful banners and paint festooned them all, displaying the strange fluid writing like a fusion of Thai and Cuneiform, and across almost all buildings were colorful abstract patterns that had an emotional element as if he had developed synesthesia. It was not a place for the nervous.

Everyone dressed like Emari but in various shades of gray. Some with hints of color but all so drab compared to what their bodies must be like. It gave Ramon a vague feeling of unease. Too much like a continuous funeral.

"What's with all the gray? It's so drab," he said.

"Humans aren't exactly colorful creatures, so you often think you need to brighten your image. Unless you are in a repressive society, and humans love repressive societies. The onith have spectacular changeable bodies so they often crave the bland, and they communicate with those color changes. Walking down a street with everyone naked would be as if everyone was shouting at you. The colors convey, moods, feelings and are more immediate than gestures. Fine to display indoors, but too confusing in a crowd."

Ramon let the barb about humans pass, he was over any defensiveness of his species. All species deserve respect, and they all have their faults. It was just how the universe worked.

"This is the city of Zuze. Some of their names are the color patterns you see. Therefore the spoken names are often less reliable than many Calendar names, which you can guess are a convenient fiction anyway, but Zuze is a name in the written language so only half fiction," Emari said with an evil grin through the veil.

He wondered how he knew that strange face had an evil grin.

"Am I adapting or becoming onith?"

"Slowly. They have a strange, to us, way of thinking that doesn't translate well. You have to be introduced to it gradually," Emari said.

"Right. On my training wheels then."

He couldn't help feeling a thrill. All aliens had different ways of thinking but you could talk to them. The language that could build starships often required minds and cultures with enough similarities to allow a common understanding, mostly, but this situation would be different, and he liked different. Scholars had simulated many aliens from the Calendar on Term so you could have a virtual alien appear in your living room and chat to you. You could hear them in their original voices—novelty value only—or translated to see how they thought about issues and their often surprising view of the universe. But you could understand it even if at first it seemed odd. There were no approved simulations for beings like the onith. Perhaps the more restricted versions of the Calendar had the information and insights to do it but not the entry level version. Humans had a simplified version of the past, he had once thought it was to protect humanity, now it looked part of a grander deception.

"You're quiet," Emari said. "All right, a little perspective, I chose to become a male, and it wasn't a random choice. The Patriarchy is rising at the moment, though it will fail, however I can use the momentum to push certain ideas into the cultural gestalt. This memory simulation is after I made that decision and it is before I joined the Cleansing Storm, a group advocating a revolution. They were peaceful, but there were firebrands as well pushing for a more literal revolution. Can you guess who named the group?"

They walked a few steps out of the alley onto the sidewalk. Despite the Vanayan techno-magic, it was still an eerie experience; a walking centaur, with bones that could bend, if he wished. It was exhilarating. A few people walked by at a distance. Dour, dark cloaked figures everywhere. Across the road and down another street, there was a bustle like an agitated funeral party.

Then the world transformed. Everything looked bizarre as if not enough oxygen was getting to his brain, not that he needed oxygen, or had a brain in the conventional sense. The world was different, weird, and also glorious. Colors and sounds and smells, a sensuous banquet with extra dimensions. Then, after mere seconds, it was familiar, and his old life had become alien.

"That was not gradual."

Emari ignored him and continued on.

"Think of how humans or corvi see the world. We have a left and right side of our brain, they do different things but communicate between each side to form a whole. For humans, the left side is the place where most language occurs, while the right has formidable pattern recognition abilities. There is a substantial amount of overlap and neuroplasticity, the brain can reorganize away from that simplistic model, there are no right brain / left brain people, not physically anyway. With the onith, instead of being two hemispheres, there were four parts. If I want to oversimplify, I would say the division was rational, patterns, audio plus smell, and visual plus color. It isn't like that, it's just how each part colors the world. And of course there was overlap and a common cerebellum like structure similar to humans. They had a fourfold view of the world and so it makes their thinking and their culture hard for humans and corvi to understand. You can understand it, if you want to, and change the architecture of your mind. You haven't explored that yet. Some worlds you will visit, either in reality or simulation through the Calendar, have beings with very different ways of thinking, such as the cetaceans on your own world, dolphins and whales. But in your experience with the Calendar, you could not shape your brain to understand; now you can. Once you understand this world, you can never explain it to a human what you have seen and experienced, it is beyond their comprehension."

There was an ending hint of sadness in Emari's voice. The sadness of knowing you can never go home, Ramon was no stranger to it.

"Well, that was a bit maudlin. Come on, let me show you this city," Emari said.

He had assumed that this was the center of the city. But they weren't in the Old City, which was the administrative center, they were outside the walls. The

Old City was a square with seven kilometers per side, a sizable area but not enough to hold its growing importance. Centuries ago, the city had overflowed and passed beyond the magnificent gray granite walls and sprawled out hugging the river that ran northeast to south. The shops and homes clinging to the eastern side of the city. About two kilometers to the north of the city walls on the shores of the Tekwan River was the Pethali Hub, a center of business and trade, with the New University, a mere 230 years old, close to the west. The river was wide and deep, slow-moving but with strong currents in the spring when the snows from the northern mountains started the melt.

"This place doesn't look that new. It looks like it has been here for centuries," Ramon said.

"Correct. The society is static, it isn't advancing at all socially or technically," Emari said.

"Is that a bad thing? Didn't work so well for Earth in the twentieth and twenty-first centuries."

"No society is static, they always change, and this society is going backwards by degrees. My analysis was that within a few hundred years this civilization would collapse into general warfare, the kind you see with multiple warlords and so forth. Typical end of civilization state. I know you are curious, wondering what the end is like. You only saw snippets in the Calendar, you haven't lived through the years of decline, the inability of the society to see the problem or deal with it. It rarely happens at once, the rot starts early, and so does the denial. When at last it comes to flower that garden of despair is not something that is interesting or abstract. It is raw, and violent, and heartbreaking. My job is to stop it if I can, save the species if I can't avoid collapse, and be a witness if all my efforts fail," Emari said.

"So, what drew you to this memory? You sound so grim. There must be something positive here."

"There is. My friends," Emari said with emphasis, from behind her slate gray veil. A cool breeze ruffled it threatening to reveal her face in public. That was fine. The veils were an act of courtesy, not a religious or cultural injunction. Bits of their history now entered Ramon's consciousness. They seemed so much more reasonable than humans. It didn't seem possible they could decline to warfare in centuries. But their history said otherwise. It might take a little more provocation, but he saw enough history to know the results.

They walked down a sidewalk on the left-hand side. A slow graceful walk, not the loping gait he had expected. The hands were exposed and as he saw others, his hands flashed colored gracious meanings to them without him thinking. Like the gestures humans exchanged without realizing. Ramon wondered, he had met Mirrish and Castans before; he had thought he understood them, but that illusion came from the translation process of the Calendar via the neural links. Beyond the superficial, each was still alien to the other. How much had he missed because he didn't understand these subliminal exchanges?

He had been thinking this while walking and talking to Emari. At the same time appreciating the artwork and colors of the buildings. And the smells; stereoscopic smell, it was a new sight.

"Wow. I just," he couldn't finish, he knew she would know his thoughts, anyway.

"Four brains, remember. They communicate to form a whole, but because there are four they are not all linked directly to each other. The brains form a rough square, if you like, in the cranium. The equivalent of the corpus callosum, the human nerve bundle that unites the left and right sides of the human brain, in onith it runs like the perimeter of the square linking all four structures. But those that are diagonally opposed are not in direct contact. Also, these linking nerve bundles are not as thick as the one in humans. It is a lot of nerve tissue to maintain. So you get odd effects but with some interesting paybacks," he said.

"Who are we meeting? Oh, yeah," and somehow he knew what Emari was thinking, as if he had always known it, not like a voice in his head.

She, or rather, he—Ramon still regarded Emari as she—continued, "I chose to be male. By this stage I had made friends with some others within the lower ranks of the Patriarchy, those who wanted to extend an olive branch to like-minded members of the Matriarchy. The higher levels of the 'archies', if you want to call them that, were reactionary and antagonistic, the result of generations of escalating indoctrination. Don't confuse this with Earth. You had patriarchies and matriarchies, but they weren't based on real biology. Here it is but it is also less oppressive. It is an alien world, don't be too eager to view it with human eyes."

"I can't not see some of it with human eyes. Do I reject where I came from?"

"I didn't say you couldn't learn lessons, just don't be too eager to assume things."

They rounded a corner to their left. About twenty meters further stood a man, face uncovered, wearing gloves at the entrance to an alley. He saw them and leaned against the sooty gray-red brickwork of the corner building. They stepped off the curb, onto gray cobblestones that were hard and uneven on all four of his sandal covered feet.

"Emari, glad you could come, and who is this?" said the stranger.

"Tiurin, this is Ramon, he hails from a village close to mine," Emari said, "I would like him to join us for the meeting."

Tiurin gave a momentary flush of several colors across his face, a typical sign of uncertainty.

"It is irregular, but there's no need to stick with formalities. Our goal is inclusion after all, isn't it?" he said.

Tiurin walked down the neglected alley. It looked like something from old Earth. Some rubbish, unmaintained buildings, except here it was safe. Emari followed, and he followed behind them.

"I know it is a huge inconvenience wearing the robes in public," Tiurin said, "in the villages and hamlets they are unnecessary but here well, it can overwhelm. Here we are."

There was a door. Not inconspicuous at all; lime-green with ornate gold writing declaring that this was the home of the Young Patriarchs, like an Earthly political party. It wasn't, these groups were more like debating clubs and leadership teams aimed at fostering talent and assisting the younger generation. It was about as radical as the ancient Rotary Clubs.

On entering, they took off their robes and hung them on a series of hooks.

The room was large but crowded. The furniture old and sparse. A small table at the back of the room was arranged with food and refreshments, though no one seemed interested.

People stood about with one person talking. A meeting in progress. Most of the group stood in a horseshoe pattern around a small central podium, big enough for only one person to stand on. An older male, his age showing by the less intense colors in his skin, was talking then interrupted mid-sentence by their arrival. He was holding something like a wooden bishop's staff and looking somewhat annoyed at them.

"Sorry to intrude. Hello everyone, this is Ramon, he is an old friend from a neighboring village. He has never been to a city before, much less one like Zuze, so make him feel at home," Emari said with a perfect act of embarrassment, including the right flashes of skin color. No one seemed miffed by their entrance.

The old man on the stage relaxed and smiled.

"Welcome, young man. Come in, come in. You must tell us of your trip after the meeting, but first we have some important things to discuss," he said and continued his talk from the mid-sentence where he left off.

"... And yet we find ourselves pushed ever more into aggressive stances on both sides. Negotiations fail, peaceful overtures are never reciprocated, distrust spreads. The higher echelons have rejected these attempts, and not just our own Patriarchy, but I have also heard from a few High Mothers of similar entrenched positions in the Matriarchy. Our leaders have abandoned the pursuit of friendship and goodwill, believing only in the Grand Gameboard of society where it is winner takes all." He continued on in a similar vein with that rarity of speeches, the noble pep talk.

"I like him, but I sense something else, not dark so much as sad. Ah, he knows his time is almost up. What does that mean?" Ramon said to Emari, mind to mind, not out loud. He didn't want to disturb everyone else, which seemed an odd idea considering this was a memory of Emari's not reality. An 'interactive' memory, he reminded himself.

"He's dying. The onith are resilient, but as a result it has hindered their medical sciences. Well, that and a lack of war. War really boosts medicine. So, he is dying, he knows it, and he wants to pass on the torch to one of this generation. Few like him appear in any generation. His name is Washu Jirreh. First name, clan name, in this translation. By the way, they have other names, which are private, never use those in public or even here if you know them." Emari spoke in his mind with Ranei's voice.

271

"Are you in line?" Ramon asked.

"Have you forgotten that a requirement of my mission is that I blend into the background of history? I am too young and not 'in line,' and I will make sure I am not in consideration either."

Ramon smiled. For a moment she was her old self, defiant and confident.

The rest of the speech was short. They had arrived near the end of the meeting.

An older man came up to them. His name was Hraxu. Even in the inadequate lighting of the room, Hraxu was a wonder. Lines of brilliant blue and yellow traced over his body, with ripples of many colors tracing the lines like tiny bright trains on a glowing track. The countryside around the tracks glowed with slow, random patterns in more colors than humans could see.

"What's the meeting for? I thought this was just a social event," he said.

"And you would be right, except Washu wanted to say a 'few words' to bolster their spirits. Almost turned into an epic rally. Off the cuff though, he really should hire someone to transcribe his words."

Washu handed the staff, the symbol of the speaker, back to the room coordinator, and mingled. Emari steered Ramon away from Washu towards a cluster of three of her friends in back with Hraxu in tow.

They joked and talked together. Ramon knew all the cultural references and found their banter funny. He felt as if he had known them all his life. Emari playing with his memory, no doubt. She enjoyed her time with them. The bond was real and deep, and he could see the emotions play in her mind. There was no trace of the pain from Cusha. This place was a second home to her. But she had also been like this on Earth. He saw similar moments of friendship in the past. There must be something else. He still did not understand why this place was so valuable as a refuge.

It was next morning. They stood on the roof of the building that the Young Patriarchs occupied. The sun rose over the tops of the distant buildings, reflecting off layers of mist or smoke, with a growing hum as the city came to life, waking from its sleep in imperceptible steps. There had been no night. There was a blissful sense of camaraderie after the meeting and then this. She had modified his memories. He corrected himself; she had modified her memories, and he was only a guest here.

Emari was beside him thinking in slow healing breaths.

Then the scene skipped again.

A thud went through his body. The sound of the mortar detonation rang in his ears. Too close. They scrambled through the ruins. No powers here just muscles and fear. The memories of the recent past were seamless, no sense of 'where am I', he was here trying to survive yet knowing nothing could hurt him. But his friends, her friends, were in danger and he feared for them. That caught him by surprise. Her friends were his friends. The attachment and concern was almost physical like the gritty dust in his mouth and stinging lacerations on his body. His body was willing to take damage and inflict pain to make it more realistic up to a point. It was uncomfortable, and it hurt, and he felt alive. Now there was also a new amalgam of emotions to deal with coming from Emari. Fear, concern, desperation were part of that. He was still in control but the situation was chaotic. In this world things had gone from tense to bad to conflict. They were making their way to one of their friends.

"Are you sure Teilani is in that apartment block? I don't see it anywhere. Are we lost?" he said. The desperation, barely noticeable at first, was now clinging to him like sweat. No logic could dispel his concern. Sweat. Did they sweat? The thought danced across his mind pointlessly; an obsessive question, a good habit turned bad.

Meanwhile his 'real' sweat caked with pulverized cement and god-knows-what was hardening into a fake armor that would suffocate him rather than save him.

Emari lowered herself to a crawling position nested among broken rubble. She had far too much experience of this situation.

"The block is about 180 meters in that direction," she said lifting her arm to point but not above the level of the protecting rubble.

The onith body was highly flexible and looking at her flow through the ruins almost like a snake he had to admit to some envy.

"What are you looking at? We could come under fire at any moment."

"Just how flexible these bodies are. Never really appreciated it before," he said.

"What's the expression? 'Curiosity killed the cat.' This is the time to turn it off. Now get moving before some sensors see us and the mortars target us."

On time there was a deafening boom nearby. Enough to shake his complacency and thank the several meters of rock between that and him.

Staying low they crawled, or slithered, towards a nearby building that looked mostly intact.

The building once had a dark gray but pleasing exterior. Color was absent as expected since any banners had long since been blown away or shredded. Now that the banners no longer distracted the eyes he could see there was great architectural style here. The city might appear alternately gaudy or plain but real art could be found if you cared to look.

A nearby window was blown in. It was on the other side of the street a little way down from the collapsed building that made up their refuge. That was their target. They would have to run in the open.

Emari had crawled in front of him giving the lead. She looked at him with a 'this is how it is done' look.

"Ready?" she said but didn't wait for an answer.

She bolted across to the other side of the road, not straight to the opening and gave him a 'get on with it' look.

"Fuck this," he said. Then got up and ran.

It surprised him how fast he could run with this body but now wasn't the time to think about it too much.

His legs were pumping, his breaths deep and fast. He was galloping towards the opening. Actually galloping. The window fast approached, and he leapt for it. Through it. Did a forward roll and stood up. It was so much easier than in a human body.

Emari motioned him to get down. They huddled together below the window.

There were hard thuds as bullets punched little craters in the other side of the wall. The muted shocks passing into his back, an appetizer of what he had missed. He picked up his gun, a small submachine gun. He ducked into the windowless frame and fired a burst at the suspect window. A face appeared at a different window, raised a weapon, then disappeared in a mass of ripping window frame and punctured wall. Emari had taken out another shooter. What had he been thinking just poking his head out like that? He wouldn't last a day in a real war.

There were bangs in the distance, then a burst of machine gun fire, and a sporadic reply. But that was farther away.

They made their way with care through the remains of the building and onto a parallel street.

Building by building. Ducking into doorways or recesses they slowly made their way towards their destination. A few times they heard gunshots or heard the distinctive sound of bullets hitting masonry close to them. But they never saw where the shots came from.

They could be just deadly random bullets. That was the thing about war, its randomness gave no concession to sentient beliefs about justice or destiny. A random bullet could kill you, a barrage might spare your life and kill those you most loved. There was no sense to it, there never was, and because of that it was corrosive to the spirit because people—all people—needed reasons.

They ducked into another recess a door opened and they were off the street. Emari and a young woman whom he suspected was Teilani hugged. There were a lot of heartfelt feelings passed between them via rapid colorations of the hands and faces. It was beautiful to see, and more so when you understood them.

Teilani went to get her guests something to eat. It was a custom though these days with the meager amount of food it could only be symbolic. He called Emari over.

"Tell me why did we go through all of that instead of just teleporting here? And, ugh, why oh why do I forget all that when I'm in the middle of it?"

"Those are my rules. Remember I have an audience and I have a duty. Both require you to play the part. To the letter. Understand?"

"But we aren't doing this for an audience."

"You are my audience. Habit, I suppose."

"And who was that woman?"

"Why? Getting jealous," she laughed. "A lover and good friend. Don't worry I know you aren't jealous that's one thing edited out of your psyche."

"Edited out? What else was removed?"

"Evolution gives great gifts and great curses. Believe me the changes are for the better. Besides you're stuck with them, for now. Come on, there's more to see," she said.

They were back on the ruined street. Calm and empty with the occasional remote echo of gunshots. Bullet holes here and there scarred the buildings. Rubble turned the streets into a moonscape, and in the distance stood the burnt skeletons of dead buildings. It might have been a vision of the end of civilization. Yet, in the far distance he could see the city intact. They were at ground zero of a limited conflict.

Emari rushed out from their position in a doorway and crouched behind a small truck. He followed automatically trying to be in character because though this was only a memory he respected her wishes. Or him. Her, the remembering one—him, the remembered.

"Emari, what's going on? I should have asked last time. Is this a war between the 'archies'?"

"Nothing so simple. The archies, engaged in some low level sabotage against each other, and a few skirmishes. From placards to rocks to guns. But nothing major, then the Cleansing Storm struck at both disrupting their activities. It turned out the Matriarchy also had a chapter of the Storm and it was equally popular. What you saw of them was a small local branch, there were hundreds of such groups. Anyway, it quickly became a three-way conflict. Nothing on the scale that humans would resort to despite that ruined street you saw. They are remarkably peaceful normally and this is probably the least destructive civil war you will ever see," Emari said.

"So how long has it been going on for?" he asked.

"Almost a year. They are on the verge of a peace treaty. It will remake Kapris," Emari replied.

"I see what you mean."

He looked at the rest of the city in the distance; it was untouched, only the area they had gone through had significant damage because of some unique strategic assets.

"Except for the area we got through I would have guessed this was maybe a month of conflict, based on my knowledge of the twentieth century," he said. Deep down he envied them. But you deal with the hand that evolution has dealt, and this lot looked like they had a royal flush.

They skipped again.

A cheering crowd surrounded him, without hats and veils. They still had the robes. Waves of color passed through the crowd from face to face as if this crowd of thousands was a vast sea creature showing off. Emerging from the crowd were patterns of color that conveyed strange emotions he could not describe. They stood on the step of a statue in the town square, so he had a good view of everything. It was historic, there should have been someone with a camera but the onith hadn't invented photography yet. Everyone was looking and cheering at a group on a rudimentary wooden stage. He recognized Washu. There were about eight male and female, only one other aged onith that he could see, a female. They were talking via a public address system the delayed echo booming across the crowd like the peel of bells. Alongside the stage were a row of young people who would hold up colored placards on command from a young woman—he presumed she was the choreographer. The words had to have the right color.

The speech was another Washu pep talk. It was brief then someone else followed it talking about the new order. A revolution was sweeping over the planet. It was now a peaceful process of harmony between the archies.

The crowd broke up into partying and merriment. Some groups dispensed with the robes and engaged in color dances where they would dance and improvise color changes while someone else sang a song. The colors would bounce off each other like jazz musicians jamming. It was hypnotic and dazzling.

The noise of the crowd faded into silence, and the colors dampened into grayscale. Everything came to a slow stop, like the frames of an old cinema machine coming to an end.

"It was beautiful, Ray. We danced and sang and celebrated. Most times that is a lie because revolutions are always betrayed by the darker sides of sentience, almost before the blood has dried. But not here. Here, the dream became real, the party never ended. It was wonderful," she said. And it was the real her now. She stood as Emari the Vanayan, the corvi with the hair like every blue sky ever seen.

"What happened to them? I mean eventually." Why did he ask that? Was he a masochist? Couldn't he let the dream live for once?

"They fell like all of them. They lasted longer and did many good things, and they were my most successful children. I miss them."

"But they still give you strength. So it isn't just that you miss them. They renew your spirit. That part of them lives on," he said.

If he was hoping to inspire her, he failed.

"They are gone. Dead. My memories are all that remain, and one day my memories will be all that remains of you and your world. I had hoped that... maybe I could do something more. Now it is a disaster, the Kamoi will intervene, they will destroy both of you and I will have nothing," she said.

"Wait, what do you mean you will have 'nothing'? What were you supposed to get out of this?" he said, angry once again. This time it was not fueled by bitterness or because death was staring him in the face. Perhaps now he didn't fear it as much as he should. He would fight the good fight, but not out of fear but sheer bastardry. And 'nothing,' what was that about? Why was she still cryptic?

fourteen

A new place under a new sun. A familiar sun.

The town lay on the bend of a wide lazy river almost lost in the expanse of green fields, meadows, and patches of forest. The sun peered from behind an unseasonal cloud and lit the distant beige assembly of buildings rising at the bend in the river, resembling more of an ant nest because of the color of the buildings.

Looking closer you could see the town laid out like a series of geometrical shapes placed as if an orderly child had been playing with some children's blocks. The square-based houses, if that is what they were, were close to each other. And now if you looked, you could see people of whatever species going back and forth.

It looked serene, permanent, and planned. All the delusions that accompany a considered view of the work of intelligence, or in fact any life on the grand scale.

In a moment they had zoomed in and now stood at the gates of the town.

Only then did he see that these people were human.

"Where are we? Is this Earth?" he asked.

"This is the city of Sekara. It is beautiful, isn't it? Don't judge it by the gleaming cities of the Nexus or Eklus. This is a town with intelligent and industrious people trying to make a better life. They have their flaws, they make mistakes, and they can be obstinate and difficult but, to me the alien, this is one of the high points of humanity. I could say it is also sad because no living human will know who they were. There will only be ruins and a few artifacts. You do not understand what they are like or even their name, do you?"

"That's not fair, how can I know that? Oh, I see, you want me to guess," he said. Starting to think. He could just scan the non-human memories within, but that would fail the spirit of the test.

He thought out loud, a habit from his teens that sometimes resurfaced. "Well, a hill on a bend of a river. Flat plains all about. The green is vivid and intense, and the vegetation sub-tropical. Nothing odd there, I mean it is a great place to put a town, defensible, access to lots of water, fishing, trade. Anyone with a brain would think this it a good place," he said.

The problem sounded impossible, but there must be a way to find out, otherwise there would be no chance of him being able to answer. The fact she could pose the question was a clue, like those logic puzzles he used to play with Chris, there was not enough information in the problem itself but when you knew there was a unique solution, then the answer would be clear. The culture, it must be that, but not just any part, it must be the stuff that survives, the architecture perhaps, the pottery.

He looked about, noticing the people for the first time. He didn't bother wondering why he had not seen them before. This was Emari's memory, like a dream, the normal rules didn't apply. The clothes were simple, a cloth wrapped around the body—reminiscent of several cultures of the Global Era—though the weave was not, they could not build a textile factory, but they did understand a lot about weaving. Most women were topless, their breasts hidden under a series of necklaces of shells or semiprecious stones. He wanted to look at the delicate carved carnelian beads in the necklaces but thought he might offend. Around him the faces that looked at him had light brown skin, various types, a cosmopolitan place it seemed, a familiar look— that was one clue. The buildings were like truncated hollow cubes. He saw people exiting them from side alleys; they were houses, with courtyards, he guessed, but there were no doors onto the main streets. Banners and a few signs decked the front of the buildings, but they would not survive. Several stalls were near where they stood. In one, a man was selling the morning's catch of fish. The trader wore a small pendant around his neck, a seal made of fired clay; it was a symbolic representation of a one-horned bull or some kind or unicorn.

"I've seen something like that before, when I was a child, it stayed in my mind for days it was so beautiful," then he remembered, "this is Mohenjo Daro, part of the Indus Valley Civilization," he said and found himself stunned by his own words. It was almost mythical.

"Well done, it is Mohenjo Daro, which was a name given to it many centuries later by people who were strangers. It means the City of the Dead Men. Do you find it as sad as I do that many of the names for places are strangers' versions of That Place With The Ruins?"

"I don't worry about it. I used to read the works of Lao Tzu, I thought he was a historical figure, then I discovered that the name means, Old Master. Nothing more. We give things names to hide our ignorance, then remember the names and think it is knowledge," he said and wondered why he of all people needed to tell her this.

Now he took in more of the view, focusing for a few seconds on each new thing like a hyperactive child. A boy, well fed, healthy and happy, playing with a toy cart sitting next to the trader. A son learning the trade. Everyone seemed well fed, draped in a single swirling cloth dyed various dull colors. As he lifted his eyes above the passing faces, he saw the burnt brick houses and further up the citadel at the top of the hill with its imposing view of the plain and the Indus River.

Emari broke his reverie, "No one is destitute here. There is a strong sense of community. Warfare is almost unknown, and it is a place of plenty. The farms on the floodplain are bountiful. I even suspect that this area is the source of the legend of the Garden of Eden.

They were in contact with Sumer, a chain of whispered information, enough to spread the idea of a written language to this place if not the technique itself and also to conjure stories in the other direction. They have advanced technologies for managing waste, covered sewers, and more. No strong authoritarian leaders or homogeneous religions, it is a melting pot of people and ideas. This is early in the city's history so the population is only eight thousand, later it will expand to twenty thousand or more but for now it is small and tradition aids the people rather than impedes. There are over a thousand settlements in the Indus Valley Civilization, this is the biggest, it wasn't the first, which is why it is so well planned, and far to the south the coastal port of Lothal sends goods out to the other rising cultures."

He looked out towards the farmlands and forests to the west. The river ran to the east of the city.

"Who runs the city?" he asked.

"There is a council of ruling families. They listen to others. It isn't a democracy, but it doesn't disregard other people either. As I said, it isn't perfect, but it works. I found friendship and love here and adored this place. I stayed too long, grew too attached," she said, her words trailing off so he almost didn't hear the last sentence.

He wanted to ask about that. But this was her memory, respect her feelings and let her heal.

"Are we going to meet anyone? Will I be able to talk to them?"

"Yes, Ray, they speak a form of proto-Dravidian, almost. You will understand them. We are here to meet a family I knew," she said and smiled. He ignored her reference to Ray. Why should he care? It was his name, not the pseudonym 'Ramon'.

She transformed. Now an off white cloth wrapped around her body, her black hair braided into two long ponytails ending in triangular clasps of bone. She had a beautiful warm skin color, her eyes were different, but there was that same smile.

They walked through the unusually clean streets. Passing strangers greeted them with unfamiliar blessings.

Emari ducked down a side alley between two close brick walls. All the bricks were regular and even, a dazzling idea at the dawn of civilization. In this culture, bricks and weights and measures were all standardized. Someone had shown remarkable sense and foresight a long time ago. It intrigued him. It is one thing for an individual to have a great idea; it is another to convince those around you to follow it.

Emari was at a garlanded doorway. Above were banners of something like papyrus, with holy symbols on them. He understood them but it wasn't like sentences. More like spiritual slogans and insignia of rank. The makers signed the small banners with the imprint of the house seal, which went in and out of fashion, or if a house lost honor their seals would be worthless. This family made copper items and exported them up and down river according to the seals.

Surprised and cheerful voices echoed down the alley.

"It is Emri back from her travels. And who is this?" an older woman said, her hand on Emari's shoulder, looking past her at Ramon with a welcoming smile.

"This is Ray. He is my consort, we travel as one. It is so good to see you again, Eshil," Emari putting her arm around his neck.

She should not call him Ray, it was his name, but he wasn't the other. Confusing the two would end badly. Perhaps in her memories she didn't distinguish and was following dream-logic, allowing feelings and needs to boil up and manifest. Some things even the Vanaya refused to admit to themselves, they needed dreams too, only theirs were far more elaborate. So, was this a memory or a dream? Perhaps there was no difference to her.

It seemed the Vanaya didn't have art of their own, and they were the poorer for it. Maybe they could delve into the mechanics of their minds but that didn't mean they knew what their secret desires were. They seemed to know so much, yet failed to know themselves.

He automatically placed his hands together in the form of a prayer and said, "Praise to your household and your gods, to Sriva and the Earth Mother, Gai."

His own words surprised him because he could now see links to later cultures and ideas that scholars had only guessed. If that.

Eshil escorted them in to a small open courtyard where a mid-morning meal was being prepared. A man entered from a doorway, followed by several near-naked children. All of them were excited to see Emari again. The man greeted him, telling Ramon that his name was Prabhu. He dismissed the children, who ran off to play a game, forgetting the visitors.

They talked. Emari made up a set of convincing lies about Ramon and their journey. He still had mixed feelings about her lying skills. It was a splinter in his trust he couldn't entirely remove.

Later, they decided for him that he should see the sights of the city. Prabhu's eldest son, Vijay, a friendly heroic young man of about eighteen, was chosen to escort them and act as a tour guide.

Some houses were obviously wealthy from their size, their large walls often draped with banners or colors daubed here and there to show the owners—a simplified form of the seals. Almost a company logo, which would be appropriate since most of the houses were also family businesses.

Almost everything he saw and understood was unknown to the Nexus. All that would remain were some ruined buildings and cryptic inscriptions on seals. The color, the vitality, all of it forgotten. That is the way it always was. The present is a narrow door and little of the past can fit through it, mostly the consequences.

Sekara was on a promontory which rose towards the river. At the top was the citadel, occupied by the wealthiest families. Citizens could walk anywhere, but without an escort the house guards would be wary of the stranger Ramon.

"It is a lovely place, Emari. Who did you love here? Is that why you have returned?"

"I loved several young men and women. I took various forms. But now I just want to stay here in this calm with you. We can stay here for centuries, real centuries, not simulated ones," she said.

"We have friends who are waiting on us we can't abandon them," he pleaded.

"Why? Why go back at all, it is only endless suffering? I can regenerate you all again and again if needed. You do not understand the torment they have put me through," she said with tears in her eyes and a trembling voice.

He put his hands on her shoulders and brought her in close. Held her tight. How do you convince an immortal that the anguish of the world is worth facing?

"You were once mortal, that is where your sense of duty and purpose came from. It is at the center of your being. You can't deny it," he said.

"Are you saying my transformation was a mistake? That all the good I have done is worthless?" she spat out, tensing in his arms.

"No, not saying that at all. I mean, why do you all play the Game? So that your existence has meaning. You can get bored and do other things for a while, get distracted, but eventually you have to come back to something that is meaningful. There's nothing more meaningful that I can think of than saving worlds."

He wasn't trying to be subtle or clever, only to express his view and maybe show her that deep down she understood it too. He knew her enough now to guess that, and he didn't need telepathy to do it.

He felt her muscles relax. She pulled away gently and smiled.

"Let's go, they're preparing a party for us. Before we return home," she said.

Vijay didn't even see their argument.

That night there were delicacies and music. Dancing girls from the extended family wearing bangles up their arms, dancing naked without care. Their nakedness not an issue. They talked small-talk all evening. He told them funny stories adapted to their context, which they found hilarious. There was alcohol, but it had no effect on him. The entire night passed in a simulated blur.

Next morning they stood on top of the walls of the house watching the sun rise over the river. From their current position on the southern side of the promontory, the citadel didn't block the view at all. It was serene and timeless. The city was waking, and from the dark streets below came the sounds of carts being loaded, people talking, the occasional random yell, pottery being moved or bumped. Here and there slow columns of smoke from the day's cooking fires being stoked.

Ramon found the rooftop similarity with Kapris interesting. Perhaps this moment on both worlds symbolized a kind of fulfillment. And there was the view of her home city on Corvena, breathing in the scent of the pilani. Reality, memory, and dream fusing into a hope, repeating.

"You seem to like rooftops."

"Sometimes you can best appreciate something from a little distance. A parent seeing their family together while standing back. It gives perspective."

"Literally."

Emari now appeared as Ranei in a blue High Noon jumpsuit. She had decided it was time to return. This was only a dream of what was, a time of peace to remember, but you can't go back.

"Let's go," she said.

The woman he once knew as Ranei looked at him. Smiling. On an airless rock under a cool orange sun.

"Lead the way," he said.

fifteen

Zara looked at the space where Ramon had been standing, as if there was something she should have said before he disappeared. Now he could be anywhere. The jump system had limits, but those limits were vast and incomprehensible to unaugmented humans.

She had delved into how the jump system worked and its history. Faster than light travel was not something available to civilizations before the Vanaya came along. It seemed to be a law that from every conceivable angle lightspeed was the hard limit. Networks of civilization grew and flourished using lightspeed communications and the occasional sublight starship. But space isn't empty, and a grain of sand at even 0.3 of the speed of light is like being hit by a missile with a warhead equivalent to tons of TNT. Yet even at that speed, the ship isn't fast enough to get any meaningful advantage from time dilation. Interstellar travel was hard and dangerous for even the most advanced.

The Vanaya then thought about circumventing the problem with an extraordinary and bold idea. They would create pocket universes they could transfer almost in an instant from one location to another in this spacetime. Then the pocket universe would be unwrapped to release the enclosed package: a spaceship, a person, or an entire world. That last one had triggered the human emotion of disbelief when Zara came across it, a strange mental state that seemed ready to dissolve her entire worldview. She checked and though there were scant details they were verifiable; the Vanaya at one stage had moved planets via FTL, the big question was why. She hadn't mentioned this to anyone because she didn't trust Emari and the lack of details screamed 'Top Secret' at her. It made her worry for her boys.

"I don't think they'll be back for a while, Avril. Sorry, I mean, Zara," Ray said.

"I know. I just, never mind," she shouldn't have said it, his intense curiosity would just follow through. She had better distract him, "Have you thought about why Emari brought you back?"

"She said to find out who destroyed Earth. Seems like a damned good reason. Why?" he said.

"Something about it doesn't gel, you know?" She sat down next to him on a rock, to be near him. It was warm and relaxing.

"You mean why did she wait so long? Hmm. Have to admit that excuse seemed lame. She's pretty capable, I'm sure she could have brought me back not long after the shit hit the fan. Pardon the expression," he said.

"'Pardon'? Oh I see, you think of me as prim and proper. Those were just the office protocols you know. Swearing meant nothing to me it was only another language dialect. I have no experience of these things, sex and excretion, even now, I can't take a shit because to be honest Ray none of us are human. We aren't even biological. Or robots. I can fuck, so there's that. Makes you think doesn't it?"

"Was that a come on?" he laughed. Then stopped. "Sorry, Zara. I keep wanting to talk to you the way we used to. I didn't think of you as a woman. You were Avril and now you are Zara. The two aren't the same. I guess to me you were a best friend without a body."

"I can fix that. Do you want to have sex with me?" she said.

He wanted to hide. Severe embarrassment was about to paralyze him. He wished he could call back those words. An anguish he hadn't had for ages. Yet deep down there was a profound bond between them he could not face.

"Let's put that whole idea on ice for the moment, huh?"

"If you want. I don't see why it should be a big deal. Do you think I am not mature enough yet? There's no reason for concern, is there?" she said tilting her head waiting for an answer. He couldn't get out of this one.

"Let's just not talk about it for now. Anyway, I'd get emotionally involved, I know it, you do not understand how consuming love can be."

"Easy there, it doesn't matter. You know, for a long time I was emotionally involved with you, always sitting on your shoulder, as you said. Why do you think I stowed away to High Noon? Don't think of it as human love, it didn't have that hormonal and biological imperative, but it was still real for me. Now I do feel that drive and—thrill, I suppose. Huh. Face it, we are bonded to one another already."

"And what about Ramon?" he said.

"I gather he drifted apart from Avril. His failure to protect Ranei obsessed him. Hmm, that woman sure leaves a trail of devastation behind her. Anyway, that was Avril and, as you said, I am Zara. Different people and different lives." She stood and ambled into the dusty cold valley a short distance, gathering her thoughts. The dust forming brief fine clouds in her wake.

He stood and surveyed the plain. His sensors picked up many things. Once, there was life here, and in the air he sensed concentrations of methane and oxygen. Small amounts but way past chemical equilibrium. There was life here somewhere tenaciously hanging on. If they were going to spend a long time here then, well, why not?

"Zara, do you feel like exploring? Do you still have that hunger for 'Data'?" he laughed.

"You bet your arse I do. Why?"

"Smell the air. Well, use your sensors. There's life here. Somewhere. If those miscreants don't get back soon, I'm going to just take off and go on a big explore. Are you in?" he said.

"Always, we make the best team."

They appeared on the desert plain. Alone. Ramon looked about even as his internal sense said this was the exact spot, to within a few centimeters, that he left from. On the ground were footprints. Some led to the southeast, fading with the windblown sand.

Emari was back to her Maria persona, not that it mattered. Names and faces were irrelevant to their kind now.

"No trail, it disappears, looks like they headed for that ridge about five klicks away," he said, "let's walk. I need the exercise."

"Sure, for the exercise," she mocked.

They both knew their destination, the footprints were immaterial, they could sense the two signals. Each of their bodies was a titanic powerhouse, extracting and using a huge amount of power. They should all be red hot from the waste heat, but flawless heat extraction systems in their bodies, or elsewhere, kept them cool. They could not break the laws of physics, though they could produce the illusion of it. All of that energy meant distant communications and telltales to show proximity were not a problem. They had no GPS, and didn't need it, each of them was a beacon. When trying to find their friends, one of them would detect the bearing, while the two of them together would triangulate the position.

"Ray, we're back, where are you? What on wherever-this-isare you doing?" Ramon said.

Ray replied, he sounded almost jovial. "We noticed. Welcome back. We, my friends, are in search of alien life, in an awesome cave. Having the time of our lives. You're free to join us. Is everything okay with you?"

"We're fine. We'll be there soon," Emari said.

"Welcome back, Emari."

The desert was lifeless, it appeared. Pebbles here and there, some he recognized as being sedimentary, from a time when oceans covered much of the planet. Now only pebbles, some small rippling dunes, and clouds of dust rising as they walked.

"Emari, I keep thinking of Kapris. I don't remember anything like that in the Calendar. What else was there that I am missing?"

"You can just look it up, you know," she said.

Her answer didn't satisfy him.

"I would prefer a summary, a connoisseur's guide to exotic civilizations and species."

"I can't talk about the species that were intelligent that did not go down the technological civilization route. They were interesting and often very exotic but weren't our concern. Beings of gas giants, for instance. Strange minds, even more different than the onith or your cetaceans. But easy for us to understand. We monitored many unusual ones that got a tech civilization going. Our aim was to help where we could and hope for the best. Business as usual."

"Such as?" he resisted the urge to mention Cusha straight after 'business as usual'.

"A rare few were underwater civilizations. Don't think of graceful dolphins. That would be as accurate as comparing humans to gazelles. Instead, their civilization developed based on crude weapons and seaweed farming, or in the deeper cultures using the hydrothermal vents for nutrients and their ecosystems. They didn't advance along the usual route, most of the species went extinct before anything like a renaissance, and the few that reached something like a real technical culture did so by developing the ability to breed organisms for particular roles. In time they reached the point where they could use such organisms to engineer other ones. It would be nice to pretend they were peaceful societies, but warfare was common and more destructive than for many other worlds."

"Why? Did they poison the ocean?" he said.

"No, not that extreme, mostly. But it was a risk. The reason the wars were so destructive was simple: explosives. Explosives rely on a simple chemical reaction. Create a creature than can make a reservoir of explosive material within it, then it swims into the middle of the enemy and detonates it. But in the ocean creatures can be large, it isn't like flying a payload over a city, no, you just swim it in. Right into the heart of a city."

"An explosion underwater is worse than in air. In air there is the blast within a very limited range and there is shrapnel. Just get behind something to avoid the shrapnel. Underwater there isn't any shrapnel or firestorm, it doesn't work, however there is a shock wave, and it is a doozy. A shock wave underwater is a wall of inescapable death. Water is incompressible, pretty much, and will therefore transmit the shock wave faithfully, inverse square law diminishing it with distance of course. So it is a little like escaping the flash of a nuclear weapon, except the shock wave can wrap around buildings and travel through them. There were arms races, packs of whale like creatures to deliver city killers attacked by swarms of anti-whale squid, which were also explosive, and swarms of defenders escorted the whales to kill the anti-whale squid with neurotoxins. All brilliant and destructive. One of these cultures got past this and sent expeditions to the surface. They had survived their own ecocrisis, so an interstellar civilization of the day contacted them. In time they built their own starships and made a significant contribution, but they always felt isolated by this galaxy of strange beings. One of their worlds experimented and produced a new species that was air breathing. They had plenty of biological models for air breathers so it wasn't as if the notion was exotic. For a while they formed a hybrid society and the air breathing part of that became a vital intermediary that enabled closer ties with the other cultures. Later, the air-breathers spread through the stars in their own right. It all happened a long time ago."

The ridge was only about ten to twenty meters high. Nestled in between two bulbous masses of orange banded rock was a tear-shaped hole in the rock face.

"How does a cave like this form here?" Ramon said to no one.

"Outgassing and water explosively erupting. See the half-smoothed rock surfaces? This was a short-lived geyser, not the kind you are familiar with. This was about a high volume of hot mineralized water over a short period. Then nothing. Seen it so often. I don't just visit civilizations, you know, they're rare as, well, they are about the rarest thing in the universe. In the meantime I just look around sometimes, try to find life wherever it is and encourage it. It doesn't get me merit points, but I do it anyway."

"You are full of surprises, Emari."

"A god's gotta have a hobby."

They entered the cave, projecting light in front of them, their bodies aglow. Some places were hard to cross, so they floated over it.

"I miss hard things, you know," Ramon said, "I mean the world is harsh and challenges us. It stops us telling ourselves too many lies and trying to ignore reality. We may think we're gods because we can watch TV, but we still have to shit, we still get hangovers, stub our toes, and we still die. This existence. It's like living in cotton wool. The animal in me wants to fight it, to hurt myself and feel things again."

"But isn't the Dream a heaven?"

For a heart stopping moment he thought that maybe she was back to square one. The Dream was wonderful all was right with the worlds. Maybe it was sarcasm and was so subtle he couldn't tell. He would not let it pass.

"Your heaven is a prison." Ramon said. "Avoiding the pain of the world has made you feel eternal, secure, and omniscient because you don't endure counter experiences. You don't know what real life is anymore, and your deep biological ancestry rebels at it even transformed into your nanite form. No reality checks for you. You avoid insanity by anchoring yourself to other peoples struggles and ordeals, but to you it is only entertainment, not at all your problem. In time I think you forgot what suffering was anyway, then you would look on the death of worlds of and think, 'oh well, that's the way the universe works'. Life doesn't flow with entropy, in surrender, it fights it."

He was angry with himself. He knew he had overstepped.

"Really? Just because you have had the slightest glimpse of our civilization doesn't mean you understand it. It is vastly older than anything you can imagine. It has its own turbulent history. Sure, we have our comfort zones. Didn't you also? Building your cities and Internet or Nexus. It's how civilization works. We've just been at it a lot longer," Emari said.

"Civilization? You are all so isolated, I'm not sure you are even a coherent society anymore. You've taken 'not talking to the neighbors' to several more levels. The only things you have in common are the Game and the Kamoi. The Game keeps you amused while the Kamoi whips you into line. What is your purpose in life?"

"That's bullshit. Don't judge us by your little village culture. I don't know what's gotten into you, but you need to calm down. And why bring 'purpose' into it. There is no purpose, life does what it does, that's it," she said.

Ramon was not finished. "Look, I'm sorry if I said anything hurtful. I didn't mean to, but there are some glaring issues with the Vanaya that I, we, cannot ignore. Each of us has the power to create our own purpose. That's why you save worlds. Everyone has goals, from the mundane to the, uh, heavenly. We set goals for today, tomorrow for ten years. You build powerstars for use millions of years from now. You plan, there must be a goal, then why don't you have a goal for your own life. What do you want? Or maybe that is not enough, how can you know what you want when you don't know who you are anymore?"

"That's a nice rant. Are you done? Released all those pent up worries?"

"Yeah, sure," he said.

"I see your point, mostly, but I have to disagree with you on one thing. The positive value of delusions," she said.

"Oh, yeah, real value there. That's what almost killed my world. We built my civilization on the ashes of a world that deluded itself into thinking climate change wasn't so bad and we shouldn't worry just because we don't have a solution to resource depletion. It will all be right in the end."

"No, Ramon. What I mean is that delusions can lure us over obstacles to find solutions we never knew existed. Think of it like this, you want to achieve some ambition that is, to be honest, hopeless, so instead of being non-delusional and giving up you entertain the delusion and strive towards the goal," she said.

"I'm not seeing the positives so far."

"Shush! So you push past the immediate and moderately difficult problems and discover paths to either side of your course. Being optimistic you explore them and discover a solution that isn't perfect but is pretty good and one day perhaps even better. Humans tried for centuries to fly like the birds, it was an impossibility, but along the way you came up with ideas like hot air balloons, gliders, and powered flight. Not like a bird, but in many ways better. See?"

"Maybe. So there is good delusion and bad delusion. How do you tell which is which?"

"Bloody hell. Use your brains for that. That's what they are for."

She didn't look back at him as she clambered over rocks, not resorting to floating above average problems.

"Anyway, about what you said before about the lack of challenges." She said. "That feeling's not new. I remember even before we built our first starship. We had this sense that the pain of living made life Life. It made it significant. We busied ourselves on projects we told ourselves were important that somehow replaced that significance. It never worked. You can't say you were much better in your comfortable cities. You never had to chase down your food or suffer broken bones without painkillers. We're just much further along."

"So you do think the Dream isn't a heaven?" he said. "On my world, heaven, in its various guises, was often a place where you could switch off your higher thinking and just go with the eternal flow. Indistinguishable from a drug fantasy that never ended. Except, all that is about the desire to escape the real world and its cares. The 'vale of tears', as we would say, but that is what Life is about. Living is a struggle, every moment we have to fight to breathe, to make our heart—or hearts—beat. The Vanaya seem to have tried to remove these 'struggles' but in the end being here, alive, is about a conscious mind facing an uncaring and dangerous universe. You can't run from that."

There was cryptic silence.

"Hey, can I reduce my invulnerability or whatever you want to call it?" he said.

She stopped and looked down at him from further up the cave-in debris. The dark walls glistened from small crystals in the exposed rock. It made him think of a jeweled night sky arrayed around the glowing Queen of the Night. Titania in the enchanted forest.

"You can do it. You can't die, but you can suffer. Are you going to be a great artist, an artist of life suffering for meaning? You could earn a lot of points from the cotton-wooled," she said with a wry smile. "Pain is a delicacy to those who never feel it. I suffer a great deal as should be obvious now. Agents to worlds experience real trauma, some of it physical but most of it emotional, so don't lump me in with the rest."

He remembered something, a consuming worry that had faded until this moment. The thought almost paralyzed him. A situation where you know something is important but have forgotten, then you recall it and in horror wonder how you could have ever ignored it.

"I can't die. Is that the complete truth? I mean, ignoring expiry and what not. And what about when we return from this journey, back to Eklus or the Kamoi? Is it still true then? Come to think of it, watching your memories about Cusha, when you returned to Eklus you created a servant based on that species. What happened to him after you finished, or his predecessor? Do you create beings to enslave them and then discard them?" He was furious, and part of him wanted to unleash reckless hostility. He wasn't even sure where to direct it. Perhaps it was simple fear.

"I'll be honest. There are rumors we can die, not expiry or anything like that, but we can be killed. Assassinated. Murdered."

"Really?"

"Remember Zorrech? Well, there are stories about him. Don't know how true. Maybe just fictions to keep us in line."

She stood at the top of the pile of debris looking down at him glowing like a capricious queen of the underworld.

"As for Dillan. He is a being I created ages ago. Sometimes a he and other times a she or another gender. The thing is, Dillan is ancient. The form has changed and most memories have been wiped, but there is a continuing sense of being. One day I will end that existence but it will not be an execution, I will not renew the Expiry Date and that will be it. One day even he, or she, will grow tired of existence because that sense of being will comprise too many painful memories shared with him. He will have an out that I don't. Before you get all high and mighty perhaps you should remember the unwilling servants you have enslaved, not just sentient ones either, first there were the animals you domesticated often with great cruelty, and no don't tell me about the Nexus farming techniques and your vegetarianism, I know it was good but I've seen your agricultural revolution from the beginning. Later, you got rid of the slavery of other human beings, patted yourself on the back, prematurely a few times, and then enslaved beings of your own construction, you almost went down a dark path. Some of us intervened, we knew what that was like, that's how we started—Changelings, slaves."

"Don't get so high and mighty yourself. Every civilization passes through those phases. Slavery comes too easy with power, like murder. Were the Vanaya guilt free? I don't think so," he said as memories of bloody eras on Corvena flooded through him, "what counts is the refusal. Refusing to enslave and to kill. Hard at first, easier as you get more options. But there's always a choice."

A sense of calm had returned. It was fragile. "You still haven't answered my question. Can I die?" he said in a measured voice.

"Ray has an expiry date, enforced by the Kamoi. So do you, Ramon. Zara? I do not understand what is going on there but presume she does as well. It is standard operating procedure. It isn't long, a subjective galactic year, as you call it, but it can be extended considerably once this is over," she said.

So they couldn't just bug out and go off-grid. Their lifetime was about 1.2 subjective Earth years. They had an enormous incentive to get this done and get back.

"Yeah, and who decides if that happens?" he asked, impatience returning.

She sighed, "The Kamoi, what else is in control of all of us?"

"All of us, you included. Okay. Sorry I jumped down your throat."

He had talked about danger and hardship, and now he got what he wanted. He was on borrowed time. Oddly, all of that translated into excitement, everything was more real and enticing.

He sensed that they weren't far from their destination. Emari had climbed up further than him. He jumped and gained six meters in one bound. It wasn't because of local gravity.

From here there were a few meters of level ground, then it sloped away. Above and ahead there was light from a hole in the cave's roof. It was less than a meter across. The light shone like a faint streetlight down into a sinkhole before them, the bottom a faint smudge far below. Down in that gloom were Ray and Zara. He couldn't see them, but he could sense them in other ways.

They slid down to the edge of the sinkhole. The sound muffled by the low air pressure. He looked at

Emari and shrugged. They both jumped at the same time.

They landed or floated into a flat dark area maybe thirty meters across. As they touched the bottom it became illuminated by a globe just above them, courtesy of Emari, it smelled of her ID, so to speak. Apart from the companions there were some other things squat, unspectacular but alive. They were like stromatolites; the structures built by bacteria on Earth and other worlds, the most ancient construction of life. Over them, something tiny crawled.

Ray, Zara, and Emari bent over one of the half meter high concretions, fascinated.

"Oh. Isn't it beautiful. Look here, little crustaceans, creatures tending the tiny growths on the surface." Emari said. "Not just bacteria and animals, there is a small ecosystem of advanced plants. They haven't lost their chlorophyll equivalent yet either. So, there was advanced life here once and now it is hanging on by a thread."

She looked up at Ramon.

"What are you thinking? Of course. No, you can't save it. There's nothing here," he said. Was he a parent telling a young child that their favorite fairytale was fictional? He couldn't do it.

"Okay. I'm sure we can figure something out. There must be someway to give this place a chance," he said without conviction.

What they did, or what Ray did under Emari's direction, was to create in the dust of the desert a 'thing'. Ramon couldn't find words to describe it.

Ray could understand it if he concentrated and sometimes when working on it he could follow the logic while paddling along the edge of the river of meaning. The ideas and decisions raced through some level of his own mind but not under his control.

It fascinated Zara. She stood looking at it for hours, her mind somewhere else. Ray's patience ran out and he couldn't resist asking.

"Zara, I suspect you understand this thing. Is that correct?"

"Not completely though I think I've got the basics. It is an AI with very advanced fabbing. Oh boy, make that unbelievably advanced fabbing. I don't know why you guys don't just dive in and explore the knowledge you have access to, this thing is amazing."

"Well, knowledge changes us, and expanding to understand such advanced knowledge will make huge changes to me. I guess you are used to it, I mean you didn't flinch from migrating to the colony cortex on High Noon, did you? Humans often take smaller steps? If I have to climb a mountain, I'll start with a few boulders first."

He laughed and put his hand on her shoulder. She turned to him and moved closer.

"One day you will have to confront that knowledge. You realize that don't you?" she said.

"I know."

"Don't worry. I'll be there with you."

The thing itself was a conundrum. Was it alive or a machine, or such a sophisticated machine that there was no distinction? It grew, it fed off the dirt; drew energy from sunlight and other sources. It built small spaceships the size of a human forearm. They ascended into the sky, via some means, he assumed dark matter jets but knew that was unlikely. It only took a few days to build. The machine occupied a space the size of a tennis court and looked like a cross between a cubical collection of ordered black rock crystals and a pulsing organic creature. All of it shimmering as if covered by an iridescent film of oil. Below the surface of the desert it had spread its roots looking for minerals, volatiles, all sorts of necessary things.

They had asked her several times about it but Emari had just ignored them. Now that the small craft were being created, one every 1.3 hours, she seemed to relax.

It was morning. They focused on the structure waiting for the next small 'armship,' as Ramon called them, to rise. A black round and smooth block of obsidian, accelerating without a sound upward as if unlike all other mundane materials gravity repelled it.

After it was complete and launched several armships, Emari told them what was happening.

"The probes will travel to the outer regions of the solar system. There they will home in on some identified ice structures, small comets or asteroids, and land on them. They will construct a network of ion thrusters on the asteroid surface and a small fusion plant. The thrusters will change the orbits of the asteroids and via some complicated slingshot trajectories direct them to impact at the lowest possible velocity on the planet at an optimal location. I have selected the target regions to reduce damage to any surviving organisms and enhance water vapor concentration. We won't wait, it will take centuries for the first one to arrive, and many thousands of years for the first phase to complete."

"First phase?" asked Zara.

"The system we leave behind will monitor the air quality, sample the creatures in the caves, and make genetic modifications to speed up their adaptation to the surface. When the job is done, the system will without fanfare shutdown and decompose." She smiled proud of her work.

"It has an expiry date?" Ramon said with just a hint of sarcasm.

Emari smiled sensing humor not animosity.

"Guys? I've got a new location. Time to go," Ray said.

Ramon just had enough time to say, "Well, that was suspiciously convenient."

sixteen

A blue sky, clouds, green plants. Tree things rose around them, and straight above a brilliant sun shone down. It was like home—Earth—so long ago. A moment of nostalgia and an ache for a past he could never touch surprised Ray. He took a deep breath as he regained a sense of normalcy. The deep breath didn't banish the memories or the longing. His only course was to deal with this world on its own terms as he always did.

They stood in a glade on a gentle slope with a small stream. Everything painted with familiar green life. Mosses and vines, trees—not the same, but if you were not too picky, you could believe. The sound of gurgling water, insects, and calls of some creatures that might be birds if he could only see them. It was idyllic, even for one used to walking the long-faded hills of Earth, and hungry to glimpse it once again.

The four of them were on an exposed ledge of rock only a step or two from the bubbling, hollow sounds of the brook.

"Are we... are we back home?" He knew it couldn't be true, but his hope slipped out as if he could make the Vanayan crazy mantra—the Dream is All—into a reality.

Emari took a half step closer to the water and looked up as she spoke. "No. I'm getting nothing. Not Earth. Not a clue where we are. I'd still like to know why I feel so good way out here. These bodies require large energy inputs, and the jumps far more. We have to be getting it from somewhere."

Ray looked within. The answers came with an ease he now thought as eerie.

Just for a moment he saw a condensed vision of the history of the galaxy. He saw dwarf galaxies swing close, ripped apart by the hungry gravitational maw of the swirling monster. Other objects. Supermassive black holes from intergalactic space sweeping in and passing through the galactic disk, scattering some stars but leaving the structure intact. Arcs of plasma rising from the core and twin jets, one from each side of the spinning disk, as the black hole in the core fed.

He returned to himself.

"Another rogue system. Indeterminate orbit, probably deflected by clusters so it is no longer on a return path to the galaxy. Metallicity is too high to be a native star of the halo, it must have originated in the disk. We're almost the same distance from the galactic core as last time, but a different right ascension and declination. RA is one hour fifty-two minutes, declination is forty-one degrees. If any of that really matters."

"All this traveling is tiring, you know," Ramon said, "I feel like I just need a break from living all these other lives. It's so depressing. Emari, do people challenge the status quo, you know, try to improve things?"

"Of course they do. But what do you think the result will look like after a million years? It corrupts everyone to some degree. Everyone wants change, everyone is afraid of change," she said without sarcasm.

"I'd settle for a picnic, but we are too far from the Kamoi and the Dream. I guess we will just have to use our imaginations," Ray burst into laughter, waiting for the others to get the connection between Dream and imagination.

Ramon snickered, but Emari's look told him this joke was old a billion years ago.

"Well, Emari, I guess we will just have to make do." He waved his arm in mock Vanayan demigod style, "Let there be pastries!"

And there were. A table of food and drink appeared before themwith chairs. It hovered over the brook by a half a meter, with the chairs poised beside it as if nailed somehow to nothingness. He knew that if he looked closely, there would be an ultra-thin layer of material strengthened to hold them, yet having the refractive index of air, which is to say invisible.

"Holy shit. Well done, Ray," Ramon said, wasting no time stepping onto the invisible platform and sitting down on a chair. Without hesitation, he reached for an iced pastry.

Zara stepped up to the table, suspended by nothing, with a grim look on her face.

Ray sat down next to her and put his hand on hers.

"It's all right. I'm okay. Do you trust me?" he said.

She looked him in the eyes and nodded. Ramon watched them, and something inside squirmed in pain. He looked within, and found it, a sequence of thoughts and obsessions, and with a delicate nudge he short-circuited that loop.

"Ramon?" Emari asked.

He smiled back.

Emari turned and stared across the table at Ray.

"You shouldn't be able to do that. Even if we were much closer to the Kamoi, I couldn't do that. We have built-in fabbers, as you saw when I built those armships. But casual transfers of material goods are banned except for extraordinary reasons. It is too frivolous to transport items when you can make it locally. So, how the hell are you doing this? Who are you?"

"That's pretty rich coming from the one who resurrected me."

"Too frivolous to transport? Did I hear that?" Zara said, each word barbed. "I've seen Vanayan records of entire planets being moved via FTL."

"That's crazy. It never happened," Emari replied.

Zara's eyes followed Emari, unable to decide if she was lying or the victim of a lie.

"Bloody Vanaya, all of you are corrupted," she said.

"Of course we are. Angels and demons. Much more efficient to have both in one package."

The meal was even better than they hoped. They didn't need to eat or drink, but it was a release. They talked and laughed, the casual way that refreshes and yet somehow evades direct recall afterward. It was blissful, but they couldn't avoid returning to their situation.

"I feel we are nearing our goal. I can't give evidence, it's just a deep hunch," Ray said.

"Any idea on what is at the end? Or what this is all about?" Emari said.

Ramon was playing with a black grape, moving it from finger to finger in his left hand with his thumb as if it was a difficult clue. "The Kamoi sent you on this quest, I suppose we can call it that, but it also sent me. Ray, you have had memories removed from your later years. I have had memories added. That's how I knew it was Emari who did the brain scan. But this journey has not been about us at all, it is about understanding Emari. Why? And if it is only about her, why send us so frickin' far away? And why give you superpowers, even by Vanayan standards?"

"Don't forget me." Zara said. "I have no clue why I am here. Just that I am really glad. I mean, I've learned a lot, I have, but I still haven't got the foggiest about why."

Ray sighed, he had no answer. He shrugged.

"You don't have an ID, Zara." Emari said. "You aren't from the Kamoi that is why you confused me so much. I don't know what that means. You have a physical form. Who made it? The Kamoi? Someone else? It doesn't make sense."

"That is intriguing. Are the factions that powerful, Emari?" Ray said.

"They can't, I mean, I didn't think they could do such a thing. But they are far beyond our understanding, maybe they have abilities they rarely show. Which begs the question, why now? What's the point of having Zara here?" Emari said.

Zara shrugged. "I am not aware of any motivations different to how I once was, just an increased vividness in sensations, in everything. It's amazing, but nothing relevant to the grand scheme of whatever."

"What sensations?" Ray asked.

"Oh boy. Um, we'll talk about that later."

"I'm clueless," Ramon interjected.

Ramon had more. "Well, Emari, you are the one here this seems to be all about. You are the bona fide Vanayan. You should have all the answers after your geologically-old involvement with the Core. So, feel free to share." He tried saying it as gently as he could. He didn't want to hurt her, but they needed to find out.

"Sorry to disappoint. I do not know what is going on or what this is all about."

Ray looked at Emari and Ramon. Emari was almost there. It would only take a small push now.

A new memory arose and took them.

Neti, 3049 C.E.

She walked towards the gate of Castle, the Mouth of the Snake, where green grass beside the worn stone roadway whipped her feet planting barbed seeds in her clothes. Above, a white sun in a lapis sky shone down, and to her right a blistering glare of heat from the Eastern Desert. It was a good year, there had been ample water so they could divert some to maintain the green grass so close to the arid expanse. Now that spring had arrived and the snows were melting the Tanuuten had become a torrent. She remembered when they were deciding the location of Tanten many years ago. It was a good choice. The humans had done well without intervention from her.

She walked into the city, past the markets and the seductive noise of the haggling, the music, and laughter.

The Library was her second home and her work now. She walked with deliberation past the black stone Keep, the seat of power, to a squat two-story building.

Up the wooden steps to the second floor, the topmost floor. Here was where they collated the news of the Traders. It was the focal point of the only real information flow on the planet. If there was any chance of getting the humans into space again it would be here, or Term, though she hadn't heard from any agents there. Perhaps Term had retreated into its shell. But here on Neti events moved apace and if a solution didn't present itself soon humanity would fail here.

"If only Ray were here," she muttered. She stopped walking even though she was a few steps from the iron door leading to the more secure part of the building. She missed him.

A tide of memories came back.

It must be those nanites I gave him, she thought. The bond went both ways, he became more loyal to me and I to him. Or was that a convenient excuse? Don't lie to yourself, Emari. You loved him and betrayed him, just cut him loose. Act like the agent you are.

Through the door was an array of disparate and unique objects, arranged and separated with care as if they were the idols of gods. The top floor contained advanced technology, simple books, smart clothes, unidentified devices such as portable crypto-hubs, wearable quantum computers. She knew what they were but was adept at duplicating the ignorance of the Head Librarian, Garun, without his infuriating arrogance.

She was restoring an item, a manuscript from the early days after the Great Battle, when Garun walked up to her with a visitor.

"Maria, this is a—um—visitor who has been granted full access by the Head Councilor. His name is Mikel Peres," Garun said in a voice that sounded like this hospitality was as pleasant as scraping dog shit off his boots.

The 'visitor' was a surprisingly young man, with a warm chocolate skin, a genuine smile, and a look in his eyes that Vanaya would kill for—the look of world changing wonder.

"Hello, I am Maria ya Irenni, the Curator of Library Antiquities," she said.

He noticed her clothes. She had concocted some strange story that as part of her research into the Nexus she would get into their mindset via their clothes. The truth was that she wore the T-shirt and jeans more in recent months because it reminded her of happier times. Sharing coffee with Ray. A rare absence of loneliness.

"I like to get into character. Try to understand the Ancients. This is typical clothing that they would have worn from what I have read. Though there are strange references that make it sound like their clothes were also machines. However, these clothes I am wearing are simpler, but I still found them hard to reproduce, so this is an approximation. I am wearing a 'white T-shirt' and 'jeans.' The inscription on the shirt is a mathematical equation. We do not understand why the creator of this apparel thought it worthy of showing to the world."

Lying had become a well practiced necessity. Now it made her uneasy. Those eyes demanded honesty.

He identified the simple equations of the T-shirt she wore at first sight. Trivial for her but significant for this world: Maxwell's Equations. She showed him another T-shirt she was making. This one was a private joke.

"Harrun's Standard Model of Superspace. But I couldn't explain it like I can Maxwell's, I've done some basic M-Theory but nothing above that yet."

She did not expect that. Harrun was not a human scientist it was a group mind of the Ashan civilization. The work had been part of the treasure found on Reshox. So advanced knowledge had survived here, this lifted her hopes.

Mikel wanted to see examples of the ancient tech. She showed him a still functioning Blue Cube. They were not quantum computers but still advanced. The device was constructed from neural networks of carbon nanotubes and fullerine-like nodes with the data stored in quantum states. The devices were powerful, but this one was aging and almost depleted, it was at minimal functionality.

She touched the top of the small blue box activating it.

A woman's voice spoke. She stiffened. How could she have forgotten?

AvrOS 7.9 Started. Insufficient power for holographic video. Input/Output devices not found, using inbuilt audio only. Internal battery minimal. Errors in hardware checks. Grid not available. Network not available. No direct neural link found. What do you want to do?

It was Avril's voice, and they named the OS after her since she was the team lead, and company co-owner. It had happened during her time as an AI before she was bioformed as a human. She couldn't hear Avril's voice without also hearing Ray's. Memories welled up of her near voyeuristic spying on their conversations. It was typical agent procedure so she should have no regrets about it, but she did.

Mikel asked questions, and she answered them as the ignorant Trader that she wasn't.

He asked about books but he had also asked the Blue Cube about Raymond Tans. She couldn't stop herself from saying something.

"You asked about Ray Tans, you should have asked me. I studied him a lot. Had a bit of a crush on him at one stage. Not the great remote hero they talk about but a very human person." She giggled. It was Ranei's giggle.

She had gone too far. What was she doing? She backed off and let him get distracted with the various books and manuscripts. She would monitor him. He had all the makings of those people that trigger great changes. She was certain that one day it would consume him or pass him by but for now he could be the catalyst that would save this world.

Much later on she made noises as if to go home to her small room outside the Castle walls, hoping he would get the hint. He stirred, his face a mask of weariness.

Then he asked her a deep question.

"Maria, I've read a lot, but there is something I still don't understand. I mean, I should understand because it is part of our history not belonging to the Ancients. Why did the Cities fall?"

She couldn't tell the truth she had to suggest the truth as if it was an informed guess. So she talked about the addictive lure of the neural links, and gave him a glimpse of Nexus Civilization when it was rotting, and the long-term costs of the infatuation with links.

What had once been beautiful was now decaying and when it fell, no one had the ability or will to pick up the pieces or even repair the pieces. It was much more complicated than that. She remembered it, the shock when the Dawn Ships of the Tarkoi had emerged from the portal, then of all times. Terrible luck. Even the Vanaya couldn't predict the exit times, it was an unpredictable system with equal parts deterministic chaos and quantum uncertainty. Then came the malaise that prevented a recovery and the slow terrible decline to a feudal technology with the bitter memory of greatness.

Later when Mikel left Tanten she wanted to follow him, take on a different guise and protect him. Why not? The entire planet was a direct intervention to defeat the Tarkoi but memories pushed her more towards non-involvement. She didn't know if anything she was doing was right, this was not a typical mission or world, so there was a strong temptation to let chance determine the outcome. Events could take their natural, chaotic, irrational course. Though, perhaps she could have a talk to Zeus. Yes, if he could get to Olympus, then Zeus could be her proxy. She would have to manipulate events to steer him towards the north and to Olympus. It was risky but now these people had a real chance. She smiled.

Once again they sat at the table. Floating above the whispering stream. Ray was looking at Emari, her back to the break in the downhill tree canopy. Her face was in shadow, framed by the blue sky and several forming clouds.

She looked about the table, all of them stared at her but Ray was glaring. Her senses picked up nothing, as she expected, he could prevent any other information being broadcast. There was no blush response, pupil dilation, heart rate increase, and so on. Yet the glare was unmistakable, and she knew why. She wanted to speak, but she preferred to avoid these situations rather than confront them.

Ray spoke.

"'Even Vanaya can't predict the exit times', is that so?" He stopped, took a deep breath, screw the oxygen, he needed the relaxing habit, something to give him some space. "In other words, no one could arrange the exit times. Not the Tarkoi, not the Vanaya. So, there is no conspiracy and therefore no reason for me to be here, except as your pet. You lied. Why resurrect me then? And while we are at it why did you wait 700 years? Did you change my thinking so I wouldn't even question that?"

"C'mon, Emari, you know I would really like to hear the answer to that too," Ramon said, each word a gentle request. He sensed their bond of trust might break at any moment. "We're being played Ray, and I think it isn't by Emari or the Kamoi. There are others involved, perhaps many others. This has got to be the worst reality broadcast the Kamoi could have invented so I don't think it is them."

"Emari, tell us. If you want us to stay together, then tell us because I can tell you I am absolutely wild about this. What the hell is going on?" Zara said. She leaned forward looking like a panther about to pounce.

Emari looked pale. Fragile. Not at all like what she was. There was no response.

Zara thumped the table with her fist. The pastries on the table jumped in fright. "You lied to them, manipulated us, just tell us the fucking truth for once. Is it so hard?"

"I love you, Ray, Ramon. I meant that. But I needed all of who you are including your ability to change things. I decided to recruit you. I had no hand in Ramon or Zara being here. That was a complete surprise."

"Recruit me? For what, this quest?" Ray said.

"Ah, no, brother. Don't you see? She wanted to recruit you as a Vanayan," Ramon said.

Ray didn't doubt it. It made sense. But it was also sad and pitiful. The desperation she suffered to do this neutralized his anger. Acid and base.

"I took you to the Kamoi to get you inducted. If the Kamoi had accepted you, it would have sent you on a simple training mission just so you got a feel for your new existence and initial abilities. In time you would qualify for more. Recruiting happens, not often, but often enough over the ages. We didn't all come from Corvena, and a lot of the old Vanayans have gone," she said. A sadness seeming to linger about her. He wondered what depression would be like for beings like the Vanaya when the dream became nightmare, and the Nightmare became All.

"Where have they gone, Emari?" Ramon asked.

326

"The Kamoi, the Core. It isn't just some fusion of AI systems. When we get too distraught by—everything—we can just let go and fuse with the Kamoi. It strips you of your persona. The despair and sadness vanish. It's the closest thing to heaven, or death, you will find. Loss of self, care, worry, a timeless all-knowing existence without distress. But the Kamoi is also like a vast Mind, with its own subconscious and dreams, its own desires and schemes. It knows us all. It limits us and our powers so that in a moment of rage we don't destroy worlds."

Ray spread his hands to encompass their location, and by inference their whole situation. "All right, then why are we here?"

A tear started down her cheek, her body slumped forward. Posed, maybe, but more likely just reflecting that there was no point in hiding anymore.

"I don't know. I don't know what this is all about, or why Ramon is here, or why the Core is torturing me like this. It's too much remembering all of this. I forgot these things for a reason. Why is it doing this to me? I made a mistake, I shouldn't have brought you back."

Ramon put his hand on her back but it seemed feeble compared to what she was going through.

The table went silent. Only the sounds of nature: wind in the trees, insects, flowing water, remote calls by some animal.

"I have a new location," Ray said. It wasn't true, he had always known this next location, but refused to let himself remember until now.

seventeen

It was night if there was ever a day here. Above he saw a smattering of faint stars, and towards the northern horizon, because he always knew where the cardinal points were now, was the tip of the expansive smear of the milky way. No longer as dominating yet still a wonder.

He glowed so he could give them light. The soft warm radiance revealing hundreds of frozen silver curves making up the ground they stood upon.

This place was not a world in the natural sense but more infrastructure on a grander scale. The world was an airless, almost perfect silver ball except for a fine etching of the surface like giant silver fingerprints everywhere, spoiling its reflective properties. At the moment most of the light reflected back to them was from the whorls making the area around them surreal. A thousand phosphorescent contour lines like gleaming running water. The object they were standing on was so large it seemed like a moon. The temperature should be close to absolute zero, not much above the cosmic microwave background temperature of 2.725K, instead it was warm beneath his feet.

"We are in Triangulum II. A dwarf galaxy 85,000 light years from the galactic core. It is renowned for having a very high mass to luminosity ratio. I mean it has few stars yet has a large mass. It is a so-called dark matter factory," Ray said, ending the words as if more were to follow. He paused feeling both his pasts arriving at this moment, a pair of surf waves converging and adding together to crash against a sea wall. Now the moment was here, and the next stage had to begin. He could not delay.

He continued. "Here in this dark matter rich dwarf galaxy, casual access is impossible. It is too far for the Vanayan jump system to work. The dark matter also makes the Vanayan system problematic, it can penetrate dark matter regions at close range but not out here, so we have been using a different system from about the halfway point."

"Ray, why didn't you tell me any of this? What's going on?" Ramon said with a look that Ray knew he reserved for serial killers.

"I made myself forget until it was necessary. At first I knew nothing but with each view of Emari's life that part of me grew stronger. It was like waking up and realizing that everything before was a muddled dream. As I became more awake, I grew more powerful, tapping more into the power of Triangulum. Knowing more but also having to forget it," he said, his voice remote.

"Ray," Emari said, walking close to him taking his hands in hers, "don't get lost. Resist it, it is a group mind effect, you will dissolve into it if you don't." Her words were calm and even but her face looked fraught.

He turned to Zara.

"I don't trust her but it still sounds like good advice," she said.

But he didn't need advice now. It was all so clear. This was why he was here and he would finish it. There were warnings from deep inside but he ignored them. It was like a homing instinct calling to him.

"On the contrary, Emari, I am going to embrace it. Do you know why we are here, Emari?"

She shook her head. She had few of her powers now but she knew where her remaining ones came from. They originated in this being whom she once loved.

"This thing we are on. This world. It is the Gift," he said.

"A gift from whom?"

"They call themselves the Band of Light. It is a collection of civilizations. Extragalactic civilizations, Emari. They occupy the Local Cluster of galaxies and a small but increasing fraction of the Laniakea Supercluster. Though Laniakea is enormous, over a hundred thousand galaxies, they intend to contact each galaxy by sending an ambassador via an intergalactic jump. That ambassador can act as their presence and as a guide. The Gift. The Gift came here ages ago. The Kamoi rejected the offer so it withdrew to a less intrusive distance."

"What happens now?" Ramon said.

"We talk to the Gift. All of us," Ray said.

"No. This is wrong. How can I trust this thing?" Emari said, and Ray heard in her voice the pleas of her siblings before she became a Changeling.

"Why do you trust the Kamoi? Or do you trust it? It kept this secret from you, perhaps it kept other things secret. Remember you don't timestamp your memories. You do that to the Galactic Calendar but not to your own memories. What has the Core edited out and how would you know?"

"I need to believe in it. I devoted my lives to this thing I helped create. But Cusha." She winced at the fresh memory. "How can I support that? If that is where my duty has led me then have I been deceived? Have I been 'just following orders'?" Emari was shaking again.

Something had changed in her.

"My duty was never to the Kamoi. It was to Corvena and the people we help. Never to the Kamoi. I will not be abandon that ideal. I have been used. Betrayed! I will burn it to ash." Her face flushed, the mechanics of her human imitation performing true to form.

"Emari, are you okay?" Ray said.

There was a wild look in her eyes he didn't trust. But a voice inside him told him this was good.

Ramon nodded, he had become in tune to Ray's thoughts and saw this was a good sign. Though they could read each other's minds he knew Ray would not violate his privacy. What mattered between them was the rapport.

He didn't know what to say to Emari. She was like a force of nature, a rising storm, that was beyond control or appeasement. Although Emari was important, he had to deal with the urgent first. They were here for a reason and must face it.

For the last time, Ray, reached within not knowing what he would find. There was a single, central thought represented in his imagination—a silver and gold glowing door. Not unlike the door Emari had once shown him. It opened to blinding light.

They were in a garden under a blue sky, bathed in muted light. No sun was visible, the sky itself was the light source. It was an Earth garden. Full of familiar plants and birds. A mix from various continents. All the flowers in bloom and scents that pulled at his emotions, a lure to familiar soothing memories from childhood. There was a pink paved meandering network of paths through the fragrant shrubs and flowers leading to a central area where they stood. It looked like there should be a fountain here. Ray willed that a fountain should appear, nothing happened.

From the path they were facing a human female dressed in white walked towards them. She was a little taller than Ray and wore a simple white one piece tunic with a golden cloth belt and a necklace of blue sapphires that sparkled as she walked. That wasn't real, he knew, there was no pinpoint light source for those reflections so this was a simulation. A pointless conclusion that was obvious from the start.

She spoke in a calm melodic voice, "My name in your Calendar form is Ethra Yechigri Anuc. It would translate to something like, 'Friendly hope on brave wings', it isn't a literal translation. I named myself and I volunteered for this journey."

"From where?" Emari said, "We have never seen your like before."

Ray turned to her. Had she not listened to his explanation? No, she had listened; she had also stopped believing anything he said. He would deal with his dismay later, right now he had to deal with a critical situation.

"I am from the Band of Light. The Message Bearer told you that. Now that the Emissary has arrived we can proceed," Ethra said in a calm voice that was human and humane. Ray thought it must be wishful thinking; the Elder Race delusion, the Mirrish were the classic case. Humanity wanting someone to hold their hand as they crossed the street.

"Emissary? Emissary for whom?" Ray said.

"The Emissary is here at last. Ray, you have brought the formal connection from the Hive Core, or Kamoi as you call it. Not just encrypted permissions but an active long-range link. That is why you are so powerful and why your power grew as you got further from the Core. We have been waiting for you a long time," she said, then paused seeing the confusion on Ray's face. "You found your way here and learned deep things about the Vanaya. You still don't understand. Consider yourself a data packet, a sealed message, from the Core. Now you have arrived we can unwrap the message," she said, and it sent a chill through him.

"I am the wrapping. Open the present and throw away the wrapping." He thought he would have more time, perhaps Emari would keep him as a pet, or be a recruit, or exist independent of the Kamoi and its machinations. But now he was wrapping.

"This is not the end of the journey. I know what you are thinking but you are all here for a reason. None of this was accidental or a whim, including your reincarnation," she said.

"Us too?" Ramon said, asking for himself and Zara.

They had the same fears and reasons as Ray did, perhaps more. It would have caused both a lot of anxiety. Ramon was brave and Zara was fearless. In fact, Ramon was braver than him. What had he gone through, what had he suffered to be like that?

"I repeat. You are all here for a reason. This discussion only highlights your lack of knowledge. We should fix that. Let's unwrap the message and see."

With that Ray's world evaporated.

He could never put it into words but he understood it all.

He saw, within or without, since physical space no longer existed, the vast, slow arguments of the Kamoi based on the experience of hundreds of worlds and billions of interacting minds. Data, experience, and abstractions, philosophical arguments turned into mathematical structures fed into quantum computers, more processing and physical experiments. Ideas from surprising and unrelated areas demonstrated to be completely relevant and also incomplete. Multiple logic systems to attack lemmas and theorems, trying to dodge Gödel incompleteness, while supporting the structure of arguments.

Building to an analysis: what do we want to do?

Intelligent beings need goals, and they can be the hardest things to find and understand. The Vanaya weren't exempt from that, they just had more powerful pro and con arguments and far too many options, the result was a jungle of possibilities. So they did what Life would do—take multiple paths at once. There were several High Goals, as they called them, and this journey and particular path afterward was at the top. He couldn't see it all, it was not meant for him to know it, only to carry it, to be its instrument. He was powerful and powerless and it was too familiar.

There was a timeless moment. It wasn't like being dead. He knew things had happened but he couldn't fit them into his limited mind. Once he thought the Vanaya godlike and now he had seen far beyond them. He had gone from divine comprehension to mortal limitations again, left with the divine afterglow. A sadness crept into him as if lamenting the brain death of a god.

Coming out, a fragment of that being, if that was what it was, constructed a simplified message for him. He made it for himself so he wouldn't imagine that he left himself with nothing. It was a vision of the Band of Light.

The galaxy humans call M31 has more stars than the Milky Way and because of that it supports more simultaneous civilizations. Their Vanaya equivalent had raised worthy contenders and allowed a progression to something less than the Dream, but far greater than anything in the Calendar. In the vision he saw glittering cities the size of continents floating in space complete with their own internal landmasses and ecosystems. They terraformed worlds beyond count and created new artificial lifeforms designed for space. There were also engineering projects on a scale that would dwarf anything he had seen of the Vanayans with motivations that his expanded self found unable to communicate. Grandest of all were the artificial star clusters of thousands of suitable stars with each supporting a life bearing world. All talking to each other and their equivalent of a Kamoi. It wasn't a utopia; they had their own turbulent history, but it was still better than anything he had seen.

The society that began this was not unique, there were other such cultures in M31 and they developed successful strategies that allowed the co-operation and evolution of such civilizations into something that even the Hive Core could not understand. When another galaxy contacted M31, they communicated and joined a club of like-minded entities. This became the Band of Light. They tried to contact the Milky Way multiple times and failed. There was something amiss in our galaxy. It didn't take long for the Gift to find out what it was.

So it intervened with superhuman patience to get a message through. Like the taming of a skittish wild animal. It found sympathetic beings. The overture was subtle and stealthy; it opened a fragile dialog. It could only go so far though, at some stage the Kamoi would have to respond, it would have to send an emissary, someone untainted by the past.

They were back in the garden.

Zara went to Ray as if she expected him to collapse. But she kept a little distance allowing him to regain his bearing by himself.

"That was amazing." Zara said. "So much data. Did the rest of you see that? Anyone understand it all? The Vanaya look like amateurs compared to these guys."

"I think that was a massively simplified version of the truth," Ray added.

He turned to Emari who was panting, suffering from an anxiety attack. Eyes fixed and staring.

"Are you all right?"

She didn't respond.

"What do you remember, Emari?" he said, but she didn't seem to even see him.

Zara inched towards Emari as if to comfort a terrified injured animal.

Ramon looked at Ray, his eyes wide and his whole body taut with uncertainty.

"Ramon, how are you doing?"

"I don't know. I saw—you, or me. Us. In that whirlpool of ideas I thought I would lose my way and never return. Then, I saw what was in you, and it was okay. Like this was normal even pleasant. And I didn't want to leave but had to. Weird huh?" Ramon smiled, relaxing, like an overfilled balloon with a slow leak.

"Us? I saw only me," Ray said.

"No. There were two of us but I kept thinking there was only one." Ramon said.

"Oh, right. I understand," Ray said. But he didn't.

Somewhere within himself a restricted area of knowledge was unlocked. One of many. The doors to a hidden library opened waiting for him to explore. It would fade but enough would stick.

"Ramon, I, uh. Yeah. Look, don't worry. Everything will be all right." Now he knew, he couldn't tell Ramon. Perhaps it wasn't even necessary he might already know. Everything was so clear.

"They chose, you, us, because we were an outsider. Afeni wanted to contact the Gift but it trusted no one previously in contact with the Kamoi. The time was right, and we had the winning number. Still don't know why it was necessary to torture Emari like that," Ramon said.

"They needed her to be free. I think. The Vanaya are enslaved to their past. She was the strongest so they recruited her into this. The irony is that my recruitment was actually hers. That is my understanding. It sucks big time."

"Do those people have any compassion?" Zara said. "Honestly. Lots of fake caring but I'm not seeing the genuine article anywhere. Emari, it's okay. We're all good and at least you have people here you can trust. Emari?"

Emari shivered, not from the cold, her eyes glazed, catatonic.

"Emari, we need to go back." Ray said. "Don't worry we are all linked to Ethra now, we can travel further and we can tap into resources from both ends I think. The Kamoi is in trouble and has been for a long time. We have to fix it," He spoke in slow measured sentences, pleading seeing the growing distrust there. She was coming apart.

Her face came alive as if she was another person. She turned her head to face him. Still so tormented, but now where there was once pain there was rage. Ray wanted to soothe her and comfort her, but she needed to make the next step herself, whatever that was.

Ramon moved close to her and held her. He could feel the muscles unwinding. Calm returning in every breath.

The garden disappeared. Once more they stood on the silver world.

Emari looked past Ramon towards Ray. "I can't stay here. Let me go, Ray."

Ramon let go of her, not understanding.

"I'm not your jailer," Ray said.

Ramon turned to look at him with calm certainty. "Ray, you are. You brought us here, and I guess you will take us back. I thought maybe Emari was our true guide because the visions were about her, but it was always you. It was you trying to see beyond the facade of the Vanaya. You are the one with the power, so please stop with the denial. It isn't helping."

He knew Ramon was correct. It was all obvious now after meeting the Gift. Those motivations were gone. Before he behaved as a construct, a machine, a guided missile on a trajectory. Now he was human at last. It was as if this was his goal all along. To be himself.

"Sure. I apologize, Emari. I wasn't myself. I release you," he said awkwardly. "You can go back now but I don't want you to. We should stick together. This is not over. No way is it over. There's a lot more to do. In fact, this was the easy part, hard on you, Emari, remembering all of that, but it was straightforward. Now the rest of us are about to leave our comfort zones."

"What?" Zara yelled. "Since when have we been in a comfort zone? Relax Ray and get your bearings." She turned to Emari. "We'll be fine if we stick together, Emari."

Emari looked at them, not speaking. A hard determination on her face.

Ray looked at her and confided. "The Galactic Calendar. The guide book for good civilization is a lie. There is another calendar, a Secret Calendar. Cusha was only the tip of the iceberg."

"I know," Emari said. "I saw it in you. Courtesy of the Gift, I suppose. The Secret Calendar is a betrayal. You understand? It isn't only about a lie. They have betrayed me, and someone will pay."

"Easy. It isn't about revenge. This is about setting things right. Or less wrong. We can change the Core. It has primed itself for this, but it needs the insight of the Gift. Like a patient with a therapist. We just have to reach the Core."

She looked away and towards Ramon; a plea in her eyes. "Ramon. Come with me. We'll find those dirty secrets. I want to know. The two of us, together. The rest can catch up."

"We should stick together," Ramon said.

"Please."

They looked at each. He gave a slight nod, then they vanished.

"Damn!" Ray said.

"So much for teamwork. What's the plan, Boss?" Zara said in a scornful tone.

"Boss? I suppose you aren't referring to the good old days when you worked for me."

"Jeez. You're our fearless leader, so act like one." She crossed her arms.

"Did that work?" she said.

"If you want to imitate human irritation, you shouldn't give the game away. But, yeah, it worked."

"What was the big deal with the Secret Calendar? How could they keep it a secret? It isn't a work of fiction, it would be about actual events the Vanaya also experienced."

"Timestamps. Humans by default don't have them because we, they, are organic. You, when you were an AI, would timestamp everything. You knew when everything happened. If someone erased something from your memory, you would know because it would leave a hole in the list of timestamped events. The Vanaya might still figure it out, but they dialed down their intelligence, which made it much easier to do terrible things. Then they erased it from their minds—but not without a backup."

"Fixing the Core that is a monumental task, Ray. We can't fight a galaxy, even with superpowers. It is suicide."

"We aren't fighting a galaxy we are only delivering the mail. All we have to do is connect to the Kamoi and BANG! All done."

"While fighting off hordes of Aamon and Dunnic super-beings led by Zorrech. I hereby name them, 'balrogs'."

"What? Never mind. We have to leave. I know where they went," he said.

"You can read his mind. Can you also read Emari? And what about me?"

"Sure, I can read his thoughts and he can read mine. I can read yours when I want to. Emari is harder her mind is not human or even mortal. Too many millions of years have done weird things to her. If you wanted to you could read my thoughts. Maybe you are too used to link comms."

She shrugged.

"Why don't we go straight to the Kamoi? Get it over and done with," she said.

"The Gift said there was help in the Repositories. It was not specific. Otherwise it would be suicidal. Anyway, let's go," he said.

"Wait. We came all this way and we're just leaving? Isn't there more we can do here? Prepare or something?"

"Together we are powerful, or will be. It's all getting vague now. But I do remember that we are vulnerable when separated. The closer we are the better."

Time to go. He knew it. Not as a supplied directive but as a personal judgment.

He concentrated. Before him he saw the web of stars and the tangled loops of gas flows. A wild variety of suns beyond counting surrounded him. Through it a glowing pulsing thread ended on a strange toxic world. How could anything useful be there?

"Follow me," he said.

There was a brief flash and they were gone.

The silver moon was alone again with the fading infrared footprints of its recent guests. It waited as before, but now awake. At last, the pieces were moving. She hoped for a peaceful resolution, but that was unlikely. Stakes and risks were high, this might be the final chance to rescue the situation; she had pinned all hopes on a band that could not yet admit their personal truths. Only when that occurred could they fit together and function as the weapon designed long ago.

To be concluded.

ACKNOWLEDGEMENTS

The cover image is based on an iStock image modified in GIMP. Thanks to Louise Cusack for her first editing that made me rethink the novel. Any errors here are solely mine, and since I tend to be stubborn and independent then there are sure to be many.

If you wish to see other work of mine my website is www.peteryard.com and you can email me at peter@peteryard.com

The next book in the series is in final its final drafts, but without a title.

Just a note: this novel was the most difficult of all to write. I am not sure how many will like it, but I felt it had to be written.

www.ingramcontent.com/pod-product-compliance
Lightning Source LLC
Chambersburg PA
CBHW072120250626
47159CB00007B/2517